Agent

Paul N. Lazarus, III

Authors Choice Press

San Jose New York Lincoln Shanghai

Agent

Authors Choice Press
an imprint of iUniverse.com, Inc.

For information address:
iUniverse.com, Inc.
5220 S 16th, Ste. 200
Lincoln, NE 68512
www.iuniverse.com

ISBN: 0-595-16663-6

Printed in the United States of America

Agent

TO JUDY

ACKNOWLEDGEMENTS

I would like to thank my mentors who taught me about the agency business and the movie industry. Although both get curiouser and curiouser over time, their lessons are as applicable today as they were when they imparted them to me.

To Dianne Cowan, my gratitude for your editorial contributions and unflagging support. Engaging in semantic debates with her was one of the joys of the writing process.

To Danelle McCafferty, whose comments offered valuable insights into how the novel should be structured.

To Sandy Davidson, designer extraordinaire, who furnished invaluable advice about what my protagonist would wear.

Finally, to my wife Judy who patiently read all of the drafts of Agent and had the genius to offer objective criticism without threatening our relationship.

I am profoundly grateful to all of them, but accept full responsibility for any shortcomings or weaknesses *Agent* may have.

PROLOGUE

March 10, 1988

It was a beautiful spring day, the sun bringing the season's first real warmth to what had been a miserable winter. Forsythia and lilacs were in bloom and Marcie Sandmore was supremely happy. Happy with her husband Bob, her 15 month toddler Rob, and that they had decided to rent a home in suburban Harrison to go along with their New York apartment.

Rob was a contented child. He zipped past the development stages before the books predicted and brought unceasing joy to his parents. Life was good, thought Marcie.

Marcie came into Rob's room as Hannah, the nanny, was getting him dressed. Marcie suggested he wear a light cotton sweater when he went out. Hannah selected the tiny Ralph Lauren tennis sweater that Marcie had recently bought. It made no difference to Rob who bubbled with excitement, as he always did, when going out to play with Hannah.

The backyard of their rental house had a fenced-in area with a sand box, a swing and see-saw set, and some fanciful bright color plastic shapes that fascinated Rob. Marcie gave Rob a big hug and kiss and told Hannah she'd be back from the beauty parlor and her few appointments in a couple of hours. She felt perhaps too suburban as she put the list of things to do in her purse. She tried to remember the plot of *The Stepford Wives* as she went through the kitchen into the garage and climbed into the Volvo in which she felt so secure. Something about suburban robot women, but she had lost the details. She pushed the automatic garage door opener clipped to the visor and watched as the sunlight flooded in.

She turned the radio to the National Public Radio station and backed up toward the street. Driving no more than five miles an hour, she felt the car run over some object in the driveway. Her first thoughts were of a toy or a newspaper. Then, Hannah's horrified scream pierced the quiet of the spring morning. "Oh god," she thought, "I've run over someone's dog." As she slammed on the brakes and leapt from the car, the awful pieces began to come together. Hannah isn't in the back with Rob. "Rob! ROB!" Her voice was not her own. She glimpsed her next door neighbor, Patricia Sullivan, running across the street toward her.

At first, she couldn't see him. Then, panicked and terrified, she saw his little legs sticking out from under the car. Sliding him out, she saw the soft white cotton tennis sweater turn red with blood. She covered him with her jacket and screamed to Hannah to call 911. Even with a quick police response, nothing could be done. She had begged him to wake up, pleading with him to hang on for a few more minutes. Rob never heard her.

Hannah had come out to the front with Rob to pick up the mail and turned her back for a minute to see whether her rose bush showed any signs of insects. In that instant, Rob had taken his favorite car to the driveway to push it on the paved surface. Hannah checked the rear and side view mirrors before backing up, but Hannah had been off to one side, and Rob had been too close to the garage and too low to the ground to be seen.

They told Marcie at the emergency room that death had been instantaneous. They might have thought it would make her feel better to know he had not suffered, but she was inconsolable. The adrenaline that sustained her in the ambulance ride to the hospital ran out and she slumped to the floor unconscious. Hannah, totally stricken by the tragedy unfolding before her, called Bob in New York.

Bob was able to decipher her hysterical wailing enough to comprehend that something terrible had happened to Rob and that Marcie was unable to come to the phone. It took him 45 minutes to get to the hospital where he found his sedated wife admitted to a private room and his son removed to a holding area for the deceased. Bob completely lost it with the doctors who tried to comfort him. Hannah had the misfortune to enter the room at the height of his emotional outburst and he turned on her in an out of control rage that brought orderlies running. Hannah would carry the emotional scars of that moment for the rest of her life. The scars from that day would also be with Bob and Marcie forever.

CHAPTER I

March 26, 2000

The stretch limousine glided to a halt in front of the Dorothy Chandler Pavilion.

Chandler Pavilion. Marcie could see the temporary bleachers, filled with fans and celebrity freaks, waiting to scream for their favorites. The traditional red carpet ushered the greats and near-greats from the sidewalk into the cavernous building.

It was Academy Award night. Hollywood's annual display of self-congratulation, presented to a huge global television audience. She'd been there six times before in her capacity as talent agent, but never with an escort like Sam. Usually she'd been the date of a studio executive, unknown to the general public, but good for her business. Talent agents needed to be mindful of such things, even if the evening turned out to be a social disaster.

Sam was different. Drop-dead good-looking, ten years younger than her tanned, long-legged, quite striking 35 years, Sam was blond with piercing blue eyes, sort of a cross between a younger Paul Newman and Robert Redford. She took in the gasp from the crowd as he stepped from the car and waved. She heard the yells all around her. "Just one picture, Sam!" "I love you Sam!" "Look at me! Over here!" That feeling must have been what the Beatles felt. Imagine, this response and he had only done one movie.

If only these eager young women, their faces contorted as they screamed to get Sam to notice them, knew how she had made his career. As they tried to attract his attention, he held her tightly for support. He flashed his now famous smile at the crowd and they returned the favor with a loud roar.

It was that smile that first had knocked her out as well. He'd gotten an upgrade on an American flight from New York to L.A. and was seated next to her in first class. With three scripts to wade through, she'd been looking forward to sitting alone. His "Gee Whiz" demeanor made no attempt to hide the fact that this was the first time he had ever sat in the front of the plane. It was one of the perks of her job that she enjoyed the most. Sure, the coach section got to the destination at the same time as first class, but the flight was one helluva lot more comfortable.

Her dismay gave way to instant interest when she looked up to see him stowing his knapsack in the overhead compartment. "Hi," he said, sitting down and offering his hand. "Sam Glass." She shook it, aware that the strength of her handshake would elicit some reaction. Her hands seemed simply long and graceful, but were in fact the powerful hands of an athlete. She loved to create the initial surprise of conveying a strength and confidence that would catch people, especially men, completely off-guard.

None of the screenplays was read that trip. Instead, even before take-off, they spoke about Sam's life, his half-hearted pursuit of an M.B.A., and his uninspiring relationship with one of his Columbia Business School classmates. Sam was a Manhattan Beach, California kid with permanently sun-bleached hair from surfing and beach volleyball. He had been handed the notion that business was the way to go by his father, a health care administrator, and chose Columbia because of its New York location. "Go where the money is," his father counseled him. And that took him to New York.

He had stumbled once over her name, Marcie, calling her Marsha instead. Was Marcie such a difficult name? Why did so many people have trouble remembering it? It did click in before they lifted off the ground, and with the arrival of a glass of complimentary champagne, a lesser make than used to be served, Marcie noted, Marcie began to look at him with her experienced talent agent's eyes.

With the passing of Schwabbs Drug Store from its perch high atop Sunset Boulevard, actors just weren't "discovered" anymore. Still, this ingenuous young man was perfect for the part of Josh in the new Sydney Pollack thriller *Whiplash*. When Brad Pitt had a change of heart, the studio went ballistic and threatened to put the whole project into turnaround. Agents scurried to replace him, but all the available names seemed tired and unexciting. Even her trip to New York to see Broadway's latest heartthrob had proven worthless. Forget the press saying he'd been manly and commanding, he had struck her as effeminate and bitchy. Good acting can take a person only so far. But Sam, God he was perfect.

She had broached the subject casually, measuring his interest carefully. By the time they flew over the Midwest, his curiosity had turned to passion. The suggestion that he go up for the part had clicked. It was the detour in his life he'd subconsciously been seeking. A new direction for him. Back to the West Coast, away from the dirt and despair of New York. "What do I have to do?" he asked, with his completely persuasive innocence.

In her bag, she carried the latest draft of *Whiplash*. She gave it to him to glance over. After a couple of questions about how to get through the format of a screenplay, he began to read. She closed her eyes for what she thought was a brief second, and was surprised when she awoke and found that he had finished. She'd been asleep for an hour, enough time for him to fly through the pages. He was brimming over with confidence. "Of course, I can play Joshua," he told her. As if inventing the cliché, he insisted, "I was born to play this part." His whole presence, his enthusiasm, composed of equal measures of sincerity and confidence, convinced her.

Partly for show and partly out of conviction, she called the studio from the plane and was fortunate enough to be put through to Pollack. She had long ago discovered the importance of being on the best of terms with secretaries. It was astounding what flowers, champagne, or a pair of hard-to-get tickets did to establish productive relationships with even the toughest gatekeepers on the Hollywood scene. "I'm kind of busy," Sydney said, "but if you're that excited, I'll make some time around four."

The rest was a slam dunk. Sydney flipped when he met Sam. He rushed him over to meet studio head Sherry Lansing, who tried to be restrained when she told Marcie she'd like to test him. Sydney kept saying to Marcie, "I owe you one! Don't forget, I owe you one." No, she wouldn't forget. She never did.

It didn't take very long to call Pollack on his commitment. The studio tried to low-ball Sam's deal, offering Screen Actors Guild minimum, plus 10% for the agent's share. Marcie knew that the whole picture hung in the balance and that she had plenty of chips to play in the negotiation. Invoking Sydney's support, she got the studio up to $250,000, plus $100,000 deferred, plus a probably meaningless two percent of the net profits. Not bad for a kid she'd sat next to on a plane.

From there, it had moved with blinding speed. Sam dazzled them in the test. He took direction easily and was what the veterans called a "natural". He signed agency representation papers with Allied where Marcie worked. The signing created only a minor stir, even when it was announced he had landed the coveted Joshua role. Fresh faces come and go; it was impossible to get worked up about all of them.

But Sam *was* special. The buzz from Paramount was immediate and more than the standard pre-release hype. Paramount, seeing Sydney's dailies, knew it first. Then the other agents in town got the word. At the other agencies, agents were besieged by their employers with the inevitable pointed questions why *they* hadn't signed Sam instead of Allied. And finally the public began to hear. The picture was still a month from general release, but Sam had already been featured on *E.T.* and in *People* magazine. Only a page on his discovery; covers would come later. Marcie put him with her lawyer, Ira Lang, one of the town's most respected show business attorneys, and convinced P.R. veteran Jane Pratt, to add him to her exclusive client list. The team was growing, and Marcie was enjoying herself more than she had in several years.

Now, as they walked down the red carpet toward the open doors of the Dorothy Chandler, the familiar face of *Variety* columnist Army Archerd loomed before them, speaking energetically into his mike, getting a few words of wisdom from Jodie Foster. In front of them, to Sam's enormous pleasure, walked Burt Reynolds and his current Loni Anderson lookalike. From Marcie's angle, she could only question why people as wealthy as Burt had such horrible toupees. This one seemed to have fallen on his head from a great height and appeared rather precariously perched there. Sam didn't notice, so swept up was he in the excitement of the moment.

Marcie was thrilled at the response Sam drew from the fans in the packed bleachers. Their shouts built in a rising crescendo as the word spread that it was Sam Glass. *Whiplash* had been in release for only a month but it was a monster. It had opened to strong reviews and instantly proved itself an audience favorite. It climbed to $100 million in box office gross and developed a potent word of mouth as thousands of moviegoers told their friends about this great new picture with a leading man "you're not going to believe". Sam's next picture, and he was down to selecting between two scripts, could catapult him into the million per picture club, and from there, it was anybody's guess.

Army's staff person was all over Sam, hustling him to the mike. Sam had done his share of interviews plugging the picture, but this was different. It was also the first time that Marcie had been at this spot, holding hands with a hot actor in front of a global audience.

"Hi, Army," she said, her voice reliably strong.

They knew each other very casually, to say hello, not even well enough for the perfunctory Hollywood "air kiss".

"Hello Marcie," he replied, his eyes looking not at her, but at Sam.

"Uh, you know my agent Marcie Sandmore, Mr. Archerd?"

"Call me Army," came the response, as Marcie could almost see the television camera moving in for a two-shot that excluded her and her smashing creamy silk charmeuse shirt, with perfectly cut tuxedo pants and jacket. Oh well, she thought, I've had my thirty seconds of celebrity. She knew her outfit was smart and appropriate, even if it was not as outlandish or revealing as those chosen by the actresses in attendance. But the gusty wind wasn't doing anything good for her hair. Her soft, carefully styled brunette hair hung just below the base of her neck. She wanted to put up her free hand to check the damage, but the moment seemed too public to take the chance. Behind them she could hear Susan Sarandon whispering small talk with the staff person, waiting to go on. Marcie glanced behind her and saw she was checking *her* hair for wind damage. It didn't seem fair.

Army congratulated Sam on *Whiplash*, shook hands, and they were ushered away into the lobby, toward the auditorium. There had been some discussion about having Sam be a presenter, he had that much heat or attention on him. But when Jeff Bridges agreed, Sam was out. Still he had been taken seriously when Marcie implored producer Richard Zanuck to give the audience someone they really wanted to see. She had agented the hell out of him, having the president of Allied personally speak to Cates on Sam's behalf. It would have been a tremendous coup had she pulled it off, but it was something of a coup to have a newcomer's name taken seriously at all.

At least it had got them good seats, Marcie thought, center orchestra and in front of the bank of television cameras. If you had the misfortune to be seated behind the cameras, you spent the whole evening watching the monitors. That had been fine when she didn't know any better, but now she preferred not going to sitting in the cheap seats. She religiously adhered to this philosophy in restaurants, at shows, in airplanes, everywhere she might be seen. Her thinking was both to create the best image of herself in the town and to derive the obvious benefits that flowed from the choicest seats.

At first, the glamour of the event was all Marcie hoped it would be. The musical numbers were fresh and inspired, the awards themselves compelling, and the patter of the presenters brief and to the point. But as the second hour eased into the third, and recipients of the minor awards felt compelled to thank everyone they had ever known, time began to stand still. Sam's attention wandered from the stage to the celebrities seated all around him. People he had never seen before, generally agents or studio executives, made eye contact and smiled or waved to him. "Who's that?" Sam whispered to Marcie. She was an excellent tour guide. Like any good agent, she didn't need a scorecard to identify the players.

When the sentimental choice for Best Supporting Actress began her speech, she paid homage to her agent, Jeff Berg of ICM. As the orchestra began playing to signal that she'd better wrap up her thank you's or face the hook, Marcie turned to Sam and said softly, "Will you thank me when you get up there?"

"Of course," he said smiling. "I owe everything to you."

Famous last words, she thought. She knew that no matter how nice actor-clients began, they all became monsters in the end. Let things go even slightly off track and they suddenly fall prey to the sweet-talking of other agents from other agencies. She no longer took it personally, nor did she believe that Sam, who still spoke with the utmost sincerity, was one iota different. No, he wouldn't leave today. Why should he? He was hot. But lose out on getting a picture, have a couple of films disappoint at the box office, and let's see where he stood then. Oh well, as her last shrink had urged her, "Enjoy the moment."

It was 9:00, and they'd been in their seats for over four hours. "Is it almost over?" Sam asked. He sounded like a little boy and she smiled at him. His adrenaline rush had subsided leaving him a little drained.

"Soon," she replied. "They only have two awards left. It's the damn commercials that drag it out."

She gave his leg a reassuring pat. He beamed at her and leaned over and gently kissed her cheek. She could feel the color creeping into her face as she imagined the people around her wondering how close she and Sam actually were. Hesitatingly, she looked around and found herself staring into the eyes of Rudy Scott, one of the town's biggest producers and biggest pricks. He acknowledged her with a subtle smile, actually more of a smirk, while she mouthed a silent hello to him. What a nest of vipers, she thought.

Mercifully, the show came to an end, the last thank you speech was given, and she and Sam filed out with the rest of the crowd to await the arrival of their limo. Being able to introduce Sam to the many players who wanted to meet him before their cars arrived took some of the pain out of waiting. Normally, waiting for a limo to arrive was her least favorite part of a gala evening. She was happy that Sam had rallied, like any good actor, and was all boyish charm and exuberance. She adored his professionalism. It was, for her, the most important of all virtues. Be a shit if you must, but at least be a professional shit.

The evening was still young on the West Coast so when their limo pulled up and they got in, it was off to Spago's for the annual celebrity bash. Sam was not keen on going but she convinced him that it was very important to mingle with this crowd, Hollywood's power brokers and most important celebrities. "Don't leave me alone," Sam begged, in an almost plaintive voice, as the driver headed west on Sunset.

"I wouldn't dream of it."

On arrival, the driver worked his way up the hill and stopped by the front door. It seemed that all the paparazzi in the world had assembled as close to the door as they could get, and Sam's arrival triggered a barrage of flashes that nearly blinded them. Ever the good trouper, Sam smiled his soon-to-be million dollar smile and waved, calling out, "How're you doing? Good to see you!" Marcie checked the drape of her jacket and ran a hand quickly through her hair. For a brief second she felt almost stunning until Julia Roberts tapped her on the arm and said, "Oh Marcie, how are you? And isn't this Sam Glass? I'd love to meet him."

As they entered Spago's, greeting proprietor Wolfgang Puck at the door, Marcie made the requested introduction. "Julia, meet Sam Glass," watching Julia light up like an incandescent bulb. Her escort, apparently accustomed to Julia's social behavior, politely hung back while Julia and Sam exchanged a few pleasantries. Marcie greeted director Richard Donner with a friendly kiss and turned back to Sam. In seconds Julia was swept deeper into the room, kissing and hugging her way across the floor to a reserved window table.

Sam turned to Marcie. "Wow," he said.

"I know. She's really something."

"Is she a client of AA?" he asked. The way Sam said the agency's initials recalled the standing Hollywood joke about AA's other meaning for substance abusers. Why didn't they change the damn name anyway, Marcie wondered?

"Uh, ICM. Why?"

"No reason," Sam said. "She told me she'd like to do something together."

"You'll be able to pick and choose, don't worry. We need to get the great material. Good scripts are everything."

He only half heard what she said as the din became a deafening roar. They followed a hostess to a table filled with Allied's clients and top agents. After the introductions were made and champagne and Evian water began flowing in copious amounts, Marcie was conscious of the fact that she was the only woman present from AA. She

knew this was only because she had signed Sam, not because of her
senior status at the agency.

She had had no expectations to the contrary when it came to
advancement to the top echelon of agency life. The major agencies,
CAA, ICM, UTA, the Morris office, and Allied, despite vigorous protests
from their managements, were men-only clubs at the level where true
power lay. But you don't come to Hollywood, as you don't join the
United States Senate, expecting equality. These were patriarchal organ-
izations to begin with and any changes over the years were merely cos-
metic. At Allied, it was never a question of respect for her abilities. She
had a tough, creative head for business and the fine art of negotiation.
Many of her colleagues frequently consulted her on strategies to bring
a desired deal to fruition. Closing deals was everything in the agency
business. Lawyers billed for their hours worked whether the deal closed
or not. Agents collected their 10% of the clients' earnings only if those
earnings materialized. If the deal didn't work out, the agent, as the
Yiddish expression went, got *bupkis.*

Sam seemed restless and anxious to have the evening come to an end.
He was fine in the hot glow of celebrity for a while, but his attention
span was short. In time, she thought, he would develop better defenses
to help him through evenings like this. For now, poor baby, he was
exhausted. Thank god he wasn't venting his anxieties by over-indulging
in the champagne that the Spago staff poured freely as they circulated
about the room. Through the famed Spago windows, the lights of the
L.A. basin twinkled. But this crowd paid attention only to each other.
Conversation dwelt on the evening's upsets and the favorites who left
the stage clutching their golden Oscar statuettes. Inevitably, the current
gossip made the rounds: who was hot and who was cold; who was sleep-
ing with whom; what deals were cooking; and, who was gay, no matter
how loudly they protested. It was the time-honored agenda for a big
Hollywood party.

Table hopping at Spago's was a tradition, and Academy Award night was its high-water mark. Normally the biggest stars remained seated and let others pay their respects to them. It resembled *The Godfather* version of Mafia life. The game was somewhat more complicated on this night as everyone had some status, as performer, agent, executive, director or producer. This was a private party, not accessible to the blue-haired matron from Iowa who had heard so much about the restaurant. If you could fight your way in past the photographers, you would be among your peers, not those who media mogul Barry Diller called "the people we fly over".

*   *   *   *

Charlie Maier, AA chairman, leaned over and whispered to Marcie. "If Sam takes the Warners deal, the agency does real well."

That's self-evident, Marcie thought. Packages, packages, packages. Put as many clients into one deal as you can and the bargaining power with the studio will increase dramatically. It will also be the quickest way to get a picture greenlighted and slated for early production. Anything to get beyond development hell. Why was he treating me like this was all a news flash, she wondered.

"He's looking at it very seriously," she said. "It's between that and the new Altman project at Fox." Marcie glanced across the table to see if Sam was all right. He was fine, very involved in a conversation with Holly Hunter who was seated next to him.

"For Christ's sake," hissed Charles, "don't let him go arty. You've got a chance at a superstar here. Don't fuck it up."

He turned back to his date, one of the agency's leading female clients. Marcie wondered whether he missed his boyfriend at times like this. On most special occasions, he could bring Dave and nobody would blink an eye. For whatever the reason, Charles had chosen not to bring Dave that night. Marcie missed him. Dave was a playwright and brilliant raconteur, who livened up any party with his acerbic wit. She wondered why Charles felt he would be inappropriate for this gathering.

As coffee was being poured, she caught Sam's eye as he gave her the unmistakable sign that he'd had enough. Quite enough really. Before dinner, and even during the meal, he'd been besieged, even with all the starpower in the room, by journalists from print and television wanting to do a piece on Hollywood's newest star. She had interceded on Sam's behalf, referring all requests to Jane Pratt. She knew better than anyone how to pick and choose interviewers so as to best further the career of her clients and still leave the public wanting more. Sam appeared grateful each time Marcie stepped in to remove the onus of refusal from him. She allowed herself only a second to ponder how long his gratitude would be there. If she wasn't careful, she could find herself developing a very unhealthy cynicism about the whole process. That certainly didn't make for effective agentry.

Finishing their coffee and saying goodbye to the Allied contingent, they stepped outside into the cool Los Angeles night. From the sidewalk outside Spago's, the crowd of photographers, fans, and the curious let out a mounting shriek for attention. Walking in front of the restraining barriers toward the limos wedged into the parking lot a few steps further up the hill, she was aware that the shouts to Sam had turned very sexual. "Do me, Sam!" "Look at me, Sam, I'm hot to trot!" Women offered up intimate apparel for his signature. As Marcie spotted their chauffeur standing by their maroon stretch limo, and moved toward him, identical twin girls rushed over and begged Sam for a late-night threesome. He colored adorably, pretending not to have heard them.

Minutes later, they were safely ensconced in the comfortable backseat heading down Sunset. Sam removed his bow tie and leaned back, exhaling deeply. "Was it that horrendous?" Marcie asked.

"Fuck me," Sam said. "What a nightmare. You know what I wish I had?"

"I haven't a clue."

"A joint."

"I didn't know you smoked," Marcie said, a little surprised.

"I don't usually, maybe a couple of j's a year. But I sure'd like one now."

Tentatively, wondering if this was a good idea, she suggested they stop over at her place for a smoke before the driver took him home.

"I thought you were opposed to all that," Sam said, looking at her questioningly.

"I am, but it doesn't mean the perfect hostess shouldn't have what her guests might order."

"Fantastic, how fast can he get us there?"

Home was not that far away. A cozy three-bedroom house with the obligatory pool and hot tub, on a small cul-de-sac just off Benedict Canyon, in the Beverly Hills post office area. The real estate agent had assured her that the Beverly Hills post office was critical for resales, but had forgotten to mention that the whole market could crash making the issue of resales, at least at a profit, moot. Still, Marcie was not looking to unload the house that had served her well. With fireplaces in the living room and master bedroom, an adorable guest room, and a surprising amount of room for entertaining, it was a great house for her. She'd entertained lavishly, mostly for business purposes, and always on her AA expense account. The agency bigwigs had made it clear that they expected her to entertain frequently.

Marcie had used a decorator in furnishing the house and the results were evident. She had wanted to make a strong statement, while preserving an essential femininity in the decor. She had little tolerance for women in the town who felt the way up the success ladder was to be more masculine than their male counterparts. Marcie's taste was eclectic, mixing old and new, different shades of wood, contemporary fine art, and early American crafts. The decorator was unsure, but the results spoke for themselves. Using the decorator for the required legwork, Marcie had done the house with an eye to comfort, soft colors, and bold accents. Her judgment was sure and confident, and it showed. The house served her well.

She punched the keypad combination, inserted her two keys, and opened the door. Sam's look of surprise at her security measures indicated that he still hadn't adjusted to the fact that the Hills were less suburbs and more extensions of the City when it came to protecting your life and your belongings. No one expected another Charles Manson to wreak havoc in the hills above L.A. ever again, but it didn't hurt to adopt some protective measures. Sam laughed when she flipped the switch by the fireplace, sending beautiful flames up from hidden gas jets among the stone logs. "I guess I shouldn't be surprised," he said, "It is Hollywood, after all." Apologetically, she offered that the one in the bedroom was real, but this one came with the house and she'd never got around to taking it out. "And anyway," she smiled at him, "this is Beverly Hills, not Hollywood."

"I couldn't care less," Sam said, "I just think it's funny."

She went into her bedroom as Sam took a seat on a comfortable, large-pillowed sofa. It was his first visit and his eye took in the artwork and the stylish decor. Stella, Johns, Rauschenberg, all signed prints, all framed in excellent taste. Sam also noticed something he had seen in very few other Hollywood homes, books. One whole wall devoted to floor-to-ceiling bookshelves. Not designer-picked leather editions of the masterpieces, but actual books, fiction and nonfiction, that gave every appearance of having been read. He called in to her, "Have you read all these?"

"Uh huh," came the reply. "There're always a few in a holding area for vacation, but mostly, yeah."

Marcie came back into the living room with a Baggie containing an ounce or so of marijuana along with papers and other paraphernalia.

"Did you think they were just for show?" she said.

"I thought no one in this town read anything unless the rights were available."

Marcie smiled, opening the Baggie.

"That's got to be right most of the time," she mused. "I'm probably the exception."

"I like it that way," Sam replied, edging closer to her on the sofa.

Marcie noted his new familiarity, but dismissed it, and set about rolling a joint. She looked at this as a skill resembling bike riding. You never forgot how. She had smoked her fair share years before, but never in a way that impeded her professional advancement. Now it was more a ceremonial pastime, like tonight, not a prelude to going out to dinner or to a movie. "Any idea what good dope costs these days?" she asked.

"To tell you the truth, no. I can't remember the last time I bought any."

"This was $750 an ounce, about twice what an ounce of gold would cost."

"You gotta be kidding me! What is it, some weird foreign shit?"

"Not at all," said Marcie. "Fact is, since Reagan closed down our borders, the best stuff has been grown right here in America."

Marcie finished her painstaking cleaning process, glued one paper to another, carefully funneled the marijuana onto the double paper and rolled a perfect joint. Sam was impressed.

"You're a pro, for Christ's sake."

"You know, if a job's worth doing…"

She took a match and lit the joint, inhaling deeply and holding her breath, before passing it to Sam. "It's pretty strong," she warned, "so you probably won't need much."

Sam nodded and tried to keep from coughing as the smoke reached his lungs. "Music," Marcie said to herself, as she rose and moved to the CD player. She turned back to Sam. "The new Mariah Carey okay?" Sam nodded, still holding his breath.

"I really like her," Sam observed, passing Marcie the joint. "Funny," Marcie went on. "I always thought I'd keep up with popular music, but I just don't get the stuff the kids play today."

Sam found this funny and burst into laughter. His unabashed good humor soon had Marcie laughing as well, and together they reveled in the warm, intimate pleasure of a shared high. Sam tried to sound cool and experienced saying, "This is really good shit." He didn't come close to pulling it off and they collapsed into gales of unrestrained laughter.

Getting their breath back, Sam's arm moved over Marcie's shoulder. "This is really fun," he said. "Much more fun than the Awards."

Finding herself getting serious, she said, "They're a necessary evil. You've got to be seen out there. Tonight was worth a lot for your career."

Normally Sam was a willing and apt pupil when Marcie instructed him on how to conquer the concrete heart of Hollywood. Now, he looked intently at her for a second and burst into laughter once more. She'd almost forgotten the importance of play. A little grass unlocked that door and threw it wide open. She relaxed into more laughter, forgetting for the moment what she had said that prompted this outburst. Any hope of bringing it back to mind disappeared in the next second as Sam reached over and kissed her on the mouth.

This wasn't a social kiss in the great Hollywood tradition. This was for real. Alarm bells went off in her mind. She had long ago resolved never to sleep with clients. There had been exceptions over the years, but clients and buyers alike knew very well that Marcie Sandmore was no "easy" conquest. She'd been horrified at the thought that women had to give up their bodies to get ahead in this town. She was very proud of the notion that she was living proof that this wasn't necessarily so. Even if she was exploited in the workplace, no one was going to put that kind of pressure on her personal life. All of this flashed through her brain in a nano-second, but was soon obscured by the excitement she felt. Maybe it was the dope. Maybe she just liked this man more than she realized. Whatever it was, although the alarm bells gave her adequate warning, she could feel herself choosing to ignore them.

"That was nice," Sam said, still holding her close. As many times as she had been with him, she had never picked up the aroma of his after-shave lotion. It was subtle, vaguely suggestive of lime, and altogether sexy and manly.

"Yes it was," Marcie whispered. Now was the decision for her. Would he be a client and a friend or, at least for this night, a lover? She adored the unpredictability of life, the moments on the edge. It was what gave her the most satisfaction with the agency business. She initiated the next kiss and Sam responded with passion and energy. His free hand slid around her blouse and cupped her breast. She sighed softly and said, "Let's go in the bedroom and get comfortable."

Sam needed no encouragement. Marcie lit the already prepared fire in the bedroom as Sam sat on the bed removing his shoes. The flames began to crackle, and the smell of the aged wood filled the room, mingling with the pleasing aroma of fresh flowers that Marcie had placed throughout her house. She lit a candle on the dresser, turned out the lamp, and headed toward the bathroom. "I'll be back in a second," she said.

She returned wearing a silky nightgown that clung enticingly to the curves of her body. Sam was already in bed, a sheet pulled over him, his eyes studying her every move. She pulled back the sheet and climbed in. It pleased her that Sam had taken off all his clothes and was eagerly awaiting her return. If he had been wearing his socks, she might have had to call this whole thing off. Fortunately, his clothes were neatly draped on her Eames chair, her favorite place to read the scripts that were so much a part of her life. Sam reached out for her and she melted into his arms.

His hands reached under her nightgown and enveloped her. She gasped with pleasure at the sensation. Sam's body was tightly muscled, not the body of a weightlifter, but very firm. Marcie had continued her fitness regimen from her competitive tennis days by using a personal trainer who arrived at her house four days a week at 6:00 in the morning for a rigorous 90-minute workout. Once, she had hoped to play tennis on the tour, but a blown-out knee ended that dream and reduced her to playing social tennis. Still, she was fiercely proud of her level of fitness and relished the moments when men discovered that she had one of those bodies that looked better and better the more clothes she took off.

Sam snuggled next to her. "Now where were we?" he asked.

Her hands began to explore his body. "We were just starting to get to know each other," she replied. She could feel his excitement build as his breath quickened and he became hard against her leg. She reached down to hold him and he moaned softly. "You're a beautiful man, Sam Glass." Any idea she had to continue her thought was lost when his hand moved between her legs and tenderly caressed her. She leaned back and closed her eyes. His touch felt fantastic, sensual and knowing. "I want you in me," Marcie whispered.

Sam slid over on top of her as Marcie moved her hand to guide him. Almost at once, his erection collapsed. Nerves, she thought, as she stroked him to restore it. But it only got smaller and softer. She moved her hand upward, embracing Sam and holding him close.

"That's all right," she said. "Just hold me for a minute. We're not in any rush." She was not fond of this kind of moment. She knew enough to be gentle and comforting and to do nothing that might aggravate a bad situation. While frustrating and unfortunate for her, it was nothing like the pain a man endured when he couldn't finish what he started. She wondered for a beat what tack he would take with her. He offered up the familiar, "This has never happened to me before" version. She held him close, her affections becoming more maternal and less amorous by the second. Quite unexpectedly, he began to speak about himself.

"You're the first person I've cared about since I split with Mandy." Marcie knew about the woman he had been going with in B-School and believed it was ancient history. "We had a pretty ugly scene when I told her I was dropping out of school to take the part. We thought maybe it would be only for a leave of absence, but I knew during shooting that I wasn't going back. She was a part of the life I left at Columbia, and she knew it even before I did. We tried to keep it going during the picture, but things were really different."

"It's okay," Marcie told him. "You don't have to say anything about it."

But Sam continued. "I felt really comfortable with you tonight. I just don't know what happened." In the flickering light, Sam looked like a small and vulnerable child to her. She held him close, rocking him back and forth, assuring him that everything was going to be fine.

Just her luck, she thought. What begins as a merry romp to cap off the Awards party becomes a goddamn therapy session. Oh well, the agent's work is never done. She smiled to herself as she recalled the old saying: "A woman's work is never done".

"Sam," Marcie continued, "trust me on this. You don't have a problem. You're a sensitive guy and it'll all work out." She felt almost a sense of relief as her role changed quickly back to agent and advisor from lover. Of course, she had to make certain that he felt no embarrassment with her, something that might lead him to seek other representation. That would be an unmitigated disaster. She was confident she could bond him to her and hold him in the nest. As a client, he was going to be huge. With a little shaping on her part, he could avoid becoming a personal monster. For the moment his child was present and she would nurture it like crazy.

Sam seemed okay with all of this, but Marcie detected a slight chill. Sensing his angst, Marcie kissed him warmly on the mouth, and held him tightly to her. Sam was cautious now, as if afraid to even begin anything intimate. She felt his body relax as they pressed close to each other. "You can stay here, if you want," Marcie said.

Sounding relieved, Sam unfolded from her embrace, pulled back the sheet, and said, "I guess I'd better go." He looked toward her now uncovered breasts and noticed, for the first time, that Marcie had no tan line on her upper body. She sported an even tan down to her bikini line on her abdomen. Recovering his playfulness somewhat, he gently ran his fingertips over her exposed breasts and said, "No tan lines, huh?"

"Very private patio where I do my weekend reading. You could join me if you want."

He smiled, appearing to have regained most of his composure and confidence. "I might just do that."

Sam climbed out bed and began getting dressed. Marcie watched him as he buttoned his shirt and slid his bow tie into his jacket pocket. After slipping on his pants, he laced his shoes sitting on the bed next to Marcie. "I'll let myself out. Thanks for being so understanding. You're not only a good agent, you're a good friend." He put his arms around her and kissed her on the mouth. Damn, she thought. He does feel good. He broke off the kiss and rose to go.

"Talk to me tomorrow, huh?" Marcie asked. "We have to give answers on those offers before they're withdrawn." What a weird world. From impotency to potent deal-making without missing a beat. Mama, don't let your children grow up to be agents. Marcie got up to lock the door behind Sam as she heard the limo leave. She secured the front door and turned off the gas in the fireplace. Remembering the dawn arrival of the trainer, she moved to empty the ashtray of the roach so as not to face a lecture on recreational drug use from him. It still had a couple of good hits left in it and she figured at these prices…She lit up and walked back to her bedroom, inhaling deeply and letting the strong smoke fill her lungs. Can this dope really be as harmless as she thought? Fuck it, one joint a year isn't going to bend anybody out of shape. She flushed the roach down the toilet, sprayed a couple of blasts of jasmine room deodorizer around the house, blew out the candle, and climbed into bed. The last thing she remembered was the crackle of the logs on the fire.

CHAPTER II

"His name is Tim Garland, and he's got plenty of money. What the hell else do you need to know?"

Marcie hated it when Charles talked to her like that. Was this all about Sam and which movie offer he would take? She knew, after his advice to her at Spago's the night before, that Charles had a vested interest of some kind in Sam's taking the Warners picture. She would get Sam's answer, which would probably be the one Charles wanted, as quickly as she could. There was no reason, Marcie thought, for him to him to treat her with that kind of attitude. Still, he was the chairman of Allied, and she did collect her bimonthly paycheck with his signature on it. Though rude and overbearing, he still was Charles Maier and Allied was one of the four largest talent agencies in the world. He had enormous power in the town and wielded it over her without a second thought.

Marcie had been told, when she joined Allied eight years before, that Charles Maier was bi-sexual. While that might be the case, as far as Marcie knew, he had maintained a long relationship with David Young with whom he lived in the Malibu Colony. It had taken her two years to return to the work force following the accident and Charles had been the one to hire her for the Allied office in New York. She had spent three years learning the art of being a talent agent, involved principally in the

theater department, before transferring to the Los Angeles office to concentrate on motion pictures.

Her client list, and therefore the commissions the agency earned, had
grown steadily in her five years in Los Angeles. The year-end bonuses
distributed by Charles and the Executive Committee, reflected, Marcie
thought, their satisfaction with her. More formal employee evaluations
were not a part of the agency business management style. The fact that
there was no discussion about grooming her for a management spot
neither surprised nor upset her.

*   *   *   *   *

Lunch with Tim Garland was later that day. Marcie had checked with
her friend Ben Kloster, a Harvard-educated literary agent of about her
age, to see if he had heard of Tim. Ben ignored the current fashion rage
in favor of traditional Ivy League style. From blue blazer to silk rep tie,
he looked as if he had stepped out of a Brooks Bros. store window. Ben
had helped Marcie find her way when she arrived in L.A., and they had
stayed professional and tennis friends ever since.

To Marcie's surprise, Ben knew of Tim Garland.

"Tim Garland," Ben said, "you know who he is."

"No, I'm pretty sure not. Who the hell is he?" Marcie asked, wondering whether she should know the answer already.

"He's supposed to have all those Las Vegas connections. Lots of
money, in with the mob, the whole nine yards."

"What's his connection to the movie business?" Marcie asked.

"I have no idea. He was rumored to be sniffing around, but I never
heard he had actually done anything."

"Well," said Marcie, "at least we know he has made contact with
Charles. I've got a lunch date with him later. I'll let you know."

"Do that," said Ben. "It could be interesting."

Marcie's morning was built around a series of meetings she had set up at Columbia Pictures, housed in the Sony Studios in Culver City. Once the home of MGM, the proudest studio of all, just thinking of its rebirth as Sony Studios caused a momentary emotional pang in Marcie. She refused to dwell on it as nothing ever stayed the same in Hollywood. Studios changed ownership, real estate developers ate into the back lots to put up high-rise buildings, hotels or condos, and change took its inexorable toll on the traditions of the town. It was too bad, thought Marcie, but there wasn't much she could do about it.

At Columbia, She met with Dan Durland, a young vice president of development to review the current status of projects. He was interested in some of her ideas for an open writing assignment, as well as some casting suggestions for an action-adventure film that was hovering nervously between being canceled and being greenlighted for production. Marcie then made the rounds of several of the production offices housed on the lot, renewing her contacts, seeing old friends, and *schmoozing* away an hour which she knew would pay dividends in the future. This was a people business and the successful agents were those who maintained strong, close relationships across the town.

She could have spent more time working the lot at Columbia, but she knew she had to make a real effort to be on time for lunch with Tim. As it was, she arrived five minutes late.

Garland's choice of the Polo Lounge of the Beverly Hills Hotel revealed little to Marcie. The Polo Lounge had become an institution many years before, and was not on the list of the "hot" restaurants in the town. If Garland was from out of town and was staying at the hotel, it did make sense.

"Charles has spoken very highly of you," Tim began, as Marcie joined him at a large table on the patio.

"Ever the gracious chairman," Marcie replied.

Tim looked at her closely. His dark, handsomely profiled face reminded Marcie of a younger, more innocent Bob Evans, the erstwhile head of Paramount and ex-husband of Ali MacGraw. Was this to be a complete waste of time, she wondered? Another successful businessman who was "seriously looking" at motion picture investments, not ready to admit that he was really looking to get laid. Marcie had never understood why they were prepared to plunk down so much cash to achieve this end. The best hookers in town, she was told, were $1,000-$2,000 a night. Even if they were more, movies involved millions, or at least hundreds of thousands of dollars. Can smart guys really believe that a good fuck is worth that kind of money? Maybe I'm in the wrong line of work, she thought. Maybe Heidi Fleiss had it right, all along.

But if he were really connected in Vegas, Marcie thought, finding girls can't really be the issue. She focused her attention on Tim who had begun the business portion of the lunch.

"Maybe what I'm looking for doesn't exist," Tim said. "I'd like to find something personal, not formula or pap, that could attract a mainstream audience. My people and I could finance it up to twenty million. Does such a thing exist?"

"Honey," said Marcie, "you better believe it. If you can put that kind of money on the table, we can do some great things together."

Tim smiled and Marcie edged a little closer to the notion that maybe this wouldn't be a total waste of time.

"How did you meet Charles?" she asked.

"A mutual friend. He met Charles when Allied went public, and I think he still has a block of the stock. Charles said you would be the right person to speak with, and here we are."

The mention of Allied stock was a sensitive point with Marcie. She had been "promised" options as part of her compensation package for two years. Somehow, they had never materialized. It might be okay if they didn't consider her management material, but they damn well should deliver on the promises they make. Marcie made a mental note to bring the matter up again at the earliest opportunity. For the present, she thought she'd better try to progress the discussion toward something more specific.

"What kind of script were you looking for?" she asked.

"Maybe horror, if it were special and not some dumb slasher film. Something that wouldn't need a major star and that could still do business around the world."

Not bad, Marcie thought. A pretty sophisticated answer. Could it be that I underestimated Mr. Tim Garland? She described a couple of projects that were at Allied, emphasizing one written by a young American Film Institute graduate who wanted to direct it.

"You should look at his thesis film before you say no," Marcie advised. "He's pretty hot."

Tim signaled the waiter for the bill. He signed his name and a house charge number, and looked back at Marcie.

"Here's my business card. Maybe you could messenger the script and the film. I'd be happy to look at both."

"Terrific," said Marcie, glancing at the Garland Enterprises card he had given her and extending her hand. "You'll have them this afternoon."

*　　*　　*　　*　　*

Marcie swung her employer-leased Lexus into the parking area of the Allied Agency. Located on Wilshire Boulevard, on the eastern edge of Beverly Hills, Allied's building was gleaming and new, but nothing like the E.M. Pei structure that Michael Ovitz had commissioned for his then company, Creative Artists Agency. Panned in the local architectural columns as sterile and cold, inside and out, Allied headquarters resembled the proverbial horse designed by a committee that came out looking like a camel. The agents' offices were barely adequate, and the secretaries and assistants were ensconced in impersonal "areas" separated by low fabric partitions. Privacy was impossible and the employee morale had been instantly lowered when the new building was opened.

That it was diagonally across the street from rival agency ICM was of no moment to the Allied staff. They fervently wished they could return to the comfortable working conditions of their old space.

"How was Garland?" Marcie's secretary Sandy asked. "Hard to say. I guess he talked the talk okay, but whether he's for real, we'll just have to see."

Sandy nodded. "Uh-huh," she said. "But what was he like? Handsome, well dressed, rich, you know?"

Marcie thought for a minute. "I guess you'd say very handsome. Sort of like a young Bob Evans." The reference soared over Sandy's head. Sandy Livingston was 21, a graduate of Hollywood High, and someone who had made living in the moment into a philosophy of life. Her sense of history, whether it pertained to cultural icons, global events or anything in the world around her defined relevance only in terms of what she had personally experienced. Thus, Bob Evans was a reference that held no interest to her.

"Did he make any moves on you?"

"No, he was all business."

"Shit, Marce, you look smashing today. No moves? Do you think he was gay?"

Marcie looked down at the beige Armani suit she had worn and concluded she did look good. Could he have been gay? "I don't know," Marcie said. "He didn't have a wedding ring, whatever that means."

"And you couldn't tell?"

Marcie laughed. "You know I'm the worst. If you weren't here to clue me in, I'd have no idea about any of that."

"Well, what about money?" asked Sandy.

"He was wearing nice clothes, and he talks about damn big numbers, but who knows? Ben seems to think he has Vegas connections. If he puts his money on the table, I'm sure we'll get along fine." Marcie started toward her office. Turning back to Sandy, she said, "Do me a favor and pull a clean script of Michael Lent's *Bent Bodies*. I'll also need his AFI video on ¼ inch. Ben may have that, and I've got to go talk to him anyway. Be back in a minute."

Marcie turned and headed down the hall.

"Is Ben in, June?" Marcie asked Ben's secretary when she reached his office.

"Sure is, hon," June Milstein said, her Brooklyn accent oozing through every pore. "He's on with New York, but he should be getting off in just a second." As June said that, the light on her phone console went out, indicating that Ben was off the phone. June stuck up one finger and buzzed him. "Marcie's here to see you," she said. She looked up. "It's cool. Go right in." "Hey Ben," Marcie began. "Anything happening with the *Bent Bodies* script?"

"And hello to you too," Ben replied. "Yes, I'm doing fine, thanks. Sold a spec script for 250 large this morning, and everything else is right on track."

Marcie nodded, acknowledging Ben's criticism. "I'm sorry, Ben, I really am. I'm racing around to pull together something for Garland and I'm forgetting to be nice to my friends."

Ben smiled. "No sweat," he said. "What are friends for? Tell me about Tim Garland. What was he like?"

"Hard to say. Came on as if money were no object, just the right material. Wants to do personal films that make a lot of money."

"Who doesn't?" laughed Ben.

"I know," said Marcie. "But he did seem genuine."

"Do you think he's playing with funny money?" asked Ben.

"I don't have the foggiest. Sandy thinks he's gay, and you think he's a gangster. This is one helluva new buyer I'm covering."

Ben smiled. "What the hell," he said, we get paid to sell 'em, not smell 'em."

"Amen," said Marcie. "And *Bent Bodies*?"

"It's available," Ben replied. He turned to his bookcase and reached for a copy of the screenplay. "Did you want his AFI tape too?"

"I mentioned it to Tim. I think it helps, don't you?"

"Yeah, I do. This is actually an interesting package, you know?"

"We'll see what our gay gangster thinks," Marcie said.

Leaving Ben's office, Marcie nearly collided with Charles.

"Well," he said impatiently, "what happened with Garland?"

"I was going to call you. He seemed interested in a small package and I'm messengering it over to him now."

"And Sam?"

"I should have his answer today or tomorrow."

"Don't slip up on this one," said Charles, walking away.

Screw you, Marcie thought. When was the last time I "slipped up" on something like this? Small wonder that the agents privately grumbled about the top management at Allied. Charles had no goddamn clue how to motivate people. Was there some other agenda going on with Tim Garland? Maybe Sandy was right, as she often seemed to be. Maybe Tim was gay and connected to Charles in some fashion. Her years in the business convinced her that the gay network was a most pervasive factor in the town, one not to be underestimated.

Marcie returned to her office and sat down at her desk. Sandy buzzed to tell her Chuck Doerge was on the line. Doerge was a personal manager who had risen from the comparative obscurity of representing interchangeable starlets to considerable prominence coattailing the success of his client Heather Ogilvy. Marcie didn't have much use for him, although she certainly didn't know him well. One of the town's better tennis players, she had seen him more on the courts than in business.

"Hey, how're you doing?" he gushed, with that false intimacy that she detested.

"Fine, Chuck, and you?"

"Couldn't be better. I can hardly wait to get to the office every day."

Give me a break, thought Marcie. As a manager, unlike agents, he was allowed to produce the films of his clients. With an "A" list performer like Heather Ogilvy, he was often able to attach himself to her pictures as executive producer for a whopping salary. Of course he was one happy man. The bucks were rolling in.

"What can I do for you?" asked Marcie, already tiring of the call.

"Your client, Sam Glass."

"Yes?"

"I think he has a real chance."

"So do we," Marcie said, a hint of irritation creeping into her voice.

"Well," Doerge continued, "the right situation with a manager could push him over the top. Frankly, Marcie, I'm interested. And, off the record, Heather is also very interested. I know you and I don't know each other all that well, but I trust my instincts. I know we'd make a formidable team."

For an instant, Marcie considered telling him to fuck off. Why make an enemy, she concluded, when she could handle it professionally just as easily?

"Let me speak to Sam about it, okay? I wouldn't be optimistic, though, because he's always resisted the notion that he needed an agent *and* a manager. Call me in a week if you haven't heard from me, but my guess is it doesn't look good."

"If he wants to meet, just let me know," Doerge added. "I have a really good feeling about this, Marcie. And I think you and I could do some great things together."

Was he aware of the double meaning? Marcie was sure it was intentional. What a pig! Of course he didn't need her to call Sam direct. But managers tried to work through agents rather than position them as enemies. Not much chance, she thought, she'd ever be working with Chuck Doerge with her hottest new client. The very idea was repugnant to her.

Calls like Doerge's were an irritant and a waste of time. Marcie checked her watch: 3:30. Her watch was always set fifteen minutes ahead, in the vain hope it would cure her perennial lateness problem. It never seemed to work. Knowing it was set ahead allowed her that much more latitude, in her mind, to continue busying herself before rushing off to her next appointment. Her ex-husband, Bob, had quarreled with her frequently over her penchant for arriving places late. She had made a sincere effort on his behalf, but it rarely proved successful. Her compromise had been allowing herself to be dragged to the airport a half hour before flight time. Left to her own devices, she would arrive as the gate was closing. Perfect timing. This approach produced such anxiety in Bob that she changed to accommodate him. Marcie reflected on the amount of time she and Bob had spent speaking about her lateness as if it were a form of pathology. Marcie saw it more as a fact of life, one that seemed stubbornly resistant to change.

The calls continued to arrive throughout the afternoon. Marcie typically received between 150 and 200 calls a day. This kept her three lines in constant use, put considerable pressure on Sandy, and forced her to leave dozens of calls unreturned. Marcie would have preferred returning everyone's call, but there simply weren't enough hours in the day. As often happened, Marcie took her phone list home and continued trying to catch up until it was too late to call people.

First thing the next morning, before the department meetings began, Sandy told her, "Your new gay blade Mr. Garland is on the phone."

"Did you pick up some juicy information since yesterday?" Marcie asked.

"No," she said, "but I can read 'em a mile away."

Marcie rolled her eyes and pushed the blinking button.

"Tim," Marcie said with considerable enthusiasm. "You're at it very early!"

"I'm a morning person, and there are always people to speak with in New York and Europe."

"Oh," said Marcie, not knowing where else to take the conversation. "Well, what can I do for you?"

"I want you to tell me what you like about *Bent Bodies*."

"You've read it already?"

"Yes, and I also ran Lent's tape, but we'll get to that."

Marcie tried to read Tim's impression of the material. There weren't many clues being put forward. He seemed kind of negative, maybe even a bit menacing, but he had responded quickly. Maybe he had no other life? Maybe he just broke up with his wife and needed the diversion? Maybe Sandy *was* right and he broke up with his boy friend? Better to answer as if he were showing interest, she thought.

"I think Lent is a real talent, a potential super-star," she began. "He knows that the best shot to break in is with the horror genre. He'd like to do it the way Ron Underwood did with *Tremors*. That got him *City Slickers* and then he was off and running. I think *Bent Bodies* has could do this for Lent, and make a pile in the process."

"Doesn't it seem a touch derivative to you?" Tim asked.

Uh-oh, thought Marcie, he *can* read a script. That was a very shrewd comment.

"Sure, it's got a derivative quality," Marcie replied, "but that's the requirement of the genre. I think Lent could be the next Wes Craven. Someone who makes the familiar seem fresh and exciting."

"Not if people think they've seen the movie before," Tim insisted.

"Do you think after looking at Michael's tape that he'd do it like it's been done before?"

"What I think is that he'd do it like a music video. I like my movies to tell a story and to entertain me. That tape you sent me did neither. Frankly, it seemed more like an acid trip than it did a narrative film."

Whew, thought Marcie, he's tough.

"It was a student film," Marcie offered.

"And it shows. I'm going to pass. I'd be happy to look at other things, but I can only hope that this one wasn't the consensus best script in your shop."

"No, no," Marcie protested, "I already know better what your taste is."

"Let me put it as simply as I can. I like quality, whatever the genre. Don't worry about the money. That's my department. If you're going to cover me, I never want to feel you're wasting my time. The project you sent over took two hours out of my life."

"I hear you," said Marcie. "You should know that even though you didn't like it, it *has* gotten a lot of favorable reactions and did win a screenwriting competition. It's not like I sent you *schlock*."

Tim paused, perhaps, Marcie surmised, unused to people who were willing to defend their positions against him.

"Okay," he said at last, "I take your point. Let's see what the next submission brings."

Sandy had walked in and sat down on the sofa during this conversation. Though she only heard Marcie's side of it, she was able to figure out that this was no easy sale.

"He's tough, huh?" Sandy said when Marcie hung up.

"Yes, he is, but more in a demanding way than in an asshole way."

"He's gay," Sandy asserted, with great conviction.

"I don't think so," said Marcie. "I've dealt with plenty of gays who were tough in business. They didn't seem like Tim."

"We'll see," Sandy replied, and walked back to her area outside Marcie's door.

Oh shit, thought Marcie, checking her watch. I'm going to be late again for my hair appointment. She quickly pulled her things together, and started to dash for the door.

"Do me a favor," she called to Sandy. "Call Ben and tell him Garland passed on *Bent Bodies*. Ask Ben to pull together some other scripts to send. Tim prefers personal films, but I think he means quality that makes money. I know, so what else is new?"

"No problem."

"I'll see you later."

As Marcie rushed to make the elevator, its door already hissing shut, she realized how much she hated the phrase "no problem." Maybe Sandy would be good enough to refrain from using it in the office.

It took Marcie ten minutes to get from Allied to her hairdresser. Marcie was one of the last of hair stylist Jose Ebert's customers. All the rage when he first opened his salon on Little Santa Monica, in Beverly Hills, in the 70s, Jose had gradually drifted out of favor, as the trend-setters found new stylists to flaunt. Marcie could still recall her confusion trying to locate Little Santa Monica, a main thoroughfare that paralleled Big Santa Monica, a mere one block to the south.

Marcie had stayed with Jose as much out of inertia as anything. He personally styled her hair, fed her the latest gossip, and talked endlessly about his evolution into a major businessman with product lines and branch salons. As she hurried in for her appointment, a smart forty minutes late, Jose was finishing up with his previous client. The woman, a stunning young redhead with too much jewelry, made the mistake of calling him Jose, as if it were a Spanish name.

"It's J-O-S-E with a hard 'J'!" he screamed.

The woman muttered something about it being only a slip of the tongue and fled into the afternoon sunshine.

"Stupid cow," Jose grumbled as he showed Marcie to the back to get changed for her shampoo.

Two hours later, Marcie emerged feeling good about her hair but anxiety-ridden over her failure to remember to buy her mother a birthday gift. She had intended to do it a week ago, but had gotten sidetracked. Now, with her mother's birthday the day after tomorrow, she'd have to purchase it and FEDEX it to her in time to avoid her mother's dreadful martyrdom performance.

"I know how terribly busy you are," she'd begin. "I don't even want anything this year. I have more than enough, and I do know you were thinking of me. That's all I've ever wanted—your love and good thoughts."

Marcie had been down that road so often there were deep ruts worn into the surface. This wouldn't be the first time she'd mailed a last-minute purchase to her by overnight delivery. Sandy was an ace at the logistics of pulling all that together and getting the package off to

Scarsdale, the suburban community twenty miles north of New York, where her parents had lived for many years. Marcie considered, on her way to pick up her car, mother's going to be 58. No great significance in that. Just a normal birthday. Maybe antique jewelry? She always liked that and Francis Klein, over a few blocks, would certainly have something "appropriate".

Marcie's decision to drive and not walk was validated when she found a place to park on Beverly Drive, across the street from Francis Klein's. She selected an art deco brooch that she would have liked herself. It was an unusual piece, done in black and white enamel, and Marcie felt good about it. She had the salesperson gift-wrap it and then wrap it again in plain brown paper. Sandy would have no trouble getting it off tonight.

Returning to Allied, Marcie deposited the present with Sandy, and pointed her Lexus toward her home off Benedict Canyon Drive. Her mind turned again to her mother, that powerful woman who had shaped so much of her life. Why hadn't she been able to please her? Whether her success had come in the classroom, on the tennis court, in business, or in her marriage, it had never been enough to gain the approval she desperately sought.

"Oh that's nice," her mother had said so often. "I'm so pleased you're doing well at your *little* job." Or course work, or tennis match, or anything else at which she had excelled. Was it simply jealousy? Was it lack of parenting skills? Some darker motivation that she could only speculate on? This was the ongoing riddle of her relationship with her mother.

How would her life have changed if her mother had acknowledged her victories and instilled a sense of confidence in her? She could only guess. For an instant, as the light changed at Sunset and she proceeded up Benedict Canyon, Marcie permitted herself to consider the possibility that her mother blamed her for the death of Rob. Of course, her mother had insisted that this was certainly not true. Ten years had passed since that terrible day, and still Marcie couldn't be sure of what her mother felt.

And Marcie's father? He had risen to a position of semi-prominence at a major New York bank and retreated discreetly into the dark wood paneling of his office. He stayed out of the firing line at home, tending his garden and paying more attention to his golf handicap than to his wife and daughter. He deferred to Marcie's mother when it came to parenting concerns, and although Marcie knew her father was indeed proud of her, she harbored more than a little resentment over his inability to tell her so.

Marcie had effectively withdrawn from the parental battleground after her marriage to Bob collapsed. Paralyzed by the tragedy that precipitated the divorce, Marcie simply had no time and no energy to confront issues with her mother. By disengaging, the game had come to a screeching halt. No, her mother was not suddenly supportive and nurturing, but the hard edges between them wore down to rounded surfaces. Maybe this working truce would have arisen inevitably, but it was the one positive benefit that Marcie could take from this darkest period of her life.

As she swung the Lexus into the small circular drive in the front of her house, her mind shifted away from her parents, back to the day's events. She'd try to get Sam to decide which picture he wanted tonight. And as for Tim, that was a hard one to call. Charles seemed pretty insistent about him, but Marcie had seen so many "wannabes" come through town. Maybe he was for real. We'll know soon enough, she thought.

Chapter III

Marcie arrived breathlessly to the meeting of the department heads. She had hoped not to be the only one late, but to her chagrin, she observed that everyone else was seated around the conference table and that she had walked in the middle of some kind of lecture by Charles.

"Excuse me," Marcie said, as she pulled up a chair to the table.

Charles glowered at her, indicating his displeasure. "We're all terribly happy you could make it," he said.

"I'm sorry," Marcie muttered, pouring herself a cup of coffee from the carafe on the table.

Seated around the table were the various department heads of Allied. Marcie was present as the head of the Talent Department, the agents representing actors and actresses. In the traditional agency terminology, talent were separated from the writers and directors who were referred to as literary clients. Marcie's title was without real authority or responsibility. She chaired the weekly meeting of the agents working in this field, but that was about it. It did not provide her with entree to the Executive Committee which shaped the agency's direction. Significantly, there were no women members of that august group. Marcie had reconciled herself to this reality, taking some comfort from the salary and perks she received from the company. The bonus structure was very liberal and she knew that a couple more clients like Sam could yield major returns for her.

"Well, Marcie," Charles said, addressing himself to her as if she were alone in the room, "we were discussing our failure to sign new clients."

This was an ongoing agency concern. While a modest game of musical chairs was always going on with the major agency clients, the tempo of the game had undergone a dramatic increase. The departure of CAA's Mike Ovitz and Ron Meyer for studio pastures had triggered a fierce competition to sign new clients. Charles's remarks suggested that he wanted a greater effort from the agency executives in this direction.

"How about you, Randy?" Charles asked, turning to Randy Goldberg. Randy was the hotshot television packager whose ambitions were matched by his tremendous success in racking up huge numbers in the television business. Handsome, with piercing dark eyes, Randy had a hardness about his mouth that inspired confidence and some degree of fear. He commanded respect not only at Allied, but also throughout the industry.

Charles continued. "Who are you working on?"

Randy took a breath, returned Charles's steely look, and responded, "Kevin Costner and Michael Douglas."

The room was suddenly very still. Marcie wondered how this had been going on and she had heard nothing about it. Not even from Sandy who normally would have rushed to her with news as dramatic as this.

"And?" Charles said, breaking the uneasy silence.

"And I have calls into both of them," said Randy, as the room erupted into laughter.

Charles waited a moment, his face never cracking a smile, then continued. "Now that we've had our moment of levity, let's get back to the business of the day."

"Maybe one of you has an idea for Catherine Sampson," Marcie said. She was referring to her client, a somewhat older leading lady who was no longer able to get the parts that used to be routinely offered to her.

"What about cable movies?" Peter Tacy, the agent in charge of that area, asked. "She's the kind of half-assed name they go for."

"I think if the project's right, she would leap at it," replied Marcie.

"Give me a break," Randy interrupted. "That cooze would be lucky to work at all."

Marcie felt herself coloring at Randy's reference. "I don't think that's appropriate language, or any way to speak about our client," she snapped.

Randy shrugged. "I give a fuck what you think," he said quietly.

Marcie looked to Charles, who remained impassive. Fine, she thought. Welcome to the Allied Boys Club.

"I'm pretty sure she's been talking to UTA," Marcie went on, "and we're in danger of losing her unless we get her something very soon. No matter what Randy thinks, she can still generate a lot of commissions for the company."

"Let me check some things and get back to you later this morning," said Tacy.

"Great, I appreciate it."

"Anything else?" asked Charles, looking around the table. Getting no answer, he went on, "Okay, let's get to work."

Marcie stood to leave. Charles rose and moved toward her. "Give me five minutes to get organized, and then come up, will you?" He didn't wait for her response.

She returned to her office to find Sandy deep in conversation on the telephone. Sandy had more information at her finger tips than the trades, and it was generally more reliable. Seeing Marcie, Sandy cut short her call saying, "Coffee?"

"No thanks, Charles has summoned me."

"Lucky you. It's all quiet on this front. See you when you get back."

Marcie left Sandy's area on her way to see Charles. She headed up the fire stairs rather than waiting for the elevator. On the next floor were the offices of the agency biggies, with Charles appropriately situated in the northwestern corner overlooking L.A. Country Club to the north and the ocean to the west. She passed through his outer office where two secretaries and an assistant tried to look busy dividing what should have been the workload of one well-trained executive secretary. In the trenches, on the lower floors, agents would kill for a little secretarial help to move the mountains of paperwork along, but these inefficiencies were simply built into the system. Marcie looked questioningly at Charles' main person, the redoubtable Edith Merrihew, the only woman addressed as "Ms." in the organization. She got back a small smile, Ms. Merrihew liked Marcie and waved her on.

Marcie knocked lightly on the closed door and peeked her head in. "Come on in," boomed out Charles Maier. "We were just speaking about you. You probably felt your ears burning." Marcie wondered whether there was anyone else left on the planet who still referred to "ears burning." She entered the office, known throughout the agency as "The Little Leather House of Horrors" after Maier's penchant for leather wall treatments and rich leather furniture. Seated around a coffee table in one corner of the large office were Maier, Derek Robinson, the agency president who was one of the biggest television packagers in the industry's history, and Maier's executive assistant, Larry Bennett.

This group also played an active role in the signing of new clients, usually those with some established credits who could be put to work immediately. The larger the agency, the less likely it was that they would sign an unknown. The large agencies left that thankless pursuit to the myriad smaller agencies, finding it more cost effective to swoop in when clients had gained some foothold in the industry. It would have been extremely difficult for Marcie to convince this group to sign Sam Glass had she not taken a shot and brought him to meet with the director Sydney Pollack first.

"Are you coffeed out after our meeting?" began Maier.

"No," said Marcie. "Black, please."

Charles looked in Larry's direction, and like the well trained servant he was, he silently rose and went to the coffee service on a credenza along the wall. Marcie accepted the cup from Larry with a smile, noting as always the beautiful bone china that graced Charles' office.

"Have you read your trades yet?" Charles asked, referring to the daily publications of *Variety* and *The Hollywood Reporter*.

"No, I've been in the meeting since I got here." Marcie hoped he wouldn't bring up her lateness again.

"There's a column item in the *Reporter* about Sam Glass signing on to do the Altman film at Fox. I thought we talked about that at Spagos."

Marcie put down her cup. "We did, Charles, and nothing's changed since then."

Charles picked up *The Hollywood Reporter* from the table and flipped through it to find the column.

"Don't tell me you've started believing what you read in the trades," Marcie quipped.

"Just checking. But seriously Marcie, Derek and I were going over again the importance to Allied of the Warners picture. With Sam as the linchpin, we think we have a real shot at Peter Weir. It'd be some kind of a coup."

"I like Weir a lot," Marcie said thoughtfully.

Charles started to cut her off, but Marcie continued. "Since we're looking at a million from Fox, I think the clincher would be if we can get Warners up to a million five."

Charles looked quickly at Derek, but his face was expressionless, the perfect poker player.

Edith buzzed Charles on the intercom.

"Yes?" Charles said, a touch of irritation in his voice.

"It's Dave."

"Tell him I'll call him back in five minutes. I'm in an important meeting."

Marcie considered that for a beat as Charles peered at her over the half-glasses he used for reading. "You're not trying to hustle a hustler, are you?"

Marcie knew she had him convinced. Time to be collegial, one of the guys. She'd drop a few choice profanities into her speech. That seemed to make them comfortable. "Shit, Charles, you know he's worth that on the open market. Fuckin' David Caruso got a mill and he was fresh out of a damn TV show. Sam is the hottest actor in Hollywood right now and you know it. If Warners wants him, with a little persuasion from you, they'll go $1.5."

Her words hung in the air. Derek seemed preoccupied, while Larry made notes on a yellow pad. Larry always made notes on a yellow pad. Charles was a believer in a clean desk. He kept his appointment calendar in front of him together with an open box of note cards with his name engraved across the top. He was famous for firing off brief notes to the employees, and moving everything else along to the overworked Larry Bennett for processing.

"I'm meeting Nat Shapiro from Warners at the Ivy at 1:00. If you can get the offer raised before then, maybe I can wrap everything up before dessert."

Larry was scribbling furiously as Charles weighed her words. After a few seconds, Charles nodded. "Call me as soon as lunch is over. I may be in the car, but Edith will patch you through."

Marcie rose to leave. "I'm sure it'll make, Charles. I'll get back to you."

"Just a second," said Charles. "Bring me up to speed on Tim Garland."

Oh yeah, thought Marcie. Tim Garland. "I think things are going okay. He passed on my first submission, but I'm still trying. Ben's been helping."

"Keep on it," said Charles, "he's important."

She left them as she had found them, staring at one another across the coffee table. I wonder what makes Tim so damn important, she thought.

Arriving downstairs at her office, Marcie found Sandy wrestling valiantly with the phones. All three of her lines were lit up, two of them blinking furiously. Marcie passed through her secretary's area into the brightness of her sun-drenched office. Decorated in white with yellow

and aqua accents, her office featured a kidney-shaped glass desk sus-
pended on a graceful pedestal. Two vases of fresh flowers, that were
changed every week, created a feeling of warmth which, along with the
general airiness and lightness, seemed quite unlike the high-powered
deals that were made there.

Already the day's call list had begun to take shape. Not counting the
thirty-odd calls left over from yesterday, there were another twenty-two
calls so far that morning. And that didn't count the three callers that
Sandy was now processing. You couldn't be an agent if you weren't willing to consider the telephone an appendage to your body. Marcie and
many other agents complained regularly how much they hated the telephone, but no one took them seriously. Indeed Marcie logged in so
much office time on the phone that she had taken to wearing a state-of-
the-art headphone and mic set to keep both hands free and to avoid
painful constrictions in her shoulders and neck.

Marcie ran her eye down the call list left by Sandy on her desk, paying special attention to the names Sandy had starred, then checked her
calendar for the rest of the day. She sat back and took a deep breath.
Great, she thought, time for a couple minutes of meditative breathing.
She inhaled deeply, extending her abdomen out as far as she could, held
her breath, and slowly let her breath out through her nose. She repeated the process several more times, pleased that it produced an immediate calming effect in her head. She was a big believer in stress reduction
techniques and spiritual pursuits, but rarely gave herself ample time to
engage in them. The best stress reducer for her remained exercise. From
her morning workouts to the satisfaction she felt when one of her first
calls of the day had confirmed her tennis match at Riviera Country
Club that night, she knew that at least the physical end of her life was
well covered.

Sandy came striding in, pad in hand. "Your ten o'clock has been waiting patiently in the lobby. Nat Shapiro asked to move lunch to the
Warners Executive Dining Room at one, something about dailies."

Sandy flopped down on the sofa next to the extension phone so that she could field incoming calls.

Looking up at Sandy, Marcie said, "Tell Nat Warners is fine and I'll meet him at the commissary. I hate getting trapped in his office. Any response from the Forum on the Lakers seats?" Sandy shook her head. "Twist their arms a little, will you? Tell them your job depends on it." That always seemed to work with civilized people on the other end of the phone. "Oh, and tell my ten o'clock to come up, please."

Marcie had agreed to see Gail Donovan, a friend of a classmate from Smith, Ms. Donovan was trying her hand at screenwriting after forging a career as a copywriter for an ad agency. She had submitted her screenplay beforehand and Marcie had read it as a favor. She would be polite, but her best advice to Ms. Donovan was to keep her daytime job.

Sandy stood, and headed out to get Gail Donovan. Marcie had the thought to dial Ben and have a brief strategy session with him regarding Tim Garland. As she reached for the telephone, Sandy opened the door and ushered a striking brunette woman into Marcie's office.

"Hello, I'm Gail Donovan," the woman said, extending her hand toward Marcie. "I'm very grateful you're seeing me."

"It's nice to meet you. Won't you sit down?"

"I know you're busy, but I'd really appreciate an opinion on my script. My friends are very positive, but they're not out here doing what you do."

Marcie took the screenplay titled *Serenade in Black* from her desk and riffled through it, as if scanning it again.

"It's nicely written, very professional in appearance."

"But-" said Gail.

"But it's too soft for this market. With the right elements, you might get some interest from Miramax, but I doubt it. It's a shame that a nice, small film won't get a reception today, but that's the bottom line. My best advice is to try to raise the money privately."

"Do you think the script is worth fighting for?"

"Frankly, no. I don't think it's special enough to hold its own out there. If I were you, I'd put it aside and start a new one. Maybe come back to it later when you've written a couple more. I'm sorry. I know that's not what you wanted to hear."

Gail rose and took the script that Marcie handed her. "No, but it's very helpful. Thank you again. I'll be sure to tell Anne I saw you."

As Gail left the room, Marcie called to Sandy, "See if you can get Ben. Then, Fred Sherman and Jane Pratt. Okay?"

She'd been a fan, along with Siskel and Ebert and many others, of Fred Sherman for a long time. Although he kept working, he had never broken through to the top of the "A" list of directors. Maybe now he could be had. Other agents had been cherry-picking ICM powerhouse agent Sam Cohn's list for some time. It wouldn't hurt a bit to take a stab at landing Sherman. She knew exactly what to say to him if he would agree to meet. As for Pratt, she wanted to run the Sam Glass situation by her. No one in town, agent, executive, or manager, understood the client advancement game like Pratt. Completely trustworthy, always circumspect, Jane was one of the town's leading public relations representatives. She had a retiring Southern manner that masked a shrewdly incisive, hugely experienced outlook on how to plot the career of talent. Operating quietly behind the scenes, she had positioned many artists into becoming mega-stars. Marcie had a profound respect for her opinion.

Marcie picked up her *Variety* and thumbed through it quickly. Required reading, she conceded, but hardly the place you would turn seeking truth. Experienced Hollywood hands were able to separate truth from rumor or simple disinformation. It was a necessary skill to possess, and one that Marcie had learned very quickly. Nothing to note in the news today, she concluded. They panned the new DiPalma film, but Hollywood watchers had written that off months ago. Several second-tier agency clients, thankfully not with Allied, had jumped ship and re-signed with another agency. Boring. And the development head for Rudy Scott had left to take a studio position. What took him so long?

Sandy buzzed her to say she had Sherman on the line. "How are you?" Marcie asked. It turned out Sandy had reached him on a mixing stage where he was posting his latest film, an unpromising remake of a Cary Grant comedy starring Michael Keaton. "It's been a long time," she went on. "I was hoping I could buy you a lunch." Sherman made some randy remark before agreeing to lunch the following Monday. Typical, Marcie thought, of most of the Aussies. You can take the boy out of Australia, but you can't take Australia out of the boy. He certainly knew the lunch invitation was not a sexual come-on, but rather part of the agency-client ritual. Yet this macho crap would allow him to hear her pitch without appearing anxious to make a move.

Jane Pratt was out, and Marcie took a call from Stan Bazelton, number two creative guy at Universal. He was a good guy, Marcie thought, but buyer or not, if he calls me "Hon" again, I'm going to make an issue of it. Sandy's double buzz meant he was on the line. She punched the lit button, and began to file a broken nail while listening through her headset.

"Hi Hon," he began.

"Stan," she said, a note of irritation in her voice. "I'd really appreciate it if you wouldn't call me Hon. Try Marcie or something more suitable. I hope you understand. Hon is not something I want to respond to."

There was a moment's pause as he fumbled for a suitable reply. Finding none, he said, in a chastened tone, "Sure, sorry if I offended you."

"No big deal," she said, taking him somewhat off the hook.

Stan had called in response to a book she'd sent over to him. Not a huge bestseller when it was published a few years before, Marcie had nonetheless enjoyed it. It was a big action thriller with a great part for a male protagonist. If Universal was in business with Stallone, then maybe this could fit into their plans. The author was an Allied client, but the literary department seemed not to think much of the notion. Fine, Marcie had concluded, she'd do it herself.

Stan allowed as he and some of the guys had read it and shown it to Stallone's people. "We like it, we do, if the price is right."

Marcie smiled. Yes! Pay dirt! "We want to be fair, Stan," she said.

"It's been around for several years, you know," Stan said hopefully.

"My problem is that its time has come. We're getting great interest submitting it this time around. I'd like to see it with Universal though, because the fit is perfect. What about $300,000 against $650,000 and 5% of the net?"

She was seeking an option on the film rights to the novel for $300,000 for one year, with an additional $350,000 required to purchase the rights, plus 5% of the net profits of the film. Pretty stiff, she knew, for a book that had been gathering dust for three years. Yet if Stallone's people liked it, her numbers were certainly in the ballpark for a Stallone picture that had to cost $75 million to make.

They danced for thirty minutes on the phone, pursuing the fine art of negotiation, one of Marcie's favorite pastimes. She knew she was good at it. Like a talented baseball pitcher, she had a large repertoire of deliveries with which to keep her adversary off guard. She could be very tough, sweet and demure, funny, or sexy, as the situation warranted. The deal was preeminent, she felt, and the rest was just posturing. Her games were always more effective with men who began such a negotiation erroneously thinking they had the upper hand because of their gender. How absurd. Marcie knew their fatal weakness was always the same. They wanted, even needed, to be liked. This allowed the disciplined negotiator for the other side to play them like a piano. Being liked, at this time, was of no moment for Marcie. She was focused on the deal and making it as good for the agency's client as possible.

In the end, they struck a deal at $250,000 for the first year's option, renewable for a second year for an additional $150,000, against a purchase price of $550,000 plus 2 1/2% of the net. Marcie knew, even if

Stan didn't, that there was no way in hell that this could be ready to go in a year. Assuming they made the picture with the option renewed once, her client would be taking home a tidy sum on a book that he'd forgotten about. The other nice part of this was that if it became a big Stallone action film, the author's paperback company would republish the novel all over the world which could bring in considerably more money to the author's coffers.

She wrote up the billing slip so the agency records would reflect the deal, and she would get credit for it when bonuses were computed at year end. When she called the literary department to report her success, she suggested that Andrea Vickers, the author's responsible agent, might want to call him to tell him the news. Marcie had never met the author and had no intention of doing so. Actors and actresses, and the occasional director, were her area. This had been a flyer that worked. "Of course," she told Andrea, "the contracts should be directed to you. You have the client responsibility." Marcie made it sound warm, generous, and supportive. Andrea would not have been wrong had she listened to the little voice within her that suggested that she was being patronized.

Marcie checked her watch, eleven o'clock. Slow day, she mused. She'd only made the company $25,000 commission. Her mood was interrupted when a beautiful woman, Cindy Ullom, popped her head into her office. An agent in the Commercials Department, Cindy said, "Caught you on the tube the other night at the Awards," Cindy said in her unfailingly sexy manner. "What a hunk Sam is."

"You're saying I was chopped liver?"

"Not at all, it's just he's to die for. Is he seeing anybody?" Cindy asked hopefully.

"He just split up with his girlfriend, as a matter of fact."

"Really? I wonder if you could arrange…"

Marcie broke in, "Actually, Cindy, there *is* another woman in the picture. But should anything change, I'll be sure you get introduced."

Cindy smiled graciously. "You're the greatest, Marce, you really are." Cindy turned and left Marcie's office, humming a tune to herself.

Marcie shook her head. It would be a long time before she put Sam together with that predator. Maybe she should have told her that, she mused. No, why go out of your way to create an enemy? Just keep them apart, and it's business as usual.

At 12:40, Marcie was in the 300 Lexus that the company leased as part of her deal, making her way to Burbank for lunch with Nat. She loved to drive, which was a good thing since agents visited buyers and the Los Angeles market was spread out over a considerable distance. She invariably had a new novel which she listened to on her CD player, while making constant use of her mobile phone, equipped with the latest in speaker attachments and call waiting. She carried a small Braun recorder in the compartment next to the driver's seat to memorialize deals she negotiated in the car, or simply to record thoughts she didn't want to forget. With the press of Los Angeles traffic, this frantic activity might have exhausted many, but the whole experience was exhilarating to Marcie. She checked her watch. "Shit," she said softly, knowing she was once again going to be late.

From the Beverly Hills office of Allied, it took about as long getting to the Valley via the San Diego Freeway as it did going through Hollywood. Marcie preferred the latter route, having a distinct aversion to the L.A. freeway system. She was convinced that with the various shortcuts she took, she could get to Burbank five to ten minutes faster her way on surface streets than by the freeways. She reckoned that over time this had made her much more productive in her work than others who squandered precious time waiting in traffic.

Nat had left her a drive-on, which allowed her to drive onto the lot and park close to the executive dining room. She was grateful for this courtesy as it shortened the distance from her car to where she expected Nat to be waiting. She strode quickly to the dining facility, threw open the door, and her eyes took in the room. Executives, agents, a few stars headed by Kevin Costner who sat with a Warners honcho, but no Nat Shapiro. He arrived seconds later, breathlessly apologizing, saying he couldn't get off an overseas call. Without waiting to be seated, he ushered them to his usual table and politely pulled her chair out for her. Marcie was pleased that he was later than she.

"Thank you, Nat," Marcie said. "I'm glad that chivalry is alive and well at Warners."

Nat smiled and summoned the waiter over. Apparently this meal fit into fairly precise time parameters. That was fine with Marcie because Nat had little if anything to talk about except the deal of the moment. A former agent himself, he was the embodiment of the notion that the deal was king. Not the material, not the director's vision, but the deal. He had been a great packager of talent in his agency days, and he was a respectable studio topper in his second year on the job at Warners. He had excellent relationships in the creative community and delighted in putting together films that looked to be blockbusters on paper. If he put half the effort into the script that he did into assembling the director and principal cast, he'd have been unstoppable.

"So," Nat began after they ordered, "I'm really happy for you." Marcie looked at him questioningly. "Your client, Mr. Glass, looks like he has a big career ahead of him."

"Yes, there's a lot of heat on him right now. The next film is critical, we think."

"Absolutely," Nat went on enthusiastically. "We've got much to talk about. Peter Weir committed this morning, and we're looking at a couple of "A" list women. Speaking very frankly, Sam is our first choice for the lead."

"He likes the script, Nat, and he's a fan of Weir. But we're sitting with another firm offer and he is very tempted. You know how it is. I really need some ammunition to sell him. I'd like nothing more than for him to have a relationship with Warners."

Their salads arrived, and Nat stared at his thoughtfully. "It's hard now," he began. "We're in the middle of an austerity drive at the studio. Shareholder concerns and all that, you know."

Marcie chewed her Cobb salad very deliberately knowing the conversation had reached its critical juncture.

"I talked it over with the guys this morning and we'd be prepared to reach for a million and a quarter, with first star billing."

Marcie took in the figure. Had Charles spoken to them, she wondered? She bet anything he had. If they'd go to $1.25 million, she was sure they'd go to $1.5. "That's a very respectable offer, Nat, I can't say it isn't. And you know I'd really like it to work." She paused and took another mouthful.

"But" Nat replied.

"But I don't know if I can make it happen for that." Marcie paused again and took a sip of her black coffee.

"They'll probably have my ass for this, but I'll go to $1.5. I'm going to leave that on the table until close of business today. Any problems?"

Marcie smiled. "No, I don't think so. I'm meeting with Sam this afternoon and I'll call you then."

"I'm out of dailies around two fifteen, and I'll have my girl put you through whenever you call. I'm counting on you, Marcie. This can be huge for everyone."

Marcie kissed Nat goodbye, and headed out into the glare of a sunny, Burbank afternoon. "His girl," she thought. Why is this politically correct stuff starting to get to me? I've got a million and a half offer on the table for Sam Glass, and I'm concerned about him calling his secretary "his girl." What the hell is the matter with me?

Marcie got back into her Lexus and turned back toward Beverly Hills. She had Sandy on the phone before she got to the Warners gate.

"All the calls can wait," she told her. "Find Sam and get him into the office right away. Yes, it's very important." Marcie asked to be switched to Charles Maier. She told Edith to please patch her through to Charles's car.

"How did it go?" he asked.

Accustomed to his brusqueness, she responded, "They offered $1.5 and first star billing. The offer's good until close of business."

"Make the goddamned deal, Marcie!"

Marcie started to reply when the dial tone informed her that Charles had already hung up. Even Mr. Warmth couldn't cheat her out of feeling good at this moment. She'd gotten Sam up to a million and a half dollars in just two pictures. If this turned out to be all that Warners thought, he could move right up there with the top male stars.

She greeted Sandy, as she arrived back at Allied, and Sandy immediately picked up on her good mood. "Sam should be here any minute," she said. "I guess things went well with Nat."

"It was a home run," said Marcie. "I just hope Sam doesn't pick this time to get cute. We need a yes today."

Sam was his bubbly self as he arrived in jeans and a tee shirt. Marcie could hear the buzz as he came down the hall after Sandy got him from the reception area. Cindy wasn't the only woman (or man) in the office who wanted to jump on Sam's bones. When he got his problems worked out, she was sure he'd be a divine lover. Until then, better to work on the business side of things. He bounced into her office, kissed her a friendly hello, and asked if he could have a diet soda. His eyes were bright and she was pleased to see that there were no ill effects from their evening together.

"What's up, boss?" he asked.

"We owe Warners an answer by this afternoon," she said.

"That's pretty quick, isn't it? I'm still thinking about both scripts. You said this was a really important decision."

"It is," Marcie agreed. "But Warners has put a million five on the table. That, and Peter Weir, and first star billing."

Sam sank back into the sofa. Marcie could see the enormity of $1.5 million flitting about his brain.

"Wow, that's a lot of money," he finally said. "Who's the female lead?"

"She's not set, but they say they're talking to "A" list actresses."

"Do you think they'll let me approve her?"

"I doubt it, but I know I can get you a right of consultation before they hire anyone. They'll want the chemistry to work between you."

"A million and a half, huh"?"

"Not bad for a B-School student I sat next to on a plane, is it?"

"You're amazing, Marcie. I can't believe they're willing to pay me that kind of money for ten weeks work. I don't think my dad made that working his whole life building airplanes. And you think it's the right move?" he asked earnestly.

"Weir is a terrific director and Warners is a fabulous place to build a relationship. Yeah, I think it's the way to go."

Sam seemed almost relieved to have the decision made for him. He beamed at Marcie. "So what are we waiting for? Let's do it."

As she rose to say goodbye, Sam bounded over to her and gave her a big embrace. He kissed her warmly saying, "Thanks, you're the greatest."

Remember you said that, Marcie thought, as Sam waved from the doorway and headed out to the elevator with Sandy running interference.

The remainder of the day moved along quickly. Charles Maier called in from Malibu for an update on the Warners situation. He seemed pleased when she reported she had just hung up with Nat and had confirmed the deal.

"Congratulations," he exclaimed. "This could be very big for Allied."

Beyond Sam's commission, wondered Marcie?

Charles continued. "I'm in the process of signing Julia Ormond. She'd be perfect for this, don't you think?"

"I do like her, Charles, but Warners says they want someone from the "A" list, and Ormond's a bit of a reach."

Even before Sam responded, Marcie grasped the larger strategy. This was a two-step dance. Charles delivers Sam, who Warners desperately wants, and they agree to take Ormond for the female lead, someone who Charles is trying to sign. Charles is then able to persuade Ormond that Allied could build her career to the next level, starting immediately. He comes back with an offer to co-star in a Warners film opposite Sam Glass. Ormond signs with Allied, Sam gets big bucks from Warners, Warners gets hot casting for their new film, and everyone's happy. It's the classic win-win situation. And maybe, if all went well, Peter Weir might be lured into the Allied fold as well. Damn, Charles was right. It *was* a big deal for Allied.

"I'll speak with Sam about Julia," Marcie went on. "You know that Sam only has a right of consultation, but I'd like him to be enthusiastic about her. I don't think there'll be any problem."

"See that there isn't."

Marcie found herself listening to a dial tone. In Charles's typical fashion, he had simply hung up. No goodbye, no compliment, just do your business and get off. She replaced the receiver, thinking that it would all work out. This was a big break for Sam, whether it worked to the benefit of Allied or not. She'd close it up with him tonight, after he came back from the gym and she finished her tennis game. A glance at her watch told her that she was on the verge of being late for the game. While Riviera Country Club wasn't that far away, she did have to contend with the rush hour traffic.

Marcie flew past Sandy telling her she'd see her in the morning. In seconds, she was in and out of the elevator, into the Lexus, and headed west to Riviera. Only a few minutes late, she observed, as she gave the keys to the parking attendant and hurried off to change her clothes in the Ladies Locker Room, before taking to the courts.

As a former ranking intercollegiate player, Marcie was always in demand for doubles games. Generally she played with three men because the level of social play, especially in the movie community, was pretty shabby. To her amusement, the town divided itself, as with the casting and director lists, into "A", "B", and "C" categories. In any other place, the "B" players would be considered "C" material, but in a town where ego ruled, this was not the case. Marcie had seriously considered a career as a touring pro until she had blown out a knee in her senior year at Smith. Now, she wore a support wrap over the knee and wished she were back on the friendly clay courts in the East where she had grown up, instead of the unforgiving hard courts of Southern California. She tended to play doubles instead of singles as it saved wear and tear on the bad knee. She had kept her game in good shape, even adding a wicked slice serve that drove her opponents crazy. Although she didn't hit with the power of one of the Williams sisters, she played a solid, heady game that rarely included unforced errors.

Tonight she and Ben Kloster were playing two motion picture agents from CAA. As they warmed up, she switched sides with Ben, taking the backhand side of the court. She could hit slice and top-spin backhands, while Ben fought to get it over the net. The rest of his game was all serve and volley, and he did that with considerable skill.

While the pretense was that this was a casual game, only for the exercise, both teams knew better. The rivalry between the two agencies was intense, and lurked very much in the background as the players warmed up. It didn't surprise her that her opponents had already heard about Sam's deal at Warners, and suspected they would be losing Julia to Allied if she headed for that project as well.

"Why don't we play for Ormond?" one of her opponents suggested.

"I don't get it," Ben said.

"I'll fill you in afterwards," Marcie said to Ben. "Let's whip their asses."

Marcie didn't believe in sharing information with her competitors, and focused completely on the game.

Ben was an acceptable player who hit his share of winners to go along with his errors. As the second set got underway, Marcie quietly suggested, "Ben, why don't you put the power game on hold for a bit?"

"Come on, Marce, it's the strongest part of my game."

"I know," she said softly, "but these guys are really in bad shape. Let's try a few lobs and drop shots. I think their tongues will be hanging out."

Ben smiled and nodded. He followed her advice and as she predicted, they went through their opponents very quickly. In short order, they
were all at the net shaking hands.

"I thought we were coming out to hit tennis balls," the more out of
shape of their opponents gasped.

"We just did," Ben answered.

"Those lobs and dinks are pussy tennis," he continued. Suddenly
conscious of Marcie's presence, he mumbled a half-hearted apology.

"Maybe you're right," Marcie said. "We were trying to win, not see
who could hit the ball harder."

Amidst the nervous laughter, Marcie declined their invitation to buy
her a drink after they had showered.

"I've still got stuff to do," she said.

Marcie stopped for a minute to speak with Ben outside the Men's
Locker Room. She quickly filled him in on the Warners situation.

"Whew!" Ben responded. "That's some kind of price for your second
picture."

"I think Charles played a role behind the scenes."

"Whatever, it's still terrific."

Marcie smiled and nodded. "What do you think we should show
Garland next?" she asked Ben.

"Let me think about it over night, and we'll talk first thing tomorrow.
Okay?"

"That's fine," Marcie said. "Oh, and good playing tonight. It was a
good win." Marcie gave Ben a friendly kiss on the cheek and moved
away toward the locker room. Stripping off her sweaty tennis clothes,
she felt the physical satisfaction of breaking a sweat in a competitive
workout. As she let the hot water in the shower beat down on her, her
mind went to the call she still had to make to Sam. I mustn't let him
think I'm hustling him into something. I've got to go as slowly as he
requires when I speak to him.

Dressed, and once more in her car, she drove out to Sunset, and headed home. With Sam's deal all but put to bed, she found herself thinking about Tim Garland. There was something about him. So far, she was unable to really read him. Something about him interested her, but even that was tough to pin down. I sure don't want to spend much more time with him if he's not for real, she concluded.

Chapter IV

Marcie felt much better. Tennis, especially winning tennis, did that for her. She had warmed a quiche, thrown together a salad, poured herself a glass of chardonnay, and climbed into bed. In her freshly laundered nightgown, she sat with her bed table on her lap feeling quite comfortable. She had the radio tuned to the classical music station, but kept the volume soft. Still work to be done before the day was completely hers.

"Hello," Sam answered on the second ring.

"Hi, it's me," Marcie said.

"What's happening with our deal? Problems?" There was a note of anxiety creeping into Sam's voice.

"No way," insisted Marcie, "this one's a slam dunk."

"That's great. Still a million five?"

"Still a million five."

"Whew," Sam sighed. "Those are like telephone book numbers."

"I know, but you deserve it. I want you to know that Warner's is starting to lean toward Julia Ormond to play opposite you." Marcie paused to gauge his reaction.

"You said they wanted an "A" list actress."

"They think the chemistry would be terrific between you. And Julia is one picture away from being on the "A" list anyway."

Sam was quiet for a moment. Marcie could hear his brain whirring. "What do you think?" he said finally.

"I'm a big fan of hers," Marcie replied. "I loved her opposite Brad Pitt in *Legends of the Fall*, and I think she'd be great with you. It looks like Peter Weir is about set as well and he's hot to put her in the picture."

"I was afraid of this."

"Of what?" Marcie asked, not liking where the conversation was headed.

"Of something like this. I don't have any control of the situation."

"Sam, come on. This is your second picture. No, you don't have control yet. That comes later when you've paid your dues. The main thing is that you're surrounded by talent. Julia Ormond and Peter Weir are the big leagues. You should be jumping up and down, not sounding depressed."

"I don't know. I feel like I'm being hustled into this."

"Come on, Sam. Trust me on this. It's a major project at a great studio with first-rate talent. You're getting one and a half, with first star billing. This is a great career move."

"I'm going to go with your judgment, Marcie. You seem very sure. But I'm not exactly a happy camper."

"This is all going to work out famously," Marcie said. "A few jitters are to be expected. By tomorrow, when the whole thing sinks in, you'll be the happiest guy in town."

"I don't know. I really don't."

Sam hung up the phone leaving Marcie with an empty feeling. She hated to say "trust me" to her clients. It invariably covered some undisclosed part of the story. Should she have told Sam that Julia was now an Allied client? Did it make any difference? She hoped it didn't, believing that the package was indeed the right step in Sam's career. That it also benefited Allied was simply a win-win outcome.

The phone rang. Oh no, Marcie thought, he's having another anxiety attack.

"Hello," Marcie said, trying to keep her voice upbeat.

"Hello, darling, I'm surprised to get you on the first try."

"Hello, mom," Marcie said, pleased it *wasn't* Sam.

"I wanted to say thank you for the lovely pin. It was a wonderful surprise."

"You're very welcome, and happy birthday! Are you having a nice one?"

"Yes, it has been a good day. I've been looking at that pin and, you know, it almost looks old."

"Mom, it is old. That's the whole idea."

"Sort of like a used car?"

"Maybe," Marcie smiled to herself, "but more like a painting from another time."

"Whatever. It's the thought that counts."

What a triumph, thought Marcie. It's great to have such an unerring sense of one's mother's taste. Always wrong.

"Well, happy birthday, mom. I love you."

"I love you too, darling."

Marcie hung up the phone feeling the same frustration she had felt so many times before with her mother. She was never able to please her. Never able to connect the way she had always assumed mothers and daughters did. Still, it was early, and it was a rare free night. She'd get another glass of wine and read something for pleasure, and not for business. Marcie went to the refrigerator and refilled her wine glass, before returning to the bedroom. She picked up the new Iris Murdoch book from her night table, settled in, and began to read.

She awakened at twelve fifteen, not certain where she was. Clearing the cobwebs, she realized she had fallen asleep, the open book resting on her legs. Reluctantly, she got out of bed to brush her teeth, wash her face, turn out the lights, and go back to sleep. She was too tired to do the usual review of what was on her calendar for the next day.

The next morning, Marcie was overjoyed that her trainer would not be there until the next day. She delighted in having the time to pamper herself getting dressed, and having her morning coffee while she read the *L.A. Times*. Looking in her closet, she moved, as she often did, to her collection of vintage 40s jackets. She chose one of her favorites, a black wool subtly ribbed jacket from Lili Ann's of San Francisco. Feeling good about the choice, Marcie put it together with a just above the knee cream gabardine skirt, with classic black Chanel pumps. Forget power wardrobes, she thought, this is my statement for the day.

Arriving at work, Marcie was pleased that Sandy noticed her outfit.

"Cool," Sandy observed, in what was a high compliment for her.

"I'll be with Ben," said Marcie, "and thanks for noticing the outfit."

June waved her into Ben's open door, and Marcie closed it behind her.

"So what do you suggest for Garland?" she began.

"You still think he's not completely full of shit?"

"It's a hard call. If he is, he plays a good game. I'd like to take him seriously and find him something in a personal film that he could make for under ten."

Ben thought for a minute. He turned toward his crowded book-shelves and ran his eyes over the titles printed on the spines of the screenplays. Snapping his fingers, he turned back to his desk and picked up a screenplay with an Allied cover.

"Do you think he'd go for a black comedy? It's really good!"

"I don't know. What's the log line?"

"Two young guys in Miami stumble over a half million worth of coke and try to unload it for cash. It's hip, very much today, and very funny."

"Any elements attached?" asked Marcie.

"The writer is some kid from NYU and he'd love his friend to direct, but he's not locked in."

"And you like it?"

"Absolute. No one's seen it yet, and I know I can sell it. Maybe not for big bucks, but I know it'll move."

"Let me try it on him. I'll make sure he knows he has it first, and can't hang us up on it. He read the last one in a day."

Marcie took the script from Ben, smiled at him, and walked back to her office.

"Would you please try Tim Garland for me?" Marcie asked Sandy, as she passed her desk.

"Sure," said Sandy, "want more coffee?"

"Thanks, anyway."

Marcie examined the title page of the screenplay. *40 Keys* by Peter Rhinethaler. Catchy, Marcie thought. Given Tim's perceptive comments about the Michael Lent submission, she figured she'd better read it before he got back to her. Tim didn't seem like the kind of buyer with whom you could wing it. That is, if he were a buyer at all. Sandy's double buzz told her he was on the line.

"Hi, Tim," she began. "I just got something very hot. I'd love to ship it over to you."

"What did you think?" he asked.

Uh-oh, moment of truth, Marcie thought. "It was handed to me about five minutes ago. No one has read it except the agent who brought it in, Ben Kloster. He's got great taste though, and he really likes it."

"If you don't like it, I don't want to see it."

"Fair enough," said Marcie. "I'll have read it by six o'clock. If it's as good as Ben thinks, you'll have it tonight."

"What are you doing tonight?" Tim asked.

"I don't have any plans."

"I'm supposed to go to political fund-raiser at Mike Medavoy's house. Would you like to come with me? If the script works out, you can bring it along."

"How do you know my politics," asked Marcie.

"I don't. But a smart woman like you is probably a liberal Democrat of some type."

"Good guess," Marcie said, wondering if it were a guess at all. Maybe he was one of those freaks who researches everybody they come in contact with. "Do you want to pick me up?"

"Sure, let's say eight o'clock. Where will you be?"

"I'll be at home, 1240 Westwanda. Just off Benedict."

"Eight o'clock, then. See you."

Marcie looked up to see Sandy standing in the doorway.

"He's gay," she said definitively.

"You don't know that."

Sandy rolled her eyes upward, turned, and went back to her desk. Between phone calls, for the rest of the morning, she read the first act of the screenplay. Ben was right. It was damned good, and he probably would be able to sell it. Before she could read further, Sandy poked her head into the office.

"You're going to be late for Ira, unless you leave now."

Marcie nodded, grabbed her purse, and headed out the door. She was meeting her attorney, Ira Lang, at the Four Seasons Hotel, his favorite haunt for meals and cocktails. He had told her once he liked the light in there, a preference that had struck her as strange, but no stranger than most preferences in the City of the Angels.

He was sipping coffee and reading the trades as she entered the dining room. She found him quickly and headed towards his table. He was a tall man, in his late 40s, darkly handsome, though seemingly always in need of a shave. He had told her once that he shaved twice a day, but even now, at lunch time, he looked like a close shave wouldn't hurt his appearance a bit. Marcie liked his intellectual honesty and the fact that he was a serious lawyer, and not an ego-driven stand-in for an agent. His personal life had been rather tumultuous, as he had chosen women who tottered on the brink of nervous breakdowns. Marcie had counseled him, as a friend, at different times in their six year friendship. She liked him as a friend and respected him as her legal advisor.

He rose to greet her. "Marcie, you're looking great, as usual."

She did feel smart in her jacket which hugged her every curve, and looked as if it were made exclusively for her. She wore a distinctive art deco gold pin of a woman tennis player that she'd found at an estate sale. It was a particular favorite of hers and was set off nicely by the black of the jacket.

This was their third try at a lunch date, regrettably, she thought, canceled twice by her. Ira wanted to discuss something about a will, as well as her Allied contract which was coming up for renewal. One of her problems, she knew, was that she was far more diligent on behalf of her clients than she was in attending to her own business.

As they discussed the subject of her will, Marcie had a flash as to why this subject was so distasteful to her. If she should predecease her parents, of course everything would be left to them. If they died first, she had no immediate family or close relatives to inherit her estate. After some discussion with Ira, she opted to give her secretary, Sandy, a bequest of $50,000, with the remainder to a leading animal welfare group. Ira was less than ecstatic with her decision but respected his client's wishes. He scrawled some notes on a yellow pad, and moved to the matter of her future negotiations with Allied.

Here, Ira had a definite agenda. "They screwed you last time, Marce, and they'll do it again, if you give them a chance. Remember, you told me not to be tough, that they had your best interest at heart. I can tell you from negotiating other deals with them, you're getting significantly less than a man would get, doing the same amount of business."

"So what are you thinking, counselor?"

"I think you should authorize me to nose around the other agencies on your behalf. This is a hot time for you with Sam taking off, and I think you'll find some very receptive people out there."

Marcie hadn't anticipated this approach. It made sense, of course, but all of Ira's ideas made sense. So why was she holding back?

Lang wondered the same thing. "What's wrong with that idea?" he asked. "At the very least you'll be testing the market and setting a value on your services."

Marcie knew he was right. It had to be fear that questioned this strategy. She was bold and decisive when it came to the representation of others, but far shakier when it came to advocating on her own behalf. Maybe it was time to start making waves—but not big ones. "Go ahead." She told Ira. "But for god's sake, be discreet. This is no time to get Charles all pissed off."

Ira nodded his agreement, but Marcie could tell he thought she should go further. It's not his life, she thought, it's mine. She was pleased that she didn't have to worry about Ira. One of his best qualities was keeping his own ego out of his clients' negotiations. It was a rarity in the town.

Marcie kissed Ira goodbye, retrieved her Lexus from the valet, and headed back to the office. Ira opted to wander by the table of a Paramount executive with whom he was in negotiation to set up a picture.

"It never hurts to *schmooze* a little," Ira volunteered to Marcie before she left the dining room.

"Give 'em hell, counselor," Marcie had replied.

Driving the short distance to Allied, Marcie was jolted by the thought that the next day was the tenth anniversary of Rob's death. My god, she thought, he'd be over eleven years old if he had lived. Odd, she reflected, that the accident was so fresh in her mind that it seemed like instant replay. What about the saying that time heals all wounds? People had told her this so many times over the years. Well not this one, you assholes, not this one.

She wondered if there was a word that describes a parent whose child predeceases them. Widow and widower popped into her head. Even orphan flitted through her mind. But what was a parent like her called? Damaged goods? Emotionally challenged?

Now she asked herself whether other languages might have a word for this condition. As she mulled that over, she pondered whether the concept was so awful that people had resisted coining a word for it. Was that possible? Were there any other states of the human condition that had no words to describe them? Or was she playing head games with herself once again instead of dealing with this painful subject? As she pulled into her reserved spot at Allied, she put her thoughts on hold until tomorrow. That day, she knew from previous experience, would be a difficult one.

As she walked toward Sandy, Sandy silently mouthed "Dick Wilhite" to her. Wilhite was evidently speaking with Sandy on the telephone, returning a call Marcie had placed to him. Wilhite was one of her special favorites. She had loved his wry, unique delivery for years. She had followed his career since his New York days, watched his hairline retreat and his importance in the feature world follow suit. He was so gifted a comic actor, she believed that it must be possible to package a television sitcom around him. The television department at Allied had been lukewarm when she brought it up at their packaging meeting. She had pressed the point and had won a grudging okay to try to sign him, if he agreed to do a series. She had called him to set up a lunch because she knew his papers had run out with his present agent and he was sitting on them. He had not yet re-signed. His days of making decent money in features were past, unless he could make it in a hit series that would give his career a new life. It had happened before with talent far less gifted than Wilhite.

But would Wilhite hold still for the cold logic of reality? Or would he go off on an ego trip, insisting that he was only one feature away from breaking out and becoming hot? She had tip-toed through this kind of mine field many times before. There was little about the fragile ego of the performer that she hadn't experienced first hand in the trenches. While she had great compassion for actors, the extended time it took to massage their egos often wore her down.

"Hey, Dick. How're you doing?"

"I'm fine, Marcie" he said warily.

Get right to the point, Marcie told herself. He knows why I'm calling. "I was hoping I could buy you a dinner. I'd like to talk with you about representation."

"I'd like to do that," said Wilhite. "I've got to make a move in that direction very soon."

"How's Tuesday?" asked Marcie, looking at her calendar for the next week.

"That should be fine," he said with more than a little seriousness.

"Suppose I call you on Tuesday, and we'll pick a place?"

"Great," he replied. "I'll wait to hear from you."

As she hung up, her private line began flashing.

"Hello?"

"I have Mr. Maier for you," Edith said.

"Marcie, I need an update on the Warners picture."

As was customary, Charles didn't linger over pleasantries like "hellos." He preferred to get right to the point. "Sam was a little jumpy over how fast things were moving with Julia Ormond. But I think he's going to be okay. I told him that he's a couple of movies away from real control."

"Ormond and Weir are both set. Derek and I signed Julia at lunch, and I want to get you together with her as soon as possible. We talked mostly about you, and how well the both of you will get along."

"That's great, Charles. Maybe tomorrow?"

"I'll be back to you with a time. Tell me what's happening with Tim Garland."

Again, thought Marcie, that strange preoccupation with a fringe player, if he was even that. Charles was not a micro-manager. His involvement in the day-to-day business of Allied meant something larger was at stake. Sam's deal was the perfect example. Julia Ormond, and perhaps Peter Weir, were on the periphery of the negotiation with Sam. This, she understood clearly. But Tim Garland? Maybe it would be clearer to her after she saw him that night.

Marcie filled Sam in on her last conversation with Tim, and let him know Tim was taking her to Medavoy's that night.

"That's good," said Charles. "I'm not going to be able to make it, so you'll be representing the company."

Charles rarely attended political events. He kept his politics and the rest of his personal life very quiet. If he gave to political causes, he did so discreetly. Now that Marcie thought about it, she couldn't be sure which side of the aisle Charles was on. She assumed he was a liberal, but she had no way of knowing for certain.

Marcie packed the *40 Keys* script into her soft leather briefcase, and left her office.

"I'm going to get out of here and read this script at home," Marcie said to Sandy.

"Works for me," Sandy replied. "Anything special you want done?"

"Thanks, but I think I'm all right. See you tomorrow."

Driving home, she was unable to form a logical response to the question what lay behind Charles's interest in Tim? Maybe Sandy was correct after all. Maybe it all could be attributed to the shadowy world of gay connections.

Arriving home, Marcie changed into a bathrobe and sat down in the Eames chair in the bedroom to finish *40 Keys*. Ben was right. It was funny, a little dark, and very hip. It did smell like a sale to her as well. Let's see how Mr. Garland responds to this submission, she thought.

At precisely eight o'clock, the door bell rang. Marcie was pleased she had gotten ready early. This evening could be dicey enough without starting it off by making him wait in the living room. She had changed into another vintage jacket, this one a brown and cream checked three-quarter flair number that had a quality reminiscent of Lauren Bacall. She wore it with a crisp white shirt, wide-legged brown trousers, a silver and leather belt, and brown suede Belgian loafers.

"Nice outfit," said Tim, as Marcie ushered him into the house.

"Thank you," she said, smiling, noticing the blue Rolls Royce parked in her driveway.

"I like your house. It seems like you."

"It's been good to me. Cozy and easy to keep up."

Tim nodded, casting an appreciative eye at the art work and the rest of Marcie's decor. "Are you ready?" he asked.

"Let's do it."

As Marcie left the house, she picked up the screenplay with its distinctive Allied Agency cover and put it under her arm. Tim opened her door for her, and in an instant, the soft purr of the Rolls engine kicked in, and he headed down Benedict Canyon toward Sunset.

"I see you brought the script with you," said Tim.

"Yes, it's a knockout. I can't be sure whether it's your taste, but I can tell you that it's going to sell. You're getting it first, and I'll see that you have forty-eight hours in the clear. Okay?"

Tim looked at her for a minute before turning back toward the road. He seemed to be gauging the sincerity of her words, Marcie thought. Well fine, she meant what she said.

"Fair enough. I'll be back to you some time tomorrow. Just one thing. Forget whether it's going to sell. *Dumb and Dumber* sold, but it's not something I would have wanted to make. What do you think of the script?"

"I think it's terrific. Funny, hip, and very fresh."

He turned into Medavoy's circular driveway, pulled to a stop, and took a ticket from the valet parker. Moving next to Marcie, he said, "That's good enough for me."

As they walked into the Medavoy house, Marcie saw the typical gathering of stars, agents, executives and other supporters of the liberal wing of the Democratic Party. After too many years of Reagan and Bush, it was nice to see these gatherings out in the open once more. While not particularly active in politics, Marcie had lent both her financial support and professional assistance to such efforts over the years. She had delivered her clients to fund raisers and had co-hosted a couple of parties for aspiring Democratic candidates.

As they walked in, Warren and Annette Beatty arrived at the same moment. Warren greeted Marcie and introduced her to his wife. Marcie introduced Tim, in turn, and noticed Warren staring at him intently. Warren seldom missed a trick, and she knew that Tim's name and face were now filed away in his head for future reference. Warren might be a tad old for a leading man, but his mind was as sharp as ever. Annette looked beautiful, as befitted the woman who had removed Warren from the ranks of Hollywood's dedicated bachelors. They walked into the living room together. Marcie was aware that even in a room packed with celebrities, from Streisand to Spielberg, eyes still turned to Warren and Annette. Sam may be hot for the moment, but he was certainly no Warren Beatty. At least not yet.

Heading toward the bar where champagne was being served, Marcie waved hello to Warners Nat Shapiro and another executive from Warners. "Very happy about the Sam Glass deal, Marcie. It's going to be a big picture for us."

"I know it will," she said. Before she could introduce Tim to him, he had gone back to his other conversation. She looked over at Tim who smiled and shrugged.

As they moved away from the bar, champagne glasses in hand, a distinguished, gray-haired man tapped Tim on the shoulder.

"Tim," he said, "good to see you."

"And you too, Fred. I'd like you to meet Marcie Sandmore. This is Fred Reker, from Bank of America, who you should know anyway. He's on their motion picture financing desk."

"Come on, Tim," Fred said, "you know we make loans, not finance pictures."

"Purely semantics," Tim chuckled as Fred turned to walk away.

"Oh, nice meeting you," he said turning back to Marcie.

"He's a little uncomfortable over a joke I told him on an airplane," Tim explained to Marcie.

"Was it that terrible?"

"I didn't think so."

"Okay," Marcie said, "try it on me."

Tim began. "Seems this woman was looking to give her husband some special birthday gift for his 50th. A male friend of hers suggested, 'I know you won't believe this, but I've got this giant toad that gives the world's best blow jobs.' 'Come on,' the woman said. 'Trust me,' said her friend. The woman was given the toad in a box and dutifully presented it to her husband. He was a little leery of the whole thing, but finally took the box upstairs to the bedroom. She waited downstairs for ten minutes, a half hour, an hour and finally two hours. Marching upstairs to find out what was going on, she opened the bedroom door to find her husband sitting on the bed with the toad, surrounded by cook books. He looked at her and said, 'You better hope this toad can't cook, because if it can, you're out of here.'"

Marcie burst out laughing.

"He found that so offensive?" she asked.

"Apparently," he replied.

"Well, he's the one with the problem."

Changing the subject, she asked Tim how much he knew about the politician they had come to support.

"More about his philosophy than any details. I'm not terribly involved in politics, I'm afraid."

"That's about where I am also," Marcie said.

Mike Medavoy picked up a microphone and asked for everyone's attention. As the room quieted, he thanked the guests for showing up, and introduced John Fairbanks, "candidate for the United States Senate, and the hope of the liberal wing of the Democratic Party."

Fairbanks spoke eloquently on the issues of the day and asked for financial and political support from those in attendance. He seemed to be an attractive candidate, Marcie thought, and she liked his message. Tim was similarly impressed. After that, there were cards to sign and more people to greet, and then it was over.

As the valet brought Tim's car over, Marcie noticed he checked it carefully for scratches and dinks. I guess owning a Rolls gives you a certain responsibility, she thought. Whatever that was, it was more than she wanted. Better to have Allied lease a smart Lexus for her use, than be burdened with that kind of baggage.

They talked recent movies they had seen, and studio politics on the way back to her house. It seemed comfortable enough to Marcie, and she was more than a little impressed by the depth of Tim's knowledge of the picture business. There was a sophistication that went far beyond the readers of *People* or the viewers of *Entertainment Tonight*. Maybe he was a player, she thought. Maybe Charles had identified a new buyer worth cultivating.

As he arrived at her house, Marcie invited him in for coffee. "No thanks," said Tim. "Tomorrow's a school day."

"Tonight was fun, thanks."

"It was," said Tim. "I'll be back to you tomorrow on the script."

Marcie unlocked the door and turned back to Tim. He gave her a friendly hug and kissed her lightly on the cheek. Marcie went into her house more curious than ever about who and what a Tim Garland was?

Chapter V

Seconds before her alarm was to go off, the telephone awakened her from a deep sleep.

"Hey, Marcie," an unfamiliar rasping voice said.

"Yes?"

"It's me, George," her trainer replied.

"God, you sound terrible."

"I think I have the flu. I'm running 101, and I don't think I can get there today."

Yes! There is a god, thought Marcie.

"Take care of yourself, okay? And if the fever keeps up, promise you'll see a doctor?"

"Sure, I'll be fine. Monday, then?"

"It's a date."

Marcie reset her alarm, thrilled with the prospect of another hour of sleep. She closed her eyes and began to drift off when it rang again. Marcie was tempted to let the machine pick up, having a solid premonition about who might call her on this particular day. She was quite correct. It was her ex-husband, Bob. The call was no great surprise. He had done this every year but one since they had separated eight years previously. It was always difficult, but she knew it always would be. There are some aches that dull with the passage of time, but this never would. They had been so young then, so full of confidence and optimism. They knew there would be bumps to negotiate, but nothing could have prepared them for the course their life together took.

After giving up her dream of making a career playing tennis, Marcie had chosen to pit her talents against the wheelers and dealers of Wall Street. It was the early 80s and gunslingers abounded in the financial circles of New York. Traders, salespeople, dealmakers, analysts—they all found opportunities to take down vast sums of money that exceeded everyone's wildest dreams. There was so much money to go around that the Wall Street chieftains allowed women to feed at the trough for the first time.

Marcie's father, a middle-level banker, had opened a couple of doors for her and she was hired by a highly successful investment banking house. She set about learning the arcane world of junk bonds and other financial instruments of the time. Marcie demonstrated an unusual aptitude for the world of finance and established herself as a quick study. Everyone on the Street seemed to be making money hand over fist, and Marcie was no exception. She approached her work with a zeal that bordered on fanaticism and the long hours at her desk paid off handsomely. She began to accumulate savings far faster than she had imagined possible.

In one of the rare moments of play she allowed herself, she was introduced at a party to a young, well-connected, Broadway producer. Coming from a wealthy New York family that had amassed a small fortune in the garment business, Bob Fisher opened her eyes to the special excitement of working in the creative world. He had access to considerable sums of risk capital from both his parents and their friends. He also had a keen sense for good quality material and how it matched up with the public's taste. His area of weakness, growing more out of indifference than incompetence, had been the financial structure of the deals. Marcie happened into his life at the precise moment when it was discovered that his partner, Ralph Cohn, the financial member of the team, was embezzling considerable sums of money from their partnership.

The allure of Broadway and Bob Fisher proved irresistible to Marcie. Without a backward glance, she left Wall Street in favor of a new career and the first serious relationship of her life. She and Bob became inseparable socially. Marcie was quickly able to master the nuances of Broadway financing and fill the shoes of Bob's former partner, who was ultimately convicted on 15 counts of fraud and embezzlement. While cooler heads warned them about the dangers of spouses or significant others working together, they were determined to prove everyone wrong. Their business flourished, as did their relationship. Two successful off-Broadway shows kept their backers smiling and happy. Money and producing opportunities were plentiful and Marcie counted her blessings. Circumstances had moved her out of the world of Michael Milken and into the world of David Merrick.

Their comparative youth was not held against them, as their successes spoke loudly and clearly for their business acumen and good taste. Inevitably, Marcie's involvement in the company stretched beyond the financial structure of the deals. An English and business major at Smith, she delighted in working with Bob on putting the shows together and showed a special flair for spotting fresh talent. Marcie was ecstatic that she had chosen this career path, and even her parents came around to being enthusiastic supporters of her new business.

She and Bob married in a large hotel wedding that satisfied the expectations of family and friends. Show business types mixed with bankers and businessmen in what the gossip pages of the New York newspapers dubbed the "Marriage of the Year." They summered in the Hamptons, and bought a showpiece co-op on Second Avenue in the 60s. Life seemed to get better and better and they, and all around them, rejoiced when Marcie became pregnant. She insisted on working into her ninth month, with her doctor's blessing and Bob's unfailing support. When she gave birth to Bob Jr., all 9 pounds 4 ounces of him, they counted his fingers and toes, then gave thanks that they were as blessed as they were.

Having sampled the lifestyle of the Hamptons, and with the raising of Robert Jr. foremost in their minds, they rented a house in Harrison, twenty-five miles north of the City, to get away on weekends and for the summer. The commute, when they did it, was about an hour and they had the sense of being grownups and dedicated parents. With live-in help both in New York and Harrison, life was extremely manageable, constantly exciting, and full of promise and opportunity. Marcie's folks were close enough in nearby Scarsdale to be doting grandparents without suffocating Marcie and Bob.

Both Marcie and Bob despised the idea of calling the baby Junior, and he gradually became known as Rob, a name that clearly distinguished him from his father and allowed conversations to flow without undue confusion. Both Marcie and Bob adored young Rob and savored each stage of his development, Marcie kept an active hand in the business, but shifted the day to day work to a trusted staff member, spending more and more time at home with her son.

It was on such a day that it had happened. How many times, over the years, she had played the scenario back in her head. If only…Had she just…But such thinking produced only a series of psychological dead-ends. None of the details had faded from her mind. Rob was dead, and he wasn't coming back.

People grieve in different ways. Bob got over the initial horror faster than Marcie, as his therapist urged him constantly to allow his grief to work itself out. "It is natural and healthy," he told Bob, "to experience the pain. It is an essential part of the healing process." But Bob was unable to confront the harsh reality fully and lapsed into a state of denial in which he maintained that it was a terrible thing, but that everything was going to be okay.

Marcie went the other way. Her cheery demeanor gave way to a dark, depressive state. She, too, began intensive therapy which was supported by anti-depressants. She cut herself off from her former life and friends, preferring the quiet of her Harrison house. She kept the curtains drawn, finding the light offensive. Family and friends tried to break through to her, to help her during this terrible time. Marcie wanted no part of them. She wept until no more tears would come. Her intellect knew she could not have seen Rob playing in the driveway and that the accident was a hideous occurrence she could not have avoided. Yet her emotions gave her no relief from the fact that she had been the driver of the car that ran over and killed her child. The loss was so primal, so close to her very being, that she could not separate herself from it. At her darkest time, she was pronounced suicidal and put into a hospital with a round-the-clock watch. With stronger medication and more intensive psychotherapy, she gradually began to rally.

Bob, while destroyed by the accident, was completely supportive of Marcie during her healing process. Their couple-of-the-year status had quickly given way to a strained and difficult relationship. Affection, play, fun, all seemed to be relics of a previous time. In addition to their individual psychotherapy, they tried marriage counseling in a good faith effort to restore some of the dynamic of their previous life. When one therapist didn't help, they tried another, and another after that. Instead of growing back to intimacy, their positions hardened and they became strangers living under the same roof, even in the same bed. They were urged to grieve and put the tragedy behind them. They were young and vital people with long lives stretching out in front of them. They could have more children, they were counseled. Start now, build a new family.

Bob was the more willing of the two to undertake this course of action. Marcie gave indications that she wanted to as well, but found herself unable to take positive steps in that direction. While she knew that Bob was the right person for her, she couldn't bear living with the memory of what had happened to their child and their marriage. The result was inevitable. As amicably as any such parting could be, they jointly agreed to call it off. A one-year trial separation evolved into a divorce. There was no acrimony and they were able to get through the legalities using a common lawyer. The business remained with Bob who had begun it. Marcie toyed with opening her own production company, but thought better of it. Instead, she accepted an offer from the theatrical department of Allied, a large talent agency, and became an agent.

She plunged herself into her professional world with a fierce dedication. Slowly, the combination of her work, a tough exercise regimen at the gym, and continued psychotherapy brought her back to being a reasonably whole person. They got out of their lease in Harrison, while Bob bought out her interest in the New York co-op. She used the money to buy a studio apartment The rough edges of her loss became worn down by the passage of time as scar tissue covered over the rawness of her wound. She dated different men but avoided any serious commitment. She reconciled herself to the fact that her healing would be a long process. She was unable to shake the notion that some vital part of her life force had been extinguished. She was functioning, but without the drive and energy that had characterized her personal and professional lives. So great had her pain been, and so alone had she felt, that she protected herself by holding back on her passions and her emotional commitments. The rewards might be less in her life, but the risks would be fewer as well. She couldn't again face the blackness of the hole into which she had fallen.

When her clients began to gravitate from the theater to films, she found herself spending more and more time on the West Coast. At first, she had the knee-jerk New Yorker's response to the glitz of Tinseltown. It seemed without substance, everything done for show and its effect on others. But as she became more enmeshed in the lifestyle and the inner workings of the town, she developed a fondness for the bolder, more innovative aspects of Los Angeles life. What she could never get used to was the notion that the creative community rooted for others to fail so that they could be perceived as prospering. This sentiment prevailed at screenings, premieres, throughout the town. Though Marcie had stopped letting it get to her, she knew it was not one of Hollywood's prettier pictures.

Both outwardly and inwardly, she grew healthy again and rose to prominence at the Allied Agency. Her problems of the past were not known by many of her colleagues, and she successfully made the transition to a new life.

Bob's call, though not unexpected, gave her a jolt. The memories of the past were still a part of the present. Too often, alone in her house, she went to her bedroom closet and took down a small framed picture from the shelf. It was of Rob at his first birthday, his smiling face a vision of innocence and happiness. Marcie wasn't sure whether holding the picture and staring at her son was healthy or not, but she knew she was unwilling to break this tenuous link to the past.

"How're you doing?" Bob asked. "I didn't wake you, did I?"

He had remarried and lived in Manhattan with his wife and their two daughters. His new wife, Pam, was not involved in his producing and focused her time and energy on raising the children and keeping their social life together. Marcie had met her on a couple of occasions and their interaction had been cordial and friendly. She felt a sincere contentment that Bob had been able to rebuild this part of his life.

"No," Marcie said. "My trainer canceled, and I was just resting."

"Should I call back later?"

"Thanks, but I'm up now."

Bob hesitated, a bit unsure. "I called to tell you I'm thinking about you and about Rob." His voice had become serious.

While pretty much of a ritual, this telephone call still had a lot of meaning to her. It was like paying respects with an annual visit to a cemetery. She knew Bob meant it and that his feelings were no more complicated than he indicated.

"I really appreciate it. You know I'll spend a lot of time today thinking about Rob and you, too. It seems like a century, but it also seems like it happened five minutes ago. It's something you and I will share forever."

Tears began to run down Marcie's cheeks. She started to say something more to Bob, but was unable to get the words out. She knew Bob too well to attempt to hide her pain. He comforted her as well as he could from 3,000 miles. He assured her that what they had, they would have forever, no matter with whom they were, or where they were. Marcie responded to his heartfelt sentiments and said, for the first time in many years, "Thank you, Bob, I love you."

"I love you too, Marcie. I hope today goes okay for you." Bob hung up the telephone, and Marcie lay back and closed her eyes. She thought again of Rob, of her life with Bob, so many years ago. She made no effort to stop the tears from coming, preferring to let them take their course.

Eventually, as she always did, she found the strength to get up, take a shower and get dressed. As she went into her closet to select her clothes for the day, she reached onto the top shelf and pulled down the picture of Rob. Was she like a junkie needing just one more fix? No, that couldn't be the case, Lots of people looked at photographs. That's what they were for, right? His precious face grinned at her familiarly. It wasn't like looking at a photograph, but at a part of herself. She rubbed the glass protecting the picture against her cheek. It felt cool to the touch. Looking at it once more, Marcie kissed her son goodbye, put the picture back in the closet and finished getting dressed.

Traffic was backed up on Benedict, but the delay only played into her mood. She continued to dwell on Rob and her former life with Bob. The closer she inched toward the Allied office on Wilshire, the more her prior life seemed to ebb away from her recall. There is little time for an agent to do anything except live in the moment. By the time she greeted Sandy, she was already focused on the day that lay before her.

Sandy informed her that she'd had three telephone calls from Sam. "What's the big problem?" she asked Sandy.

"I don't know," Sandy replied, "but he's on his way over. Should be here any second."

It starts so soon, Marcie mused. Before she could pursue the thought, Sandy buzzed to say Sam was downstairs in the lobby.

"Send him up. Let's see what his problem is."

Sam came striding into her office. In place of his usual happy grin, he had a dark and concerned look.

Sounding as upbeat as possible, Marcie said, "What's up, Sam?"

"The script, that's what. This isn't what I agreed to do. They must have been working on a new draft this whole time, just waiting to get me to commit. Well they can stuff this version! I'll be damned if I'm going to be in this piece of shit!"

"Slow down, Sam. This isn't the shooting script. It's just the next draft. Have you spoken to Peter Weir yet?"

"No," Sam admitted, "I called you as soon as I read it."

Marcie continued. "You've got to sit with Peter. He's great with story and it's in his interest, and everyone else's to get your character and the rest of this script right. This is all process. You've got to give it a chance."

Sam looked at Marcie a little sheepishly. "Maybe I over-reacted a bit."

"That's okay. It's coming out of a passion for the material and that's fine. Just don't jump the gun. I'll set up a story conference with you and Peter. Only the two of you. After that, we'll take another look at things. All right?"

The darkness had vanished from Sam's face. His smiling good looks returned and Marcie breathed an inner sigh of relief.

"How'd you get to be so smart?" asked Sam.

"It's not so much being smart as it is going through it about a million times," Marcie replied.

"No way," said Sam. "There are tons of agents out there, but I'm sure they don't have your way of seeing the situation for what it really is."

I hope you never forget that, Marcie thought as she smiled warmly at Sam.

Sam came around to her side of the desk to give her a big hug and kiss. As he left her office, he turned and waved. "You're the greatest," he said. She could hear him saying goodbye to Sandy and heading to the elevator. You are going to be a real handful, she thought. You better be worth the trouble. Marcie knew that in agency commission terms, he most assuredly was. In human terms, well, that could be a different story.

The day continued, with calls piling up and no definite answers from buyers. If only the town didn't specialize in "definite maybes," life would be a whole lot more tolerable. She met again with Ben who wanted to know all bout the function at Mike Medavoy's and where Tim was regarding *40 Keys*.

"Medavoy's was same old, same old..." Marcie replied. "Tim promised an answer on the script today. I loved it, but I have no idea how he'll come out on it."

"MGM put *Dark Horses* in turnaround late yesterday," Ben said. "Do you think he'd like that?"

"I like it a lot," Marcie said. "I always have. I hope to get a better feel for what he likes after I speak with him."

"It'll cost a bundle to do right."

"He insisted we weren't to worry about the money. Let's try to flush him out. If he's full of shit, as he probably is, we'll tell that to Charles and be rid of him."

Marcie had had her fill of Tim Garlands over the years. You expend time and energy, and almost always have zilch to show for it. No need to get exorcised, she thought, because it was a short day. She'd be cutting out early for a weekend in Palm Springs. Yes, she had a pile of scripts to get through, and this was the ostensible reason for getting away, but the Springs always had a great allure for her. She never tired of the warmth of the days and the cool of the nights. With the breathtaking scenery and the pampering her body and soul got at the better spas and watering spots, it all added up to one of her favorite weekend escapes. She had also discovered that taking a couple of days off around the time of the anniversary of Rob's death was therapeutic for her. Marcie had done this the last three years and was convinced it had helped her refocus her energies.

Returning to her office, Sandy informed her that a Mona Cleary, from Tim Garland's office, was on the phone.

"Put her through, please," Marcie said, moving to her desk.

"Hi, this is Mona Cleary, Mr. Garland's assistant."

"Hello."

"Mr. Garland left for to New York very suddenly. He took the red-eye in last night. He called from the plane to say he has the script with him and will telephone you sometime today. He'd like me to get some numbers on how to reach you."

Marcie paused, processing this information, before answering. "I should be here until the early afternoon. Then I'm driving to the Springs where I'll be staying at the Marquis."

"Fine, I have that number right in front of me. I'll pass this information along to Mr. Garland."

Marcie hung up, finding it mildly curious that Mona had the number at her fingertips.

*   *   *   *   *

She had picked the Marquis Villas and Spa because each villa offered its own private pool and hot tub. She had discovered the Marquis soon after it opened and still found its quiet luxury exactly to her liking. Most Hollywood types still preferred the Racquet Club, and Marcie found that reason enough to go elsewhere. Besides, the tennis pro was fantastic to hit with and his looks were to die for. She had booked him for the last two hours of his day on Saturday. He would be her reward for the big dent she hoped to have made by then in the pile of scripts she was bringing with her.

She arrived at the Springs in time for dinner, modestly pleased with herself that she had avoided a speeding ticket on the way. She appreciated that Traffic School was an alternative to getting a moving violation put on her license. But Traffic School was very near the top of her list of least favorite things to do in life. In fact, she thought she might just take her punishment if she got nailed again, instead of having to endure some "double digit IQ" type droning on for a whole evening about the obvious. The last time, the officious instructor had interrupted his lecture to try to humiliate her in front of the class for reading a script when she should have been attending to his heart-stopping lecture on single and double highway lines.

As she checked in at the Marquis, she was informed by the desk clerk that Tim Garland had called fifteen minutes earlier. The manager, Brian Ralston, came out of his office to greet her as the message regarding Tim was conveyed.

"You are a friend of Mr. Garland?" he asked.

"A business acquaintance, why? Does he stay here?"

Ralston smiled, "In a sense. The Marquis Spa is his development."

Marcie had always heard that the Marquis was done with Teamster money, or Vegas money, or something along those lines. She had never pressed for details because it had no relevance to her life. But if Tim was the principal in this deal, suddenly she could get interested very quickly. Maybe, he was a player after all.

Finishing checking in, Marcie confirmed her Saturday tennis lesson with the pro, Wes Snyder, and went directly to her villa. As always, the management had taken pains to make her feel welcome. A bottle of respectable California Chardonnay stood chilling in an ice bucket. A basket of fruit and hors d'oeuvres invited her to snack while pondering her dinner choice. A note from Brian Ralston welcomed her back to the

Marquis and offered his assistance in making her stay more comfortable. Great, she thought, but let me see if I can catch up with Tim.

"Tim Garland," he said, after she called the number he had left.

"Hi, it's Marcie. I guess I'm staying at your place, in a sense."

Tim laughed. "Let me know if they don't take good care of you."

"They're always great. I've been coming here since it opened."

"Glad to hear it.

"You own this?" Marcie asked, somewhat incredulously.

Tim chuckled. "It's a little more complicated than that. You know, investment groups, and all that."

What the hell did that mean, Marcie wondered. Funny money? Mr. Garland got more interesting by the minute.

"Whatever," she said. "Did you have a chance to read *40 Keys*?"

"I did, twice actually. I guess that's what five hour plane trips are good for."

"And?"

"And I understand what you like about it. I think it's a good piece and I'm sure you guys will be able to sell it."

"But," Marcie interrupted.

"But it's not me. I know enough to know that most producers like what they can sell. That's not who I am. I have to love it to want to do it. I've got plenty of other action that's about making money. Anything I do in motion pictures has to be because I connect with it, because I want some other kind of involvement with it. Do you think that's crazy?"

"Actually, I don't. Maybe a little unusual, but not crazy. If you can get more specific about what you're looking for, I may be able to come up with it for you."

"That's fair enough. Suppose I buy you dinner Monday and try to spell it out for you then. I'm impressed with your taste, and have a good feeling that you'll be able to come up with the right material."

"Monday's great."

"I'll call you in the office. Make sure they treat you right at the Marquis. Any problems, I want to know about it. Have a great weekend."

Hanging up the phone, Marcie thought, he wants to know about it? Why did it sound so ominous when he said it? Is it only the rumors that Vegas money was behind the resort? Maybe Tim Garland was more than he appeared to be. That would be a switch. He certainly had her interest piqued. But that was for Monday. For now, she could address her schedule for the weekend.

She had booked her normal session at the spa. A massage, a facial, a manicure and pedicure. With any luck, she would feel almost human again after this weekend.

Dinner. The drive down to the Springs always left her ravenous, and today was no exception. Marcie consulted the room service Menu and opted for soft shell crabs. An odd selection, perhaps, considering the location in the desert, but probably as fresh as anything else she might choose. She called the order in and was told it would be about forty-five minutes. Time enough for a shower and a change of clothes. In the round stainless steel shower, the multiple water spouts sent a warm, caressing spray all up and down her body. Bliss, she thought. She felt her muscles relaxing. This weekend was going to be exactly what she needed.

Dinner arrived at the predicted time.

"Hello Miss Sandmore," the waiter said, as she opened the door. "It's good to have you back with us."

"It's always good to be here, Maurice."

Maurice had been there since the opening, and always seemed to wait on Marcie. Conspicuously friendly and courteous, Maurice seemed to take an interest in her work at Allied.

He opened the wine she ordered asking, "Is your business going well?"

"Very well at the moment, thank you."

"I'm glad," he said. "Bon appetit."

Maurice left the room, and Marcie could feel herself begin to unwind. She flicked on the television to *Jeopardy*, and began eating. As always, she effortlessly answered most of the questions except those on science. People had told her for years that she should go on this show. It had seemed like too much trouble, especially since she wasn't desperate for money. But looking at these contestants stirred up her competitive juices and she considered giving it a shot. The feeling was reinforced as she nailed the Final Jeopardy question "Which world leader was born in Gori, Georgia?" Who is Joseph Stalin, you *putzes*.

For a weekend that was supposed to be for chilling-out, she was getting herself into a competitive frenzy. A hot tub was the answer. She wore her terry cloth robe outside to the walled-in patio where her villa's hot tub and pool were located. She brought with her the wine and a joint from her small stash. Dropping her robe to the ground, she let her body luxuriate in the soft, night breeze. She checked the temperature of the tub—a perfect 104 degrees. She slid into the bubbling water and leaned back looking up at the night sky. You couldn't see stars in Los Angeles, another reason Marcie loved Palm Springs nights. She lit the joint, inhaled deeply, and exhaled into the night air. This was more like it, worth every cent of the outrageous sum they charged for the room, not to mention the dope.

Marcie closed her eyes and let the warm, roiling water work on her muscles. As she always did, she found these solitary moments conducive to collecting her thoughts and getting herself centered. Something was starting to nag at her and she wanted to bring it into focus. She had had similar feelings before in her life and they had proven to be harbingers of change. They had been tiny indications, which ultimately bubbled to the surface and made her take a different direction in life. But now? She wasn't 21 years old any more. It made little sense to play games with her life every time she got fed up with some of the components of her job.

Maybe Lang had a point. Maybe she should be more attentive to her position in the Allied power structure and not be so accepting of "corporate policy." Maybe there was reason to take a close look at the rest of her life as well. She had exhausted her interest in therapy in the period following Rob's death. Since then, maybe she'd played things too safely. How long could she protect herself from pain? Rob had been dead for ten years. Was that what Ira was really urging her to do—take more chances? Maybe his instinct that now was the time to poke around a little *was* the best way to go. Her work had been the center of her existence for some years. It was the logical place to start any examination of her life.

Her father had been right when he accused her of being unrealistic about work. "Work is work," he said. She remembered his look of dismay when she rolled her eyes upwards at the seeming ridiculousness of his statement. What he meant, he continued, was that it was futile to hold unrealistic expectations about the level of fun and challenge in what one did for a living. He had likened it to the shift in the nature of a long-term relationship, like a marriage. The extreme passion of the first days and months inevitably gave way to a deeper but different love. "Only a fool assumes everything stays the same. If you demand that of your life, you're bound to be unhappy, both professionally and personally."

Full of herself and her 22 years, she had walked away from his advice, she recalled, mumbling about the "generation gap," and how she hoped she'd "never be that kind of person." But time had inexorably inched her closer to the truth of his statements. Was she now willing to settle? Was it fear that held her back? Fear of a commitment? Fear of success? Fear of another terrible loss? She took another sip of wine and decided she had no answers for the time being. Christ, I'm here to get away, and not sort out the meaning of life. She finished the joint, attributing her half-formed anxiety to a combination of fatigue, wine, and a very fine sensemilla.

*   *   *   *   *

Saturday, Marcie awoke from a solid eight-hour sleep to see the rays of the desert sun squeezing through a small slit in the curtain. She smiled, knowing that the day was going to be wonderful. Breakfast on the patio, a leisurely swim, knock off one script from the pile, then repair to the spa. Not terrible. As she had her second cup of coffee, she decided to do *The New York Times* Saturday crossword. She had been a devoted fan of the *Times'* crosswords in New York when Eugene T. Maleska had been the puzzle editor. She loved the logic of the puzzles and solving the Sunday puzzle had been one of her favorite weekend pastimes. For some reason, she had left this passion behind when she moved to the West Coast. As she turned to the puzzle, she noted that someone named Will Shortz was now the puzzle editor. Had Maleska died or just retired? Do puzzle editors ever get fired? She doubted that would have happened to Maleska, since he was, after all, the best of his breed. She picked up a pencil and immediately ran into difficulty in the upper left-hand corner. She smiled as she recalled that the difficulty of *The Times'* puzzles increases every day from Monday to Saturday. With some effort, the blank spaces gave way to neatly written letters as Marcie completed the puzzle in half an hour. Solving puzzles is another thing that's just like riding a bike, she mused. You never forget how.

She turned to her pile of six scripts that had to be evaluated before Monday. The first was from the literary department. Allied's reader for this project was a young UCLA grad who Marcie had never met. The daughter of a director who was one of the agency's clients, she had secured this position in the time-honored fashion of knowing the right people. Not that it was a plum job. She had to read scripts written by Allied clients and those submitted for the consideration of Allied clients. She then had to provide the responsible agents coverage consisting of a page and a half of synopsis, followed by a half page of recommendation. The system paralleled the way the studios conducted business and created a lowest-people-on-the-totem-pole class who were paid $50-$60 per script analyzed. For this royal fee, the reader

determined whether or not a script would move along to a higher echelon where something might be done with it. If the reader didn't like a
script, it was history.

The six screenplays Marcie brought with her had passed the first hur-
dle. Marcie opened the first script, titled *Texas Ranger*. The coverage
suggested that it might be a great star vehicle for Sam Glass. As Marcie
began to read she noted that the Texas Ranger was a 60-year-old weath-
ered cowboy, and that the antagonist he pursued throughout the piece
was all of 19, and half Native American. Is this reader crazy, Marcie
wondered? Looking at the recommendation she saw that the reader and
the literary agent who supported her contemplated making the Ranger
into a much younger man, suitable for Sam. Fifteen pages in, Marcie
decided that the writing was not good enough to warrant any excitement for the project. She wrote on the coverage that if the writer wanted to rewrite it with the Ranger as a younger man, she'd take another
look. Until then, the project had too far to go.

She moved to the next script on the pile, having spent approxi-
mately fifteen minutes considering the first. A writer had better grab
a busy person in the first few pages, or lose them forever. Marcie
thought of herself as one of the more literate agents, having a solid
background in and a taste for well-crafted material. She was far too
pressured to spend any significant time on scripts like this, spec
scripts without an offer for her client, and if the screenwriter didn't
understand that, he needed better guidance.

The second script led her to abandon reading in favor of a swim in
the pool. It was a project called *Pool Man*, written by her very own pool
man, who had given it to her with much fanfare and enthusiasm. She
had passed it along to a bright, young reader who was up on youth
comedies. This one defied belief. Writing without regard for grammar
or syntax, the pool man, Tag, had alternated visual jokes with sexual
conquests in a combination that should be directed at his psychiatrist
rather than a movie audience. The reader had summarized his reaction

in a single sentence. "This is unspeakable garbage!" Because of the personal connection with Tag, Marcie had felt compelled to at least glance at the script. That done, she scribbled a quick note to Tag on the coverage: "Keep your day job." Putting the script down, she dove into the pool to swim laps.

Later that morning, Marcie saw Ronnie, one of the spa's expert staff, for a massage. It was heaven. She preferred not to talk, keeping her eyes closed and letting the attendants pamper her. Her preference was a deep massage. After years of trying all of the masseuses, she had settled on a masseur, Ronnie, someone capable of digging deep enough into her tissues to loosen all the knots the stress of her world tied her into. He asked frequently if it was too painful, and her answer was always "no". After one hour with Ronnie, Marcie glided rather than walked to her next appointment. The facial made her skin feel alive and tingly. While the attendant worked on her, she tried to remember who had first introduced her to this pleasure. It wasn't her mother, who thought such activities were insanely extravagant, even decadent. Her mother's mother, growing up in the nation's heartland, must surely have held those same beliefs. Marcie had long since stopped trying to convince her mother that there might actually be health benefits derived from caring for one's skin in this fashion. There were some arguments that a child could never win.

Feeling fabulous, Marcie walked the short distance back to her villa, expecting to knock off the rest of the scripts before her tennis lesson. She ordered a salad and iced tea from room service and turned to the script pile. The telephone rang.

Marcie answered, hoping nothing would interfere with her lesson at five o'clock. It was Sandy, the only person who knew how to contact her. Sandy rarely called her when she was out of town, so competent was she at dealing with the self-described crises of her clients. What could be so important this time, Marcie wondered? If it's Sam with some ego-driven emergency, she vowed to straighten him out right away. Let them start to run all over you and they'd never let up.

"Hi Marce," said Sandy. "I'm really sorry to bother you, but Charles Maier said it wouldn't wait until Monday. He wants you to call him at his beach house as soon as you get the message."

"Did you tell him where I was?"

"Shit, no. I said I thought I could track you down."

"Know what's eating him?"

"Other than Dave, no idea…"

Marcie laughed at Sandy's customary good humor and bad taste.

"Do you have the beach house number with you?" Sandy asked, reverting to her efficient, secretarial mode.

"Uh-huh," confessed Marcie. "I did bring my book."

"Anything you want me to do?"

"No," Marcie concluded, "I'll see what the hell is so damn important it won't wait 'til Monday."

Marcie called Charles and got his impatient telephone voice. She knew that meant he was on the other line, so she asked him if he wanted her to call back. "Just hold on," came the response, "I'm getting off this other call." He must really want to speak with me, she thought, when he was back within seconds. Normally, he wouldn't hesitate to leave her hanging up to five minutes. She had hung up once when the wait seemed interminable, and he had had plenty to say about it when he rang her back. Now she knew it was part of the routine, and she would read a magazine, file her nails, or otherwise occupy herself while waiting for Charles to finish his other call.

"What do you know about this Young Lions business?" Charles demanded when he got back on.

"Is that a new film?"

"Goddamn it," Charles said, raising his voice, "this is no time to be smart!"

Marcie was genuinely perplexed. "I'm serious, Charles, I've never heard of it. What is it?"

Charles softened a bit. "You've really never heard of it?"

"Give me a clue, will you?"

In measured tones, Charles went on. "It's some of our key agents, Randy, Jack and Ben, who think they can turn Allied on its head and give themselves all the power." His voice turned flinty hard. "Well, they're fucking with the wrong person."

"Ben's in this too?" asked Marcie.

Charles ignored her question. "They think they can leverage their clients to change everything I've done!"

"Have you spoken with them?" asked Marcie.

"I can't get them on the phone. They've left town for the weekend. That's why I assumed you were a part of it."

"No. This is the first I've heard about it."

"They'd be crazy to open up their own shop now. The trend is toward big, not boutiques. They'd get buried out there. It's probably a ploy for more money." Charles paused for a beat, apparently contemplating the situation. "The hell with it. It'll be under control by Monday. See you then." He hung up.

Marcie looked at the receiver as the dial tone sounded. So she wasn't the only one with professional problems. How could it be otherwise? Agents were trained to be aggressive and with the good ones, the lessons took. Agency after agency had endured power coups engineered by the young hotshots, full of themselves and the power that flowed from their client base. "Give us the reins of power or we'll set up our own shop!" That had been the rallying cry in the town for years. The prototype was of course Mike Ovitz and his band of disgruntled William Morris cohorts who left to found CAA. They expanded that agency, from its humble beginnings, into the most powerful agency in the world. True, a Mike Ovitz doesn't come along every day. But try to tell that to any young Turk making seven figures and driving a luxury automobile. The more things change, the more they stay the same, thought Marcie.

She put the whole business out of her mind. Charles's call was most unexpected, but didn't really concern her. While she was close to Ben, she understood Monday was soon enough to catch up on the weekend's gossip. In the meanwhile, she had scripts to finish and a tennis lesson to close out a great day.

As the sun's last heat graced the grounds, Marcie made her way to the pro shop where Wes Snyder was putting the finishing touches on the sale of a top-of-the-line racquet to a very large woman who probably couldn't get the ball back over the net. His body carried the deep tan of someone who worked outdoors, while his blond hair was streaked from the sun. Wes smiled as Marcie entered the shop and indicated he would be ready in a minute. He finished his transaction with the woman, charged the racquet to her room, flashed his warmest smile and said he couldn't wait to see the difference in her game. She grinned appreciatively, and left the pro shop.

"Hey, ace, how you hittin' 'em?" Wes asked.

"Holding my own," Marcie replied.

"What'd you have in mind for today?"

"I'd like to hit a few with you, break a sweat, and maybe play some points later."

"Sounds great. Let's have at it."

They walked the few steps from the pro shop to the main court. Only one other of the eight courts was in use, a mixed doubles match that had "social tennis" written all over it. Wes carried several dozen balls in a carrier that he could stand on the court as he taught. He had played #3 singles at Pepperdine, good but not good enough for the tour. With his looks and charm, however, he had staked out a lucrative career for himself as a teaching pro. In Marcie's opinion, he had a natural bent for teaching; he had improved both her strokes and her strategies. Playing together, they had won a mixed doubles charity tournament the previous year, beating some tough competition in the process. It had been a wonderful weekend and she was proud of the trophy she had taken home.

They began to rally, gradually increasing the pace. Marcie loved to hit with men, using their power to hit the ball back without killing herself in the process. When she felt her muscles were responding and she had broken a sweat, she asked that Wes hit cross-courts at her. She couldn't take too much of this, but it was tremendous exercise. He placed them superbly, requiring her to put out maximum energy, but still be able to reach the shots on both sides. Panting, she held up a hand to indicate that she'd had enough of that drill.

"How about some volleys till you catch your breath?" Wes asked.

"Great," said Marcie, taking up a position down the center stripe a few feet from the net. Again, Wes started slowly, gradually increasing the pace of the shots and making her extend more and more toward the baselines. He passed her on some, but most she volleyed crisply from both sides. Wes was very encouraging and lavish in his praise when she hit a particularly good shot.

As the basket ran out, he picked up the balls on his side while Marcie kicked those on her side to the net where he could retrieve them. "How's that second serve coming?" Wes inquired.

"It's better, but not as much of a weapon as I'd like."

"Let's try a few," Wes suggested, walking over to Marcie's side of the court. "Are you still hitting slice serves?"

"Trying," said Marcie.

"Hit some flat ones first," Wes said, "but nice and easy. We don't want you pulling anything."

Marcie took a couple of balls from the basket and set to work on her serve. She increased the pace until she was cracking them sharply into the box on the opposite side of the net. Wes nodded, paying close attention. Marcie moved on to her slice serve, and her percentage fell off dramatically.

"It's your toss," Wes said emphatically. "Let's review the basics again."

Marcie began moving her toss to accommodate Wes's patient insistence. As she did so, her serve began to improve. Soon, she was hitting wicked slice serves that would draw her opponent out of position. The change brought a smile to her face.

"I wish you were there when I play matches." she said.

"You know you can't be coached during a match."

"Give me a break," Marcie said and laughed, "that's only for the pros."

Marcie moved to the bench at courtside and retrieved a towel. As she wiped her face, Wes said "Now what?"

"You're not getting off that easy. Let's play a set."

"Do you want a spot?" Wes asked.

"No way," came the reply.

The set score was 6-3 in favor of Wes, but the match was actually closer than that. The points were exciting, and the tennis pretty damn good. As they played the set, they had gathered a crowd of nearly twenty guests who had wandered by and stayed to watch.

Marcie gave as good as she got in the ground strokes department. She had great difficulty handling Wes's serve, the strongest part of his game, unused as she was to returning serves that came in at nearly 100 miles per hour. While she got many back, they were rarely returned with anything on them.

Sweat pouring off both of them, they rushed to the net for congratulatory handshakes. Wes draped his arm over Marcie's shoulder and told her, "Good set!"

As the two moved off the court to the water fountain on the side, Marcie asked, "How the hell does Agassi return the big ones the way he does?"

"He's one of the few who can," Wes answered. "Agassi, Chang, Connors before that, then who? It's plenty tough, Marcie."

Marcie felt better. Indeed she felt great after the workout. As they went back into the pro shop, Wes gave her a look. "Are you doing anything for dinner?"

Marcie seemed surprised, but hoped she hid it. "Actually, no. I don't make plans when I come here."

"Can I buy you dinner?" Wes continued.

"I'd like that."

"How about if I pick you up in front at about 7:30?"

"Sounds terrific," Marcie replied. "I'll see you then."

Marcie walked the short distance back to her villa, stripped off her tennis clothes, and stepped into the shower. Her mind was totally occupied with the dinner invitation, which had come out of left field. She'd known Wes for the five years she'd been coming here, and there had never been even the slightest indication that he might have any interest in her, other than as a tennis client. Did he now? Did she have any interest in him? She didn't really know if he could keep up a dinner conversation. Their entire relationship had taken place on the court and in the pro shop. As she let the warm water run over her body, she wondered if it mattered if he could talk or not. He certainly was cute. Is that who she had become at the ripe old age of 35? Would she be moving on to pool guys, cable television guys and kids from the Allied mailroom? Please, she thought, he just asked me to dinner. Maybe he wants to get into films, and not into my pants. That's a much more likely scenario. And anyway, why log in all this thought about a dinner invitation? See what happens. No reason to plan like this, unless you want to influence what it is that does happen…

Wes took her to a new Italian restaurant that was small, one step above a "family" restaurant, but softly lit and inviting. He was greeted like a relative at the door, by Giovanni, the restaurant's owner and maitre d'. They were seated in a comfortable booth and Wes ordered a bottle of Chianti. Giovanni left two menus then hurried away to greet other diners who arrived immediately behind them. Wes and Marcie turned their attention to the hand-written offerings labeled Saturday.

Looking up, as if suddenly inspired, Wes asked, "So do you have a regular person back in Los Angeles?"

Marcie smiled at his choice of words and shook her head. "How about you?"

"No," he replied, "I broke up with Jennifer, the girl who helped in the pro shop, about six months ago."

Marcie had vaguely wondered where she was. Did he want to be questioned further about her? Apparently he didn't, as he switched back to the safer topic of tennis.

"So, how much are you able to play in L.A.?"

"Two or three times a week," she said, "mostly doubles though. Not much competitive tennis any more."

He nodded and took a sip of wine.

Marcie thought that dinner could be awkward and painful in the extreme. Better to take control.

"So, Wes, how come after all this time, you decide to kill a Saturday night with me?"

He smiled. "It's not like I'm killing it."

"But why now?"

He grinned again. "It's taken me all this time to get up the nerve to ask you."

Marcie smiled back, and the ice thawed. From that moment, conversation flowed easily as they discussed a wide range of subjects, from movies to politics, to tennis, to drugs. Wes turned out to be reasonably well informed, with a sneaky sense of humor. He had a point of view all his own, and Marcie found him far more interesting than she had anticipated. The wine loosened his tongue still further and he proved an attentive and stimulating dinner partner. She offered to split the bill, but he wouldn't hear of it. "I invited you," he insisted. Wes did accept Marcie's invitation back to the villa. She suggested stopping at a liquor store and picking up a bottle of chilled champagne. Wes readily agreed, and put up no resistance when Marcie said that this was on her. She asked Wes to pick the best liquor store open at that hour and he told her that Vendome didn't close till midnight.

After purchasing the champagne, they drove the short distance back to the villa. As they sipped their first glass, Marcie asked if he felt like a tub.

"You bet," Wes answered, "I've been on the court all day." The water was always kept warm, so it was just a matter of turning on the jets. Wes took a beat to check out how this was to proceed, but when he saw Marcie peeling off her clothes and draping them over a chair, he was quick to join in. Marcie slid into the water first, bringing her glass and the bottle to the side of the tub. Wes was a couple of steps behind her and Marcie turned toward him to see him emerge from inside, two towels in his hand. His body was not a great surprise to her but his hips looked narrower and his shoulders broader than they did with clothes. He was comfortable with his nudity, as she was with hers. He dropped into the tub, then put his arms around her and pressed her to him. The cool Palm Springs night, the wine and now the champagne, and most of all the extremely attractive man who held her close, made Marcie sigh with pleasure.

"You mean we could have been doing this for the last five years?" she asked.

"No, Jennifer was around for most of that time. But for the last few months, yeah, we could have."

Marcie put her glass down, put both arms around Wes's neck and kissed him on the lips. He responded passionately and Marcie felt herself fighting for breath. Wes ran his fingers lightly over her back sending shivers of pleasure wherever he touched. She leaned back for a minute, looking at the dazzling stars overhead.

"You don't know how lucky you are to have a sky where you can see stars at night."

"But I do know," said Wes. "It's one of the things I like best about living here."

"A girl could feel very romantic in a setting like this."

"With just anybody?" asked Wes.

"No," Marcie replied. "It would take a special person."

"How would you know him?"

"I'd know him, you can be sure of that."

Wes kissed her, his body pressing tightly against hers. She marveled at the tightness of his athletic frame. She also felt the stirrings of his arousal as their bodies remained locked together.

"I'm getting that feeling now," she whispered to him.

As his hands reached to enclose her breasts, she leaned back, resting her head on the rim of the tub as a jet of water played sensuously between her legs.

Wes moved away from her, hopped from the tub, and taking the mattress off the chaise lounge, placed it on the ground. He covered it with the towels, then ducked into the villa. In a few seconds he was back, holding a wrapped condom. He climbed part way into the tub to help Marcie out and led her to the mattress. Marcie took the condom from him, pleased that they didn't have to stop for discussion at this juncture, and slipped it on his erect member. He shuddered slightly as she touched him.

His lovemaking proved to be gentle, considerate, but quite athletic. He was an accomplished lover who brought her to successive orgasms. The final one was in tandem with his, and they lost themselves in the sheer excitement of the moment. Afterwards, their bodies aglow, they climbed back into the tub, all smiles and soft caresses.

"That was wonderful," Marcie sighed. "What a perfect night."

"For me too," said Wes. "I can't believe I couldn't get up the courage before."

"When the time is right, it's right," Marcie said. She laughed. "God, I wish I hadn't said something that stupid."

Wes put his arm around her and kissed her lips. "I don't think it was stupid. What's stupid is your not having a better second serve."

Marcie grinned. "Nice talk. That's not what you told me this afternoon."

"You were a paying customer then."

"And now?"

"Now," said Wes, "now you're my friend."

Marcie picked up the bottle and poured the last of it into their glasses. She raised her glass in a toast and clicked Wes's. "Let's drink to being friends!" They drank and held one another closely. Now this is more like it, Marcie thought.

CHAPTER VI

Marcie returned home from the Springs Sunday evening, eager to plunge into her L.A. life. She felt refreshed from her wrap-up at the Villas. She had finished her scripts, whipped through the *Times* Sunday puzzle, had one more massage from Ronnie and said goodbye to Wes. He had been charming and almost grateful, although she had spoken to him in a corner of the pro shop, not exactly a place of great privacy. Grabbing a yellow pad and pen, she moved to the answering machine which was furiously blinking on her night table. The digital display said there were twenty-six calls waiting for her. She winced and considered changing her mind, but they would still be there the next day, blinking more impatiently than ever. With the help of the fast forward, she began to roll through the callers. People in search of a fourth for tennis, a late invitation to fill in at a dinner party, several calls from Sam, growing increasingly impatient, her mother, sounding normally cranky, Charles Maier, and a half-dozen calls from Randy and Ben, two-thirds of the Young Lions team.

Curiosity got the best of her and she returned Ben Kloster's call first. He answered, sounding almost breathless. When Marcie identified herself and started to come out with a witty remark, he quickly put her on hold. She fought the urge to hang up and return more of her calls. He came back on the line, even more breathless, in seconds.

"Christ, Ben," Marcie said, "you sound like you're having a stroke."

"No," Ben piped up, "just a little stressed out."

"So it's true?"

"I don't know what exactly you've heard, but I really need to see you before you go to the office tomorrow. How's about in a half-hour?"

"Slow down," Marcie answered. "I just got home and I've got to crash. I'll meet you for breakfast, if you want."

"Great! The Bel-Air at 7:00?"

"What about 7:30?" Marcie asked. "I've got my exercise guy early tomorrow."

"Deal," said Ben, hanging up so quickly it was as if he was trying to avoid the police getting a fix on his location.

Marcie decided to attack a few more of her calls to get a head start on Monday. Since her mother was on the East Coast, she reasoned she'd better call her first before she turned in for the day. She dialed her home in Scarsdale, a posh bedroom community about twenty miles north of New York.

"Hi," she said when her mother picked up. "I was away for the week-end and just got back. I hope it's not too late to call."

"No, sweetie, let me tell your father you're on."

In seconds they were all together for a telephone family reunion. They wanted to know all about the weekend, how her job was doing, any new men in her life, and had she heard that Aunt Elizabeth had had a stroke and checked out? Marcie had only met Elizabeth twice in her life, once at her wedding and once when she came through L.A. when Marcie had helped her get tickets to the Arsenio Hall Show. How the hell would she have heard, Marcie wondered? Was it written up in the Trades? Best to express her sympathy for poor Aunt Elizabeth and move on.

"What about new guys?" her mother asked. "Aren't there supposed to be so many eligible bachelors in Los Angeles?"

Marcie smiled to herself recalling her night with Wes, but told her mother there were none, and she would be the first to find out. Nice to know, she thought, that the term "eligible bachelors" was alive and well.

She got the usual sign-offs and declarations of everyone loving each other very much.

"One other thing," her mother said.

"Yes?"

"I wore your pin to a lunch with some of the girls today, and guess what, everybody loved it!"

"I'm glad, mom."

"I don't know whether they knew it was used or not. But they did say they loved it."

Oh well, thought Marcie, don't fight it.

"That's terrific. I'll talk to you guys soon,okay?"

"Take care of yourself, honey," her father said.

"We love you," her mother chimed in.

"I love you too."

She hung up and took a deep breath. Why is all the talk about how difficult children are? Maybe it's all wrong and it's parents that are the real problem. Thinking about problems, she decided to call Sam and find out what was eating him.

She dialed his number and got his answering machine. "Hi," his recorded voice said, "You've reached Sam. Leave your name and the time you called and I'll get back to you right away. Thanks."

Short and to the point. She weighed hanging up but decided to at least get credit for having called him back. "Hey, handsome, it's Marcie. Sorry I missed your calls, but I just got back…"

"Marce," Sam said, turning off his answering machine.

Oh no, she thought, already screening his calls. How do they learn the bullshit so quickly?

"I'm really glad it's you."

"What's going on? This was supposed to be a quiet weekend." "I met with Peter, and I think he's going to make the changes. He seems like a good guy. Julie Ormond came in to see him as I was leaving and I got a few words in with her. We're going to have lunch on Wednesday."

"That's great," Marcie said. "It sounds like everything's coming together."

"I don't know. They want to start in six weeks, and it could get pretty rushed."

"Come on, Sam, this one is better prepared than most. Don't get paranoid on me. Just ride along on the wave and keep making your points. You'll be listened to. I promise."

"That's fine for you to say but it's my fucking career."

Whew, thought Marcie, it starts so soon.

"Sam, it's natural that you're worried at this stage. Trust me, movies are all about crisis management. It's process, and it'll all work itself out."

"I don't know. They're not giving me the fucking time of day. And without me, their picture is nowhere."

"Sam, we've confirmed this deal to Warners. If you're even thinking about doing something rash, put it right out of your head."

Sam took a beat, a little surprised at Marcie's emphatic tone. Then he waded in again. "They've got to listen to me, especially when I'm right!"

"Look, pal, this is a collaborative business and always will be. You may have some muscle here, but not as much as you think. You've only done one picture. Do yourself a favor and don't get a reputation for being trouble. It's the fastest ticket out of the business."

Sam considered Marcie's advice. Seeming a bit chastened, he murmured, "All right, I'll keep trying to make it work."

"It's the only way to go," said Marcie.

"Thanks, Marcie. You're the best," said Sam, in a tone that Marcie found lacking in his usual conviction.

Enough, thought Marcie, as she hung up. She wistfully recalled the weekend's pleasures, now so far away. She shuddered slightly as her body recaptured the feeling of Wes inside her. It had been a magical night. As she got ready for bed, setting the alarm to be up in time for her trainer, she let her mind play on different possibilities with Wes. None seemed very realistic.

*   *   *   *   *

She was a little stiff from the weekend's exercise and took a 400-milligram Motrin before her trainer arrived. She was happy to be working out, but no sense starting the work week feeling like shit. The short ring of the doorbell announced the arrival of George. Her trainer was a bit more restrained than usual. The flu must have robbed him of his customary brimming over with life exuberance. It was almost obscene to see him that way at 5:15 in the morning. George was a walking advertisement for the healthy way, the way of exercise and discipline. Indeed, his washboard abdomen was featured in the advertisement he ran in the Trades when he first became a personal trainer. Now he was one of the inner circle—trainer to the stars.

Marcie greeted him warmly and asked how he was feeling?

"Much better, thanks. I'm still a little weak, but at least the fever's gone."

"So you didn't see a doctor?"

He looked curiously at her. "No need. Mega-doses of C and zinc, and I feel pretty good."

"Well, I'm glad," Marcie said, lying down to run through her stretches before beginning her workout. George took the exercise CD from the top of the wall unit and slid it into the player. The heavy metal beat pounded out the rhythm as Marcie was put through her paces. George employed a program of weight training and aerobics, guaranteed to make you aware you had had a serious workout. It was not for nothing that his clients referred to him as the Trainer from Hell. At precisely 6:30, he announced that she was done for the day. She looked upward and softly said, "Thank you, God." George chuckled as he gathered his gear, put it into his bag, and headed for the door.

"Wednesday?" he said, turning toward her.

"Perfect, have a good one," Marcie replied, as George let himself out. Marcie didn't take a lot of time getting ready. She peeled off her clothes on the way to the bathroom, and threw them into the hamper. She washed her hair quickly in the shower, missing the luxury of the extra time she'd had for such things over the weekend. She dried her hair, made up her face, slipped into a nearly new dress, put on accessories, and was out the door at 7:10. Plenty of time to cruise down Benedict and head west on Sunset to Stone Canyon, where she would turn off for the Bel-Air Hotel.

Traffic was heading east, as she had figured, and she was able to pull into the Bel-Air parking lot at 7:25. She knew this would shock Ben, her being not only punctual, but actually early.

As Marcie gave her Lexus to the attendant, Ben pulled up in a red Jeep Cherokee. He waved as she stopped and waited for him to surrender his keys. As he kissed her hello, Marcie wondered, as she always did, why the strange, presumed intimacy had become commonplace in this town.

"Hi," he said, "I can't believe you're here early."

Marcie smiled and said, "It's the new me."

As they headed into the dining room, Ben looked at her quizzically.

Marcie smiled mysteriously, but offered no further explanation.

As they walked into the uncrowded dining room, Ben looked around to see if he knew anyone. He didn't recognize anybody, but steered Marcie to the farthest corner, away from the morning sun streaming in the windows facing the patio. Marcie noted the precautions, but opted not to say anything. Better, she thought, to let the breakfast play out by Ben's design.

Coffee was poured and Ben asked the waiter to give them a few minutes. Ever obliging, the waiter returned to his post by the door. Ben inhaled deeply, as if suffering a sudden oxygen debt, and said, "How much do you know about what's going on?"

"Basically zilch," Marcie answered. "Charles found me in the Springs over the weekend to ask me the same thing. I didn't know anything then, and I don't now."

Ben seemed to weigh his words carefully. Then, he continued.

"I don't know what Charles said, although I'd like to, but basically Randy, Jack and I are going to go into business for ourselves. We may take one or two of the junior people and we're pretty certain that the bulk of our clients will come, too. We're making good money and all that, but we think the agency is standing still. It's all changing out there, and the agency business has to change with it."

He stopped for a beat to let the main thrust of the plan sink in. Marcie remained expressionless, too good a game player to reveal her hand this early in the conversation. She had thought she was a good friend of Ben's, and was considerably affected by his failure to discuss his plans with her.

"That's all very exciting, but what does it have to do with me?" Marcie tried to sound unemotional and open with her question.

"We want you to join us as a partner. Part of the change we see is the expanded role of women in the business. Look around Allied. The message hasn't gotten through to Charles and Derek yet. We all have tremendous respect for you, your work and your clients. We want you to join us."

A shot of adrenaline pumped through her body. This was both unexpected and very exciting. She saw he was waiting for some indication how she was taking this information. "You're thinking of four equal partnerships then?"

"Uh, no, not exactly."

"What were you thinking, Ben?" Marcie said quietly.

"Thirty, thirty, thirty and ten to start off. We'd take another look after a year and see where the equities lie."

"So it's sort of everyone is equal, but some are more equal than others?"

"Come on Marcie, we don't all make the same now."

"I thought you were arguing for an enlightened structure where women and men were paid for the work performed, not whether they had a dick or not?"

Ben colored noticeably. He seemed suddenly uncomfortable in his role as messenger. Ben signaled the waiter over and they placed their orders as if nothing had happened. As the waiter freshened their coffee and withdrew again, Ben asked Marcie if she would at least think about it.

"This is all very preliminary, and very hush-hush," he said. "We wanted you to hear it first from us, and to give some serious thought to the advantages in joining us. Shit, Marcie, we'd really have a good time. You know we would."

"Come on, Ben. You're saying give up the security and benefits of Allied because they treat me unfairly. Come and join you three guys, with none of the security, and come in as a junior partner when I've been in the business almost as long as any of you, and surely book as much business a year from my list as you do. Where's the upside for me? Am I missing something here?"

Again Ben shifted uneasily in his chair. He was pleased to see the waiter making his way over to the table from the kitchen, their orders on a tray balanced skillfully in one hand.

As the waiter again departed, Marcie asked, "Have you had your discussion with Charles yet?"

"No, that's set up for 10:00 this morning—at his apartment."

"Sounds like Charles, trying to get a little edge by having the meeting on his turf."

Ben picked at his pancakes, continuing to appear uneasy about the direction the conversation had taken.

Marcie dug into her scrambled eggs with relish. Between sips of coffee, she asked, "Ben, we're supposed to be good friends. Did you really expect me to jump all over that offer, if that's what it was?"

Ben looked her in the eyes. "I'm in a difficult seat. They approached me about this deal. They know we're friends and I was asked to speak with you. Without betraying my partners, I can honestly say they truly want you to join us. The terms will have to be hammered out."

Fair enough, thought Marcie. She felt a little better about where she stood with Ben. For the others, she'd have to see.

Ben paid the check and they walked together to the parking lot. "Do me this favor," he said, "keep all your options open. Things could get a bit hairy this week."

She smiled. "I'll do that. But you be sure to tell your team that it's got to be an equal partnership, or no deal."

Ben hugged her warmly. "I'll do that," he said.

As they split up, Marcie said, "Good luck in your meeting with Charles. Maybe he'll surprise you and it'll all work out."

Driving to the office, she ran the notion of joining the Young Lions around in her head. There would be short-term cuts in cash flow for all of them. There always were. But real money came today when you owned something that some purchaser wanted to buy. Salary and bonuses were nice, but she knew enough about the Tax Code to know that the lower tax rate for capital gains was the real key to coming up with "Fuck You Money." Most of the town was focused on accumulating enough capital to walk, their middle finger extended in the classic "Fuck You" posture. Maybe, Marcie thought, she was no different. She wasn't sure how much that would be today, but knew it had to be plenty to permit her to walk away from all this without worrying about money ever again. Ownership in the new agency would give her that opportunity. It *was* kind of flattering that they had asked her. She decided to let the game proceed a little before giving it any serious thought.

Marcie walked into her office, buoyed up by the breakfast at the Bel-Air. Games had an intrinsic appeal to her, and this one promised to be intriguing, with high stakes and careers in the balance. She smiled, waved hello to Sandy, and wasn't surprised when Sandy followed her into her office.

Never bashful, Sandy blurted out, "So what gives?"

Marcie gave the briefest thought to trying to be circumspect. But it was Sandy, and any artifice like that would never get by her.

"With the Young Lions. Come on, tell me everything."

"Okay, okay," said Marcie, instantly caving in to what would be relentless pressure. "Just do me a favor and get me some coffee, while I glance at the Trades. When you get back, we'll talk."

Sandy looked a bit apprehensive, but reluctantly put her pad down and left Marcie's office. It always amazed Marcie to discover how much Sandy and her counterparts actually knew about the inner workings of the agency and its clients. And the network didn't stop there. Staff at all the other agencies were involved in a constant game of gossip one-upmanship, so Sandy was privy to the goings on at those agencies as well. Marcie had used Sandy's pipelines of information before and wouldn't hesitate to do so again if this situation ever got serious.

There was no mention of upheavals at Allied in the *Reporter*. Moving to *Daily Variety*, Marcie found a tease in Army Archerd's column, suggesting that rumblings were being heard at one of the big agencies. This meant that Army didn't have enough facts, even for *Variety*, to print a story. He would by tomorrow, she knew; today was the last day of comparative secrecy on the whole Young Lions scenario.

The telephone rang and Marcie forgot for a moment that Sandy was not at her desk to answer it. She contemplated letting it ring through to the receptionist downstairs, but decided at the last moment to pick it up.

"Marcie Sandmore."

"Answering your own phones now," drawled the unmistakable Southern voice of her friend from public relations, Jane Pratt. "Things must really be a mess if they let poor Sandy go."

Amidst hearty laughter from both ends of the telephone, Sandy walked back in carrying two cups of steaming coffee.

Marcie held up one finger to indicate this call would be over soon and Sandy silently mouthed the word "fresh," so Marcie would know what had taken her a few minutes.

Pratt continued. "Everyone's talking about the Lions or something. It's the hottest gossip in town."

"So it seems," said Marcie. "I was away this weekend, in the Springs, and I see all hell broke loose."

"Well, we should talk about this and some of your people. How about drinks around six? You could come over to my place, if you'd like."

"That's great," Marcie replied. "I'll know much more by tonight and we can scheme and plot to take over the world."

"I don't want the whole goddamned world," Jane insisted, "just my fair share. See you at six."

Marcie put down the phone and turned to Sandy. "Well, you heard the bottom line. I don't really know shit."

"Cut the crap," said Sandy. "What about your breakfast with Ben? Is he suddenly trying to jump you, or did that have something to do with all this?"

Marcie laughed. "How did you know about that?" Sandy nodded knowledgeably. Marcie thought to herself that she ought to know better than to shortchange the info queen. She wasn't going to be let off the hook until Sandy was satisfied that she had pried out of her all that she knew. Marcie let on that Ben had tried to recruit her to the Young Lions team, but that she had not given him a definitive answer. She didn't want to go into the deal with Sandy, who, in any case, didn't ask for those details. Marcie was pleased that Sandy seemed satisfied knowing only that talks were underway.

"Can we go to work now?" asked Marcie.

"Sure," replied Sandy. "How long do you think you've got until Charles buzzes you up to his office?"

"Good question, but Charles is meeting with them at his apartment. So, let's get started."

Marcie took advantage of the absence of crises to pursue normal agency business. Clients to check in with, buyers to press for answers, an actor who she had been trying to sign for six months, all calls in the line of duty. As she hung up with her last caller, Sandy buzzed her.

"Yes?" Marcie said, picking up the phone.

"It's Charles," Sandy replied, dragging out his name. "He wants to see you right away. In his office."

"Please tell Edith I'm on my way."

Marcie headed up the stairs to see Charles. As she walked down the hall to his corner office, she passed open secretarial cubicles, with agents' offices behind them. Although the telephones were ringing off the hook in the usual fashion, Marcie thought the agency seemed a little quiet today, even a bit tense. Maybe it was her imagination, but things seemed to be progressing in hushed, anxious tones. Oh well, Charles would certainly move the game pieces in one direction or another.

She greeted Edith and was waved towards Charles' closed door. Knocking once, she opened the door and found Charles alone in his office, seated at his desk. He was wearing a power suit and tie rather than his customary sport jacket and slacks. Maybe this was to be a momentous occasion.

"Sit down," he said, gesturing absently at one of the two chairs in front of his desk. She hated this arrangement because his chair and desk were positioned on a raised platform, making the chairs in front of the desk unusually low. The result was that you were forced to look up at Charles to hold a conversation with him. It was this kind of bullshit that truly bugged Marcie. "Are you any more plugged in than you were in San Francisco?"

"Palm Springs," Marcie commented.

"Whatever," replied Charles, dismissing her correction with a wave of his hand. "What do you know?"

"Actually not much more than what you told me," Marcie said, wishing she had a better idea of Charles' agenda.

"Are you saying you haven't talked to any of the so-called Young Lions since we talked?"

"I didn't know that's what you were asking."

Charles flared with sudden anger. "Well have you?"

"Yes, I had breakfast with Ben this morning."

"Did he ask you?" Charles wanted to know.

Marcie thought that he was really reaching and considered for an instant telling him that wasn't any of his business. She decided not to antagonize her employer and instead responded, "Yes, we did talk about it over breakfast at the Bel-Air."

"And?"

"And what?"

"Marcie," Charles was now in a rage, "this is no time to be coy. These idiots are trying to tear apart this agency. The whole town is buzzing about it, and it's got to have a damaging effect on the morale of our employees, not to mention our clients. I need to know if I can count on your loyalty. We've been very good to you and this is the time to show some appreciation."

This was not exactly what she had thought would occur. He was putting the screws to her before anything had been worked out. Better to tap dance for the moment.

"Are you saying it's all over for them at Allied? I didn't get that idea at all at breakfast."

Marcie noticed that this piqued his interest. Apparently there was still play in this situation. "What exactly happened at breakfast?" he inquired gravely.

"We talked in general terms about their desire to have more control over the business. He said you were meeting with them at your apartment this morning. Then, he asked me if I would consider joining them, and I put him off. I don't even know for sure that they're leaving."

Charles considered Marcie's account of what had transpired at breakfast. He buzzed Edith and asked for a refill on his coffee. Looking at Marcie questioningly, she shook her head. "Just one," he added. Charles seemed content with her explanation, Marcie thought, as she saw the worry lines on his face relax. After a brief pause, Marcie continued.

"What can you tell me? Have they resigned? Did you fire them? Has it spread beyond Ben, Jack and Randy? How come you're not meeting with them?"

"This is very confidential, Marcie, so I'd appreciate your not talking to the others, and especially not to the press. We've adopted a 'No Comment' stand on the whole thing."

Marcie nodded her head, indicating she understood.

"I'd like to be able to work this out with them, and their attorney is meeting with ours as we speak. The principals will meet later. Money isn't the main issue, although it certainly is on the table. They want a bigger role in management, and frankly it's time they had it. There *is* an inevitability to things like this, and it always takes a push to make things happen. Well, they pushed, and we're trying to respond."

"Do you think the deal is makeable?" Marcie asked.

"Of course it's makeable," Charles snapped. "Every deal is makeable, it just depends on how much you want to give. We're willing to give plenty, but nobody is going to tell me to bend over and take it in the ass. Not them, not you, nobody."

Charles had gotten himself worked up again. His face flushed slightly, and he seemed relieved that Edith took this moment to walk in with a fresh cup of coffee for him. Marcie wasn't sure what else could be accomplished in this meeting. She decided to let Charles carry the ball, and continued to look at him as if he had more to say.

Finally Charles's face softened. "I don't mean to take this out on you. These guys have made me crazy by trying to put a gun to my head instead of talking across a table like grownups. Do me a favor, let me know if you hear anything you think I should know. Okay?"

"Sure, I'll do that," Marcie responded. She was happy to escape without having to make any bigger commitment than that. This all struck her as being somewhat bizarre since she wasn't a major player in the agency. She certainly was responsible for more than her share of commissions. Her clients were steady earners and generally loyal to her, at least as loyal as most clients could be said to be. Sure Sam was hot, but Sam was just getting off the ground. If his next two pictures bombed, no one would even remember his name. Was she really in the middle of this game, or had she simply wandered near the front where the war was being waged?

When Marcie got back to the office, Sandy was waiting expectantly for news from her meeting. "Sorry," Marcie said. "He didn't let me know anything. He only wanted to know what I knew, so I referred him to you."

Sandy's jaw dropped as Marcie grinned and said, "Just a joke. Lighten up, will you?"

"You had me for a minute there. You sure he didn't say anything that I should know?"

"Yes, I'm quite sure."

"Okay," said Sandy a little dubiously, "let's go at the call list."

Most of the calls were pretty routine, and didn't suggest any particular urgency. No new developments on the Young Lions front, although Marcie knew that much was going on behind closed doors. There was a call from Wes Snyder on his lunch break leaving a home number where he'd be after nine. Marcie reflected for a minute on that one, feeling a warm flush envelop her body. Sandy asked her who Wes was, perhaps registering the subtle change in Marcie's color. "Just the tennis pro at the Villas," Marcie answered, playing down any emotional response to the question.

Before Sandy could follow up, she answered a call and told Marcie that Tim was on the line.

"Hi!" Marcie said. "Are you back in L.A.?"

"I am," said Tim, sounding very serious. "Is dinner still on?"

"If it's still all right with you, I'm looking forward to it."

"Do you like sushi? There's a new joint on Ventura that's great."

"I do like sushi," Marcie said. "You're sure you're cool with this? We can postpone it, if you'd like."

"No, my New York trip was a bit trying, but I've been looking forward to this. Eight o'clock at your house?"

"Perfect," she said. "I'll see you then."

Sandy, sitting in Marcie's office, hearing only her end of the call, stuck her index finger in her mouth and made gagging noises.

"What's with you?" Marcie asked.

"What's with you? This gay caballero comes riding in on his white horse, and you're like buying his whole act."

"Hey, slow down. He's a buyer introduced by Charles. He can be straight, gay or bi. If his money's on the table, which remains to be seen, my job is to make nice and sell him whatever I can. Do you have a problem with that?"

Looking chastened, Sandy shook her head. "I was only watching out for you."

"And I appreciate it. I do."

"I don't know exactly what it is," Sandy said.

"I'm seeing him for dinner, and I'll keep my eyes and ears open. Okay?"

Sandy nodded.

Strange, Marcie thought, that Sandy would have this strong a view about someone who was barely a business acquaintance. Imagine what she'd think if she were informed about her activities with Wes over the weekend. Well, it wasn't such a bad thing to have someone looking out for her.

CHAPTER VII

Jane Pratt lived in Santa Monica in one of the small, 40s houses that seemed to jump out of a private detective novel. Marcie adored the house because it was what it was. No pretensions, no artifice, just a splendid example of a classic California architectural style.

"Get your ass in here and help me with this bottle of wine," said Jane, when she answered the doorbell. "Francis Coppola sent it to me as a peace offering from his vineyard. The bastard slandered one of my clients, and thinks he can get away with a case of wine. The least we can do is drink it."

Jane ushered Marcie into the living room which was tastefully decorated in a spare, modern style. The impact of the decor was clearly more *Architectural Digest* than dentist's office, and Marcie marveled at how welcoming and warm the room felt. Jane pulled the open bottle from a crystal ice bucket and poured two glasses, handing one to Marcie.

Marcie clicked glasses with her and tried a sip. "It's damn good, isn't it?"

"Maybe he should stick to wine and not try any more movies," Jane offered.

"Vicious," said Marcie. "Okay, let's talk about something else."

Jane smiled. "Great. Tell me what those wackos at your agency are doing. They've got the whole town talking."

Marcie filled Jane in, including the substance of her breakfast with Ben.

"Would you consider leaving if they upped the ante?" asked Jane.

"I don't know. What do you think?"

Jane considered the question for a minute. "Hell, I guess it depends on how adventurous you feel. You've got your client base and you can always catch on with one of the big agencies. Do you see yourself in partnership with those guys?"

"It's a tough question. I'm kind of in a cocoon at Allied, working hard, but not really moving forward. Lang thinks they're screwing me over, and he may be right. I'm pretty sure I can structure a new deal at Allied, but I'm not sure that's what I should do either. I don't know, maybe it is a time for a change."

"Too many tough questions on the table," said Jane. "Let all of that rest for a bit and see which way things break. We can't make much of a plan in a vacuum. You've got to let it work itself out for a while."

"But it doesn't hurt to take a good look at myself while all this is going on," Marcie insisted.

"No, that's right. But don't be beating up on yourself. That won't help anything. Trust me, this is a very fluid situation. Don't get sucked up in anything yet. It's going to shift almost hourly." Jane changed the subject. "So how's your boy Sam making out on the Weir picture?"

Marcie was happy for the respite from her concerns. "Okay, I think. I'm having lunch with him this week, but I know I'll hear from him before. He seems to be doing all right with Peter. He's at the stage where he takes himself very, very seriously."

Jane laughed. "Do they learn that in actors' school, I wonder?"

"It sure seems to go with the territory," said Marcie. "He was such a nice boy when I met him. Do they have to turn into monsters?"

"Only if they stay in this town. The ones like Harrison Ford and Redford keep their humanity. They were smart enough to get the hell out of here. For the others, the town chews them up and spits them out. They may make a bunch of bucks, but they sure lose something in the process."

Marcie pondered that for a minute. "Sure they move out. That's possible when you're a big, big star. It's awful tough when you're on your way up."

"No doubt." Jane agreed. "But there's still hope for Sam."

"I know there is," said Marcie. "But all the signs point in the other direction. Let's try to keep him who he is, shall we?"

"You got a deal," Jane agreed. "Now I've got to throw you out and get dressed for the theater. I have house seats for the Ahmanson."

"Have a wonderful time. I hear the show is great, and I want a full report tomorrow," said Marcie, already standing to leave. "You got it," Jane replied. "You take care of yourself. You'll know much more about everything in a day or two."

Marcie nodded and kissed her goodbye.

"Thanks for being here for me," she said.

"Any time."

*   *   *   *   *

When the doorbell rang, Marcie answered it, noting that Tim was again precisely on time. It was eight o'clock on the dot. She had had time for a quick shower and change of clothes, and, considering the turmoil of the day, was feeling pretty good. She had changed into a silk blouse and blazer, and slipped on jeans and a silver Native American belt. With black shoes and an unusual silver pin she'd found in Santa Fe, Marcie was ready for Tim, sushi, and whatever direction the evening took.

"Hi," Tim said, kissing her lightly on the cheek.

"Good to see you."

As Tim opened the door of the Rolls, Marcie added, "The Villas were great. I never had to drop your name at all."

Tim got in the driver's side, closed the door, and replied, "They'd better be doing the job right, or they'll be looking for new positions."

He said it softly, but without a trace of humor. This guy's about power, big time, thought Marcie.

"So," she said trying to inject some lightness into the conversation, "New York was a hassle?"

"Your typical Wall Street merry-go-round. But you know how that goes, don't you?"

He *has* pulled a bio on me from some place, Marcie thought. Is he thorough? Paranoid? Or a control freak?

She down-played her concern.

"That was a lot of years ago."

"Don't kid yourself, nothing's changed. It's still a big poker game, and still about trying to guess whether the other players hold the cards or not."

Marcie mulled that observation over, as the Rolls headed over the hill into the Valley.

"I hear," Tim went on, "that the natives are restless at Allied."

"Yeah, something like that."

"Are you part of the insurgent group?"

"No," Marcie said, unwilling to risk Tim's being a pipeline back to Charles.

"Charles is tough," Tim continued, "I'd think carefully before going head to head with him."

"I'm on the sidelines in this one." At least so far, thought Marcie.

They parked on Ventura Boulevard, and walked the short distance to Kouko Sushi.

"You're in for a treat," said Tim.

Before she could reply, a man holding menus came bustling over and began spouting rapid-fire Japanese to Tim. Marcie thought she heard him say "Mr. Garland," but the rest went sailing over her head. Before she could say anything, Tim responded in what she assumed to be fluent Japanese. Her mouth fell open as Tim concluded whatever he was saying, returned the slight bow of the proprietor, and took her arm, escorting her to the table that the proprietor selected.

"You speak Japanese?" Marcie asked, her voice full of surprise.

"I spent some time there a few years ago, when they seemed to have cornered the world's money supply."

"And you learned to speak like that?"

"Sort of self-defense. I wasn't too happy working with a translator."

"Well, I'm impressed," Marcie said.

Tim smiled at her. "I've always had a pretty good ear for languages."

Marcie accepted Tim's offer to order for her. Soon, *sake* and a variety of *sushi and sashimi* were brought to the table. Tim identified some of the more exotic choices, those that Marcie found unfamiliar. Tim had been right. This was a treat.

In the course of eating, Tim volunteered, "I've been giving some thought to trying to tell you what kind of material I'm looking for."

Marcie waited expectantly.

"But I find it nearly impossible to do. If one analyzes it in risk/reward terms, it's like any other business problem. But if you ask what I'm looking for, the best I can come up with is that I'll know it when I see it. It's got to be a good script, a movie I haven't seen before, and a movie that has an emotional center to it that audiences will respond to. I'm afraid all that's of no help at all."

"I don't know," said Marcie. "It sort of sounds as though you'd like to make a movie you'd like to see."

"That's actually pretty close."

"Let me go to work on it. I'm sure we can find something exciting." Marcie paused for a beat. "You seem to have developed a pretty sophisticated knowledge about the movie industry."

"You know what they say. Movies are everybody's second business."

"I'm serious," Marcie insisted. "Most investors seem drawn to the flash or their expectation of the glamour. You seem to have thought more about it."

Tim turned serious. "When I play, I play. When I do business, I do business. The movie industry interests me because it is so full of amateurs and wannabes. It's a pot limit poker game which conventional wisdom says defies logic and predictability. That's exactly the kind of market I prefer. It rewards aggressive chance-taking and focus."

Marcie smiled. "You sound like you're talking to Wall Street analysts."

"The key, as far as I can tell, is stay away from the pursuit of some magic formula for success. Give the public good movies, and they will come. The trick, of course, is to know how to find them and make them at manageable price."

Marcie took it all in as Tim spoke. This was no casual investor. And, he sure sounded like someone whose interests ran beyond producing one vanity film. Maybe it was time for her to do a little research on the mysterious Mr. Garland.

As she finished her second cup of green tea, Marcie said to Tim, "That was just incredible."

Before Tim could reply, the proprietor came by and again engaged Tim in a spirited discussion in Japanese. This time, the only words she could pick up were her own name. As Tim said, "Marcie Sandmore," the proprietor looked to her and bowed. She smiled at him saying, "This was absolutely terrific."

"Thank you very much, Miss Sandmore," he said. "We are very happy you could come with Mr. Garland. He is one of our favorite patrons."

The ride home over Benedict produced very little new information about Tim. Marcie asked whether he had an umbrella corporation or different partners in his deals. He responded elusively.

"I sort of operate by myself. I do have some friends with whom I do deals, but they're not in every one."

At Marcie's house, Tim again chose not to come in, gave Marcie a light kiss on the lips, and told her he'd enjoyed himself.

"Could we do this again?" he asked.

"I'd love to. We'll speak soon."

Marcie went into the house, and as she locked up for the night, she heard the sound of the Rolls pulling out of her driveway.

Interesting man, Marcie thought, as she moved through her house to the bedroom. Before plunging back into the mainstream of her business, the answering machine light blinking angrily, she thought she'd return Wes's call. When he answered, she was pleased at the sound of his voice.

"I'm real happy you called, Marcie. I can only imagine how busy you are. I mean it's a school night, right?"

"Yes, it is a school night." She chuckled at the recollection. "Did you just want to talk, or is there something special you wanted?" That came out much more officious than she had wanted.

Wes picked up on her line. "Is this a bad time?" he asked. "I can call you tomorrow."

"No, it's fine," said Marcie. "I didn't mean it to come out like that."

Marcie explained. "When I got home, everything hit the fan. There's a big mess at work, and"—she paused for a beat—"I miss you."

"I miss you, too," Wes said. "I keep playing back our time together in my mind. It was really special."

A thousand thoughts raced through Marcie's mind. Could she buy into what this man was telling her? Is this some tennis pro who fucks the clients because it's good for business? Was the timing right for her to contemplate a relationship? Was there even a possibility of a relationship? Go slow, she thought. When overcome with doubts, go slow.

"So, Wes," Marcie began, "I'd like to stay on the phone, but there are some calls I have to make. Forgive me if that sounds too Hollywood."

"No problem. Just one more thing. I was asked to be in a commercial, some tennis equipment thing. No big deal. They wanted me to give them the name of my agent to get the deal on paper, and I guess I didn't want to tell them I didn't have one."

Perfect, Marcie thought. If people didn't want to hear the latest Hollywood gossip, they wanted you to represent them. Some things never change.

"You want me to represent you?" Marcie asked.

"Don't you do that kind of thing?"

"To tell you the truth, you'd be better off if you let me put you in touch with a commercials agency. They do this every day, and it might lead to something else."

"Doesn't Allied have a commercials department?" asked Wes.

"They do," Marcie replied, "but it's there to service the big clients— you know for spokesperson ads and that sort of thing. Trust me on this, I'll get you set up tomorrow with a responsible shop that'll take good care of you."

"You're the expert," said Wes. "I really appreciate this."

"I'm sure I can figure out a way to have you return the favor."

Wes laughed. "So I'll wait to hear from you, right?"

Marcie said, "I'll be in touch tomorrow. You take care. I'm glad you called. Bye."

The call was natural enough, but something made Marcie uneasy. She trusted her antenna when it came to reading people in this business. Was he using her? He was charming all right, but the town was overflowing with people oozing charm. What was behind the good looks and the outward warmth? Like the rest of her life at the moment, best to go slow.

The telephone rang. She knew at once that it was Ben.

"Hello," said Marcie trying hard to be warm.

"Where the hell have you been," growled Ben. "I've been trying you all night."

"Whoa, my friend, I just walked in and I don't think I owe you an accounting of where I've been!"

"Jeez Marcie, I'm really sorry. The fucking pressure is building up like crazy and I'm so stressed I'm not even civil to friends."

"That's okay," Marcie said comfortingly. "You've got to lighten up a touch, though, if you want to get through this. So, what happened today?"

"Our lawyers met their lawyers. You know, the big guns. Charles didn't use Tony Boyle, he went to the outside counsel."

"And what happened?"

"The morning meeting was a total waste of time. Lots of yelling and no real progress. Put a bunch of lawyers in a room, and what do you expect? We suggested that the principals join the lawyers and take one more shot at it. After lunch they came back in a more conciliatory mood. I think we can get to some agreement on the money, but those guys don't want to let go of any control. They say they want to share it, but when it comes down to specifics, nothing concrete gets done."

"Did you put a time limit on the discussion?" asked Marcie.

"Kind of. We're talking about a memorandum by close of business tomorrow."

"Or?"

"Or, we're tendering our resignations."

"That's pretty final, isn't it?"

"It's not like this was just sprung on them. We've been separately negotiating with them for months. They keep dragging their heels. Anyway, I'm supposed to get back to Randy and Jack tonight with your answer."

"Did you have a chance to speak to them about dividing the equity evenly?"

"I did. They were very agreeable to modifying the deal. You know, Marcie, we really do want you in."

"Don't agent an agent," Marcie replied. "What kind of modification? Twenty-five percent around the table?"

"Not exactly. We'd each take twenty-seven and a half and you'd get seventeen and a half."

"Gee, that doesn't sound that even to me," Marcie said, putting on a little girl voice.

Ben toughened. "You haven't even said you were willing to leave Allied. We've got our asses hung out so far, there really isn't any turning back. Even if they can structure some kind of deal, it's not going to last for long."

"Let me make it as easy as I can for you Ben. I've been giving a lot of thought to all this since we last spoke. The four of us would have to sit down and really talk things through to see if we could be partners, and hopefully friends. Until we have that discussion, I can't give you any kind of answer. I can say that I wouldn't be willing to entertain the idea at less than an equal partnership. I'm worth every penny of it, otherwise we wouldn't be having this conversation right now."

"I think you're making a huge mistake, Marcie, not looking at the big picture."

"Maybe so, Ben, maybe so. I think we've gone as far as we can for now. You know where to get me if you guys want to talk. I hope you get what you want out of it. I really do." Marcie hung up the phone.

This has been one helluva day thought Marcie. She went to the kitchen and took down a snifter from one of the cupboards. She went back to the living room, poured herself a brandy, took it to the bedroom and began readying for bed.

Getting into bed, Marcie picked up the current *New Yorker* from her night table. She took a sip of brandy and wondered if she were awake enough to read anything beyond the captions to the cartoons. That was the last thought she had before falling asleep, the brandy on her night table half-finished.

The telephone awakened her. She heard her mother say "Hello" as she tried to sound as though she had been awake for hours.

"I didn't wake you, did I, dear? I know you're always up at an indecent hour."

Marcie glanced at the clock-radio. 6:00. Not this indecent unless it's of my choosing, she thought.

"Oh no, mom," she lied. "I was just reading a script." Why did she feel compelled to tell people they had not wakened her? It wasn't just her mother, and not just today.

"I was calling to tell you that Stan and Beverly's son Ed just got divorced."

Marcie was confused. "Yes? Am I missing something here, mom?"

"You always liked him, didn't you?"

"I guess so. Of course, I haven't seen him in over ten years. He could be a serial killer now, for all I know."

"That's ridiculous. He's a wonderful man who is doing very well."

"Mom, what the hell does this have to do with me? You call me at 6:00 to give me an update on Ed Fucking Barnett?"

"Now there's no reason to speak like that! That's not how you were brought up. It's all of that Hollywood business."

"Will you please tell me why you're talking to me about Ed Barnett?"

"Well, Beverly and I were chatting yesterday, and we think it would be marvelous for both families if you and Ed were to see each other. We just know that something wonderful would come of it."

Marcie took a deep breath. I'm 35 years old, she thought, and my mother is trying to fix me up—with a friend of the family, no less! God!

"Thanks" Marcie said, deciding to soft-pedal her response. "Let me think about it, okay? I'll let you know. I've got to get going now to go to a breakfast meeting. Thanks for thinking of me. Love you. Bye."

Marcie hung up before her mother had a chance to say anything else. Did other daughters have this kind of cross to bear? Probably, but it didn't make it any easier. Many of her friends did refer to their mothers as their closest friends. Wasn't that how it was supposed to be? A mother and her daughter, tied to each other in an inseparable way that no other relationship would even approach. Marcie had never felt that. It left a significant void in her life.

Marcie got up and fixed herself a cup of coffee. She brought in the *L.A. Times* from the porch, and quickly flipped through it. Another non-news day. Okay, she said to herself, finally energized, time to get my act together.

Marcie proceeded to shower and dress, thinking about the Young Lions and whether her conversations with Ben would go anyplace at all. Did she want them to? Without more details, she concluded, she couldn't answer that.

When she arrived at the office, small clusters of people, staff and agents alike, were poring over the Trades. Both *Variety* and *The Reporter* carried front page stories on the doings at Allied. One paper had the Young Lions already out the door and about to announce the formation of their new agency. The other revealed that an unnamed source had disclosed that a settlement with Allied was in the final stages and an announcement was imminent. Ah, Hollywood journalism, as unreliable as ever.

Marcie was pulled into a couple of conversations on her way to her office, but she insisted that she knew nothing. Her denials only fueled the rumor that she was in some way involved, probably exiting the agency with the Lions. As she walked past Sandy, acknowledging her with a wave, Marcie couldn't help but wonder how much Sandy had done to spread the word that the Lions were indeed after her.

Sandy brought in her morning coffee, letting the door close behind her.

"You look like shit," were the first words she uttered.

"Thanks," replied Marcie, "I needed that today."

"I don't mean it like that," said Sandy, "I mean you really look stressed. If you want a little bump, I know one of the girls in Concerts who's carrying."

Marcie smiled. The ever-helpful Sandy. "No thanks, I'll muddle through the best I can."

"What can I do to help?" asked Sandy.

"You can keep people out of here today."

"Wow, those guys have really gotten to you."

"It's not just that. I feel like I'm coming down with something."

"Want some aspirin, vitamin C, zinc? I've got it all in my desk."

"I took some Bufferin before I came in, but it's nice knowing a pharmacy is so close."

"Just say the word," said Sandy.

"Let's keep going and maybe nothing will come of it. I should put in an appearance at the Talent Meeting."

Sandy returned to her desk. In seconds, she was back in Marcie's office.

"Do yourself a favor," Sandy said, "and take one of these." She brandished a small, blue pill in her hand.

"What is it?" Marcie asked warily.

"Just a Valium, promise."

"So it's 'better living through chemistry,' huh?"

"Don't knock it. It works."

Marcie smiled, took the Evian bottle she kept on her desk and washed down the pill.

Marcie looked over her call list from yesterday, a morning ritual, while Sandy plopped down on the sofa, waiting for instructions. The phone rang and Sandy answered, "Miss Sandmore's office." Marcie paid very little attention as Sandy repeated "Uh-huh" several times and hung up.

In a dramatic, hushed tone, she said, "That was Karin, Randy's secretary. He called her from the road and asked if you would swing by his office when your meeting let out. He said to tell you it was very important." Sandy looked expectantly at Marcie. "What do you think it is? They want you to leave with them, don't they?"

"You're right, but so far they don't want me enough. And we're a long way from seeing whether that kind of deal makes any sense. But I'll go up and talk. Can't hurt, you know?" Marcie smiled at Sandy, her confidence high, enjoying, for the moment, the game.

"You get 'em, girl," said Sandy.

The Talent Department meeting was uneventful, as expected. The agents were far more interested in the machinations within the agency's power structure than in the servicing of their clients. After denying that she knew any more than they did, Marcie chose to adjourn the meeting. She also found herself growing increasingly intrigued with her coming session with Randy.

"Coffee?" Randy asked, as Marcie walked into his office in the Television Department.

"Please," Marcie responded.

Randy Goldberg's office was completely decorated in gray and black. It had a grim, almost depressing feel to it, even though the furniture and the accents were expensive and in excellent taste. It certainly said "a man lives here," and perhaps that was the purpose of the motif. She had never reached a conclusion about Randy's sexual preference. She'd have to ask Sandy who either knew or believed she knew all such things. As Randy's assistant, a strikingly handsome young man named Tad, brought in the coffee, and discreetly departed, Randy sat down on the gray sofa and indicated that Marcie should sit in one of the untempting black easy chairs. Randy was a level above her at the agency, and the presence of an assistant, to go along with a secretary, was symbolic of that status.

"Well," Randy began, "Lots of drama isn't there?"

"I'm afraid I'm pretty much watching from the sidelines."

"There's a little more urgency now to get you into the game."

"Are you saying that the talks between you guys and Allied broke down?"

"What did you think would happen? Those pigs want the trough all for themselves. They're not giving us any real choice."

Marcie looked at him closely. Probably 32 years old, Yale and Harvard Business, successful father in the textile business in New York, and a reputation for being a true sexist. Real nice person. But a very successful agent. Already a polished dealmaker and a particular favorite of the networks because of his remarkable talent for getting creative types to toe the line and not jeopardize successful shows with their temperamental outbursts. Goldberg was the number two man in the Television Department and champing at the bit to move up. He'd already been rumored to have turned down an offer for the number one job at another agency. The book on him, Marcie had learned, was that he'd been plotting the Young Lions game plan for almost two years.

"Look Randy, I wish you guys well. I made myself as clear as I can to Ben. If you guys want to sit down and explore how we fit, it has to be on an even basis. Otherwise, let's not waste each others' time."

"As I understand it," Randy began again, "we're not very far apart."

"Come on," said Marcie, a trace of irritation in her voice. "It's twenty-five per cent across the board. Then we spend as long as it takes to see if we're compatible, how the draws and the bonuses would work, what our visions for the agency would be. If we can reach agreement, terrific. We set up shop and blow this town away. If we can't, we shake hands and wish each other luck, and then try to beat each other's brains out."

"Well, I'd have to talk to the guys."

"Look, Randy"—Marcie was now bristling—"I didn't approach you, you came at me. For all I know, I was only a card you wanted to play in your talks with Allied. I made myself perfectly clear when I spoke with Ben. This is bullshit having to say the same fucking thing when I talk to you. You know where to find me if you have anything serious to say. Otherwise, I don't have time for any more of this chicken shit."

Marcie left her half-finished coffee, rose suddenly, and moved past Randy and out the door.

Tad called behind her, "See you, girl."

Without turning back, Marcie said, "Right." Dude, she added to herself.

"Should I start packing?" Sandy asked.

"I'd wait just a bit," Marcie replied.

Sandy followed Marcie into her office saying, "I thought you were asshole buddies with Ben."

Marcie smiled. "We are good friends, but I think Randy's the driving force behind the Young Lions. Do you hear anything different?"

"Shit, no. It's supposed to be Randy and his court. He's the star, Ben the brains, and Jack the movie agent who everybody loves."

"Truth is, I hardly know Jack."

"He's easy," Sandy said. "In love with his wife, doesn't screw around, doesn't party, and honest to a fault."

Marcie couldn't resist commenting, "Just your kind of guy."

"Yeah, right. But he does sound like the kind of partner you should consider."

"All in due time," said Marcie. "They still haven't come off the idea that I should be a junior partner."

"Fuck them!"

"My feelings exactly," Marcie observed.

Sandy answered the ringing telephone from her position on the couch. "Miss Sandmore's line. One minute please, I'll see if she's in." She pushed the hold button and looked up at Marcie. "It's Puff the Magic Dragon."

"Who?"

"Tim Garland."

Marcie shook her head at Sandy and picked up the phone. "Tim, how are you? That was fun last night."

"Actually, I'm upstairs finishing with Charles, and wondered if you had a minute?"

"Sure, come on down."

"Great, I'll be there right away."

"He's paying a house call? I'm impressed."

"Never mind. He was doing something with Charles, and is on his way down. Please call Dick Wilhite and get him squared away for dinner at Tutti's at eight o'clock. Oh, I don't want any calls when Tim is here."

Sandy rolled her eyes upward as she got up and went back to her desk. She was back in seconds with Tim in tow.

Sandy showed him in. His appearance in a dark blue, chalk-stripe suit with a maroon tie with white pin dots rated a nod of approval from Sandy who closed the door behind him.

Marcie came from behind the desk as Tim moved forward to kiss her hello.

"Did you want coffee or anything cold," Marcie asked.

"I'm fine, thanks. I don't have any real agenda. I was meeting with Charles and thought I might catch you in."

"Not about the Young Lions mess?"

Tim laughed. "No, I try to stay out of domestic disputes. They tend to get very dirty."

Apparently, thought Marcie, he's not going to volunteer anything. "If you don't mind me asking, what were you meeting with Charles about?"

"We've been talking about another deal," he said elusively. "It doesn't affect our dealings."

While he didn't seem to mind her attempting to pry into his affairs, Marcie noted that he was far from forthcoming with information. This is a man who plays his cards very close to the vest.

"I'll have something else for you to look at by the close of business. Do I send it to you or to Mona?"

"Send it to my attention, please."

"Will do."

"So, Marcie, one other thing. Are you free for dinner on Friday."

Marcie quickly checked her calendar before answering. "I am."

"Great. Could we have dinner again?"

"Sure, Tim, that sounds great."

"Wonderful. I'll give you a call when everything is in place. Meanwhile, I look forward to the next script you send over."

Marcie rose as Tim did, and escorted him to the door. Again, he kissed her lightly on the cheek. "See you Friday," he said. And he was gone.

CHAPTER VIII

She met Ira Lang, following her workout with George, at the Mondrian Hotel at seven-thirty. Not wasting a minute, Lang was talking animatedly on his cellular phone. He spotted her approaching his table and quickly got off the phone. The entertainment bar in Los Angeles, and Lang was one of its stars, bore a remarkable resemblance to the talent agency business. Indeed, the very agenda for this breakfast meeting was the kind of agenda that might be followed between an agent and his client. Lang had been scouting the town on his client's behalf, checking out the possibilities for other employment.

"Damn New York lawyers," he said. "They don't have a clue about how the business works."

"I'm sure you'll be able to straighten them out," Marcie said with a smile.

The waiter approached, pad in hand.

"I'd like an English muffin and coffee, please," Marcie told him.

"Just a refill on the coffee for me," Lang said. "Lots of action at Allied?" he asked, as the waiter headed toward the kitchen.

"Seems to be. Rumor has it that they're out of there. History. It's hard to say if someone is at fault, or even if either side really wanted to make a deal. But from every indication, the talks have broken down."

"And where are you in all that?"

"Nowhere, I guess. They keep coming around with low-ball equity deals, and I keep telling them that talks would have to start with an even division of the pie. Then, we'd see if we could live with one another."

"Shouldn't I be the one negotiating on your behalf?"

"When, or rather if, it comes to that, you bet. But if they're unwilling to pony up a full twenty-five percent interest, there's nothing else to talk about."

Lang smiled. "I like your style, kid. Lay out the ground-rules up front,then see if the players are still in the game. You'd make a good lawyer."

"And how are you doing as my agent? We seem to be involved in a role reversal situation here."

"I had breakfast with Jimmy Wiatt of the Morris office yesterday, and I'd say the results were very positive. They'd be receptive to bringing you in as a senior picture agent at considerably more than Allied is paying you now. They're hot at the moment and would welcome someone like you, and your clients."

Marcie was now paying close attention. She had not been involved in the musical chairs game that many agents played habitually. It had probably cost her a considerable sum of money over the years, but she had preferred staying in one place and building a secure base. Now, it seemed as though all of that was up for grabs.

"UTA is still trying to get their house in order, so I don't think that's the right place for you now. Jeff Berg at ICM was friendly, but he wanted to think about it before he got back to me. CAA seemed lukewarm. I think they're afraid the client exodus isn't over."

Marcie considered Ira's report. It made her uneasy to think that she was being "shopped" by her attorney, but she knew this was how the game was played. She also trusted that Lang would be circumspect, and in no way suggest that she "needed" another position.

"From my end," Marcie began, "I suspect we'd be in a position to beat up on Charles a bit and renegotiate my deal, if that's what I decide to do. If I had to guess, I also think the Young Lions will come up with the full twenty-five percent I said I have to have. Whether I could live with Randy as a partner is another thing. Ben is great. No problems there. I think Jack is cool, but I don't really know the man very well. Randy, I just don't know whether I could live with him."

"He would be my major concern," Lang said. "Randy may be a great agent, maybe even the next Ovitz, but I'm not sure you'd want to get into bed with him. Figuratively speaking, of course."

Marcie smiled at her attorney's way of putting things. He had identified the giant question mark in any Young Lions discussion— Randy Goldberg. Anyway, there was nothing that demanded resolution that moment.

"Let's keep all the options open, Ira," said Marcie. "I don't want to feel like a piece of meat on the auction block, but I have come around to believe you were right about this being a time for me to reassess where I am and where I'm going. Let's let the next couple of days go by. I don't have any clear sense of what would be the best situation for me. Do you?"

"No, I don't. I'm confident that where you end up, we'll be able to do significantly better for you than you're doing now."

"On that cheery note, we'll be talking…"

Marcie stood to leave as Ira took his phone out of his attaché case and began to place a call. And they say agents are addicted to the phone, thought Marcie. She kissed him goodbye, causing him to mis-enter his credit card number into his phone. For a second, a dark cloud passed over his face, then he looked up and laughed.

"We're all nuts, aren't we?" he said.

Marcie let the remark hang in the air as she walked across the dining room, into the lobby, and out of the hotel.

As she got into her Lexus and headed to work, the car phone rang. Marcie didn't ordinarily give out the number for her car phone or her cellular phone, preferring to keep them for outgoing calls only. Indeed, she professed to actively dislike the telephone and the time she spent on it. She claimed that it was a necessary if regrettable part of agenting.

Sandy, of course, was privy to all her telephone numbers but had been counseled not to give out the car phone or cellular number except in times of great urgency. Wondering what bad news lay in store for her, Marcie answered the phone. Her leased Lexus had been outfitted with an elaborate phone system which permitted her to put calls onto a speaker and informed her when there were calls waiting. By not encouraging incoming calls, there was very little use for the call waiting feature, but Marcie was glad to have it.

"Hello," she answered, at the second ring.

"Hey, Marce, it's Ben. Forgive me for calling you on the car phone, but I told Sandy it was an emergency and she gave it to me."

"Uh huh," Marcie said noncommittally.

"Look, Randy and Jack and I were wondering if we can buy you lunch today. It's pretty important."

"What's going on?"

"The talks collapsed last night and we don't think Allied has any intention of trying to get them back on the tracks."

"So you're saying you guys are out of there?"

"Man, we're gone, and let me tell you it feels great!"

Marcie found herself unable to share Ben's enthusiasm. She was unclear how she figured into their plans, if at all. "Have you reached an agreement about the partnership then?" she asked.

"As a friend, I think you should come to this lunch and hear what we have to say."

"Goddamn it, Ben, how many times to I have to give you my bottom line? I don't have any idea whether we can operate as a team yet, but I sure as hell know that I have no interest in finding out unless you're prepared to look at me as an equal!" Marcie's voice rose in anger as she went over ground that was by now a well-plowed field.

Ben continued to play it low-key, as if he held all the cards in this conversation. "Look, Marce, I know what you're feeling, and I know what you told me and told Randy. Trust me on this, come to lunch and I'm confident you'll leave satisfied."

"Why the hell should I trust you and your partners?"

"Because I've known you a long time and consider you my friend."

Marcie reacted instinctively to his response. It might work out and it might not, but there was nothing more at risk than a lunch. She considered for a beat whether Ben was trying to agent her, to promote her by saying what she wanted to hear, and decided that he sincerely believed in the message he was being asked to convey. There was little doubt in her mind that Randy was the king of the jungle with the Young Lions. She would have to reach her understanding with him if this were to work out. Still, Ben was no *schlepper*. And he was right that he was among the few people at Allied she would call a friend. Jack was something of a wildcard in all of this. A good agent, aggressive and smart, a good family man by reputation, he was somebody who Marcie knew very little about. At the least, a lunch could get some pretty interesting things out in the open.

"Where and when?" she said.

"The Bistro at one. Is that okay?"

The Bistro, she thought, how utterly passé. No one went to the Bistro anymore. Why there? Old line class? No way. The food? No chance. To avoid detection? Of course. She was sure they would have a private upstairs dining room and be far away from the prying eyes of the town's rumor mongers. That had to be it.

"Can I give you a lift?" asked Ben. "We have the private room upstairs."

"No thanks," she said. "I've got a meeting after lunch that I can't break." This wasn't true, but she felt it would be a mistake to be dependent on a ride from Ben when it came time to leave. Better to keep all her options open. "I'll meet you guys there at one."

"Terrific," said Ben. "I know you won't regret it."

By the time Marcie got to her office, she already regretted agreeing to lunch. She weighed canceling it, but decided against it. When she got to Sandy's area, she was surprised to find Peter Tacy, one of Allied's hot-shot junior agents, speaking with her. He had never, in her memory, dropped by her office. Or was it only to see Sandy?

"Sandy said," he began quickly, "that you were probably too busy to see me. I wonder if you could give me five minutes. I promise it won't take longer than that."

"Sure, Peter, come on in. Coffee?"

"No thanks," he said nervously.

Marcie nodded at Sandy, indicating she wanted her customary morning cup, and ushered Peter into her office.

"What's up? The Catherine Sampson deal?"

"No way. Winkler thinks she's yesterday's news. I wanted to talk to you about the Young Lions for a minute. Jack stopped by last night to say they might be interested in talking to me about joining them. I told him I'd be interested, but that's as far as it went. What do you think? Everybody believes you're going with them, so I thought I'd *ask you* for some career advice."

Sandy brought Marcie her coffee, looked at Peter and Marcie as if hoping to be asked to stay, and getting no invitation, left.

"First," Marcie began, "I have no deal with them. Yes, we've talked, but we're not close to an understanding yet. Second, I really don't know how to advise you. You're at the beginning of your learning curve, and you shouldn't be contemplating a move unless you're either stymied here, or the opportunity is so unusual there. Otherwise, the prudent thing to do is to stay put and work on developing your client base, learning the business and building a reputation. You're not there yet."

"It's hard to argue any of that," Peter replied. "I was so knocked out when Jack talked to me that I didn't know how to get any perspective."

"If I were you, I'd wait to see how things shook out here. You might come off smelling like a rose with those guys leaving. My inclination is to take it a little slowly."

"Hey, you've really helped me, and I appreciate it. I hope this works out for you the way you want."

"Thank you," said Marcie. "And just to help you put my advice in perspective, if I ever were to join them, I'd probably be trying to convince you the right thing to do was to leave and join us right away."

Peter laughed. "Thanks again." And he was out the door.

The morning was comprised of the usual frantic phone calls, mixed in with other agents stopping by to try to glean information about the Lions' activities. Sandy valiantly tried to shield Marcie from the onslaught, but the agents' aggression generally won out. As Beverly Donovan sashayed out of her office, Sandy buzzed Marcie and reported, in a questioning voice, there was someone named Wes Snyder in the lobby to see her.

"Okay," said Marcie, "tell him to come up."

In a few minutes, Sandy showed Wes, wearing his tennis whites and a warm-up jacket, into Marcie's office. The approving look Sandy gave him indicated she found his good looks much to her liking.

"Coffee, Mr. Snyder?" she said in her most seductive voice.

"Uh, no thanks, I'm just here for a minute."

"What a nice surprise," exclaimed Marcie, as Sandy reluctantly left her office. "What brings you by?"

He moved around the desk to Marcie's side. "I've missed this," he said, bending down to give her a kiss.

"Mmmm," said Marcie, "me too,"

Wes moved back to the other side of the desk and sat down. "Seriously, I took a week's vacation so that I could do this commercial. It shoots Wednesday, Thursday and Friday. I've got some family stuff to take care of Saturday, but Sunday is the City of Hope mixed doubles tournament. We could enter the Open category and have a pretty good chance. What do you think?"

"That sounds like fun. Let's do it. Excuse me for one sec. I was on my way to the ladies room when Sandy said you were downstairs."

Marcie walked out, closing the door behind her. Wes got up and gave Marcie's office a close look. Wandering over to her side of the desk, he saw a Twentieth-Century-Fox logo on top of a cover letter clipped to a screenplay. Glancing at it, he read that it was a submission, with a $2 million offer for Sam Glass to play the starring role in a film called *Beef Jerky*. It was signed by Frank Katz, Executive Vice President in Charge of Worldwide Production. Wes was impressed. Two million bucks for Sam Glass who only had one film released. Not bad.

At that moment, Marcie walked in as Wes continued his examination of the room, checking out two photographs hanging on the wall.

"I recognize you with President Clinton," said Wes, "but what are you doing in the other one?"

Marcie glanced toward the wall. "I was receiving an Obie for an off-Broadway show I produced. It was a hundred years ago."

"Pretty neat."

"I guess it was."

"So, Marce, I'm staying with my old roommate from Pepperdine for a couple of days, but I wondered how Saturday night was for you. I was hoping we could hang out and play in the doubles on Sunday."

"You got a date," said Marcie. "There's a screening at the Academy which should be fun."

"Terrific," said Wes, standing to leave.

Marcie got up and gave him a big hug. "Good luck on your shoot. You'll be great."

Wes got a big goodbye from Sandy before she burst into Marcie's office.

"Tell me everything! Who was that?"

"It's my tennis pro from the Springs."

"Yeah, and what else?"

"And we're playing in a tournament this weekend."

"And?"

"And," Marcie said smiling at Sandy's persistence, "we began a little something off the court as well."

"Is he as good as he looks?"

"I'm afraid that's where I draw the line on telling all. But I don't think you'd be far off if you assume the answer is yes."

"All right!" said Sandy, giving Marcie a high-five.

At 12:30, Sandy offered to walk her boss to her car. She was beside herself to learn more about Marcie's lunch with the Young Lions. Of course, she was aware that the Allied negotiations had reached a stalemate and that Randy and the boys were leaving. "Even the Trades know that much," mused Sandy. She wanted a scoop on Marcie's intentions, and was prepared to put up "her strictest confidence" in exchange for an exclusive. When Marcie told her she'd have to wait for lunch to conclude before there would be any information, she was disappointed.

"But what about me?" she asked. "If you leave, will you take me?"

Sandy had a refreshingly direct way of putting things. It certainly made it easier to respond.

"If I leave, I will happily try to work something out. It's a little early to talk about money, benefits and that sort of thing, don't you think?"

"I know, but a girl does have to look out for herself. Good luck," she said, with a big smile.

Marcie waved, got into her car, backed up and swung out toward the street.

At the Bistro, she gave the car to the valet and was directed up the stairs to the small, private dining room. The captain led her to a closed door, knocked softly, and opened it to show her in. Marcie was greeted by the Young Lions, assembled in a small pride at a round table set for four. They stood as she sat down, a marked change from office protocol, although a welcome one.

"Champagne, Mademoiselle?" asked the waiter who hovered close by. Marcie nodded, seeing the men already had been served, and watched the bubbles rise as her glass was filled with Dom Perignon. She looked up to see all eyes were on her.

"Here's to the Young Lions, whoever they may be," she said, bringing a smile to Ben's face, and a slight scowl to Randy's. Jack remained impassive, a man nearly impossible to read. Turning to Ben, she added, "You were right. This beats sending out for a sandwich." Again, a predictably mixed reaction to the comment. Whew, she thought, this is one tough room to work.

Randy abruptly changed the mood. Looking at Marcie, he said, "We've been here for a while, so maybe you'd like to look at the menu and order. Then we can talk."

"Sure," Marcie replied, conscious of the coldness that came from even the most innocuous things that Randy said. He may be a great agent, she thought, but his interpersonal skills really sucked. Marcie looked quickly over the menu, aware that all eyes were on her. She ordered a salmon salad and an iced coffee, handed the menu to the waiter, took another sip of the excellent champagne and turned to the men gathered about the table.

"Well," Marcie began, "where are we?"

Ben started to speak but Randy came in over him. Marcie glanced quickly to see Ben's reaction, but he deferred to Randy, his face impassive.

"Allied had no interest in making a deal with us," Randy said, "so we've agreed to be out of there by close of business on Friday. I don't think they negotiated in good faith, but that's ancient history now. The press release was approved this morning and the settlement papers will be done by tonight. Clients have been notified, at least those that didn't know already, and we signed on a lease this morning. There's a partner's office for you, if you want it."

Marcie looked at Randy squarely. He didn't flinch, meeting her gaze with a steely one of his own.

"Define partner," said Marcie.

"An equity participant," said Randy.

"Look Randy, if you want to seriously explore the possibility of my joining you, that's why I'm here. If you're going to be an asshole and treat me like a four-year-old, thanks for the champagne, and I'm out of here."

Randy showed no emotion and stared for a few seconds at Marcie before speaking. "The three of us would begin," he finally said, "with twenty-seven and a half percent, and you with seventeen and a half. If your commissions, received or booked, at the end of the year, exceeded the lowest of the three of us, you'd be raised to 25% and we would all be equal partners. What do you think?"

"I think I'm too old to audition for parts like this. You know what I book, and you know damn well what my futures look like. I don't intend to say it again. An equal partnership is the condition precedent to seeing whether we could structure a compatible business relationship." Marcie hoped her use of legalese would gain her an edge. Randy looked meaningfully around at his partners.

"Suppose, hypothetically," he suggested, "we agreed to twenty-five percent for each of us, what do you want to know?"

Marcie took a breath and began. "I'd need to know how each of you feel about women in general and me in particular. I don't know Jack at all, and I'd need to spend some time alone with him to get a sense of how he thinks, and how we'd work together. I guess I know Ben the best of any of you, so I have the fewest questions about him. And as for you, Randy, I'd need to find out whether your sexist attitude would extend to me or only to the other members of my sex. That it is objectionable to me is a given. But if you kept it out of your dealings with me, it might be something I could live with. Beyond that, we all know what it takes to succeed as a beginning agency. If we're on the same page as regards draws, expenses and other perks, I wouldn't anticipate any serious problems at that end."

Marcie paused, looking at each man in turn. Their faces revealed nothing except their deferral to Randy to speak for the three of them. The waiter arrived with the lunches during this pregnant silence. Jack took his first tentative bites of his Caesar salad, hesitating to look toward the participants in this discussion. Ben didn't reach for his silverware, continuing to regard Marcie, perhaps with new esteem.

"Okay," Randy said, "let's assume, for the sake of the discussion, the twenty-five percent split. Are you free to have dinner with Jack Wednesday and me Thursday?"

Well, Marcie thought, so it was all an elaborate ploy to try and beat me out of a few points. Fair enough. An opening gambit that didn't succeed. The critical talks were yet to come. And at least the playing field was level.

"That would be fine," replied Marcie. "It would be a mistake for both of us to let this drag out. We should know this week whether there is a deal to be made or not."

Ben smiled, or seemed to, for the first time. "Terrific," he said, picking up his fork, "Let's see whether they make a decent hot duck salad."

*   *   *   *   *

Sandy burst into her office, as soon as Marcie sat down.

"Sorry, I was in the ladies room. So what happened? Are we going? Should I start packing? I hear the Lions are out the door. That's right, isn't it?"

"Whoa," Marcie said. "You're getting a little ahead of the game. Yes, the Lions appear to be out of here. Yes, they seem to want me on equal terms, but we're at least two dinners away from finalizing."

"What's that all about?" asked Sandy.

"I need to find out whether I can get along with Jack and Randy."

"Hey, Jack's a pussy cat. No problems there. But Randy? You know the girls call him 'Pig Man'. He's hit on everybody in the place."

Marcie looked at her questioningly.

"Yeah, even me. I told him if he so much as touched me, I'd sue his ass for harassment so fast his head would spin. He's been okay to me since then."

"Those are the kinds of things we have to work out."

"Do you think you could be partners with him?"

"Sandy, I just don't know."

Midway through the afternoon, Marcie found the volume of the gossip to be intolerable. By now, the imminent departure of the Lions was common knowledge, and all the offices were abuzz with speculation about what other agents were going, which clients would be leaving, and how Allied would fare without the Lions. Even with Sandy running interference for her, Marcie found herself wasting time tap dancing around the inevitable questions. Finally, she'd had enough.

"Sandy, I'm getting out of here. I'm going home to read until I have dinner with Dick tonight. This place is a zoo."

"I don't blame you. You're all set at Tutti's at eight. Have a good one."

"Thanks. See you tomorrow."

*   *   *   *   *

Dick Wilhite was waiting for her at the small bar at Tutti's. His face was instantly recognizable, but he still resembled a college professor or an accountant more than an actor. While polite, and even chivalrous, to have preceded her to the restaurant, Marcie noted that his being early betrayed an anxiousness about his present position that a more confident star would never have shown.

"Darling," Marcie said, moving to where he was sitting and giving him a big kiss. "How are you? I'm really glad you were free tonight."

"I'm fine," Dick replied. "I haven't seen you in ages."

"Well, I've been keeping track of you," she said. "But it *has* been too long. Let's get a table, shall we?"

Marcie nodded to the maitre d', who picked up Dick's drink and ushered them to a private booth toward the rear of the restaurant. "Will this be all right, Ms. Sandmore?"

"It's lovely, Carlos," said Marcie. "And could I get a dry chardonnay?"

"Certainly, Madam," Carlos replied.

"Jesus!" Dick exclaimed as Carlos walked away. "Do you have a piece of this joint?"

Marcie laughed. "No, I just come here pretty often. I like the food."

As her drink arrived and Dick ordered another Campari on the rocks, Marcie broached the subject for the evening. "You know," she said, "you really ought to be working more."

"I know, I know," Dick responded, a slight tinge of desperation in his voice. "I don't even know the suits at the studios any more."

"They're for the agents to know. Your job is to do what you do best—make people laugh."

"I'd love to," he said plaintively. "I'm getting damn tired of waiting for the phone to ring."

Okay, she thought. Here goes. "Have you thought about doing a series? The people at our shop think they could package a show around you and get the networks really excited."

"God, Marcie, I don't know. I'm thinking the right feature is bound to come along."

"Dick, we've known each other for how long, ten years? You know I've always been your biggest fan."

He was caving fast. This was going to be easier than she thought.

"I think maybe it's time for a change in representation. A move to some place that really has your best interest at heart. Frankly, Dick, that agency is Allied."

Dick paused, then asked, "But would you be involved with me?"

"Of course," Marcie assured him. "I'd be your responsible agent and coordinate all the other agents so that we can implement a strategy to get you rolling again. Once the momentum is there, you'll find yourself with lots of choices. That's when the leverage of a company like Allied can do a huge job for you. That's when our muscle can get your price to what it should be, re-establish you in films, the theater, whatever you want to do."

Marcie paused to let her words sink in, Dick looked as though he wanted what Marcie had described in the worst way. She knew, as did he, that it wasn't happening with the agency where he had been. What choice does he have, she thought. It shouldn't even be a tough decision.

"Okay, okay! Let's go for it!"

Suddenly he brimmed over with excitement. Marcie could see the enthusiasm envelop him. She called over Carlos and ordered a bottle of Dom Perignon.

"This is a celebration," Marcie almost shouted as the champagne cork popped. "Let's drink to us! To changing our friendship to a working relationship, but staying friends."

Dick beamed. "I'll drink to that!"

From there, it was all down hill. Of course he'd do a series. He insisted the writing be first-rate, and Marcie assured him that Allied represented the beat comedy writers in the business. The notion that she was pushing Allied hard, while negotiating with the Lions at the same time, did not elude her. She had no choice, she felt, but to take each day as it came, and not second-guess every move. Maybe she'd be a Lion, and maybe not.

Dick said, "I'm only sorry that I didn't do this sooner."

"It's all about timing," Marcie responded. "And this is the moment."

She wondered whether the television department could deliver on the promises she'd made to Dick. They hadn't shown any enthusiasm about signing him. Maybe she should stall until the dust settled at Allied. She knew that it was her and not Allied that was the driving force in getting Dick to come over. It would sure be nice to bring a hefty commission from a series with her if she went with the Lions. But that was getting way ahead of herself.

They ordered dinner, ate and drank, coasting on a tide of optimism and enthusiasm. Marcie opted not to reveal anything to Dick about the Young Lions. Not being a dedicated reader of the Trades, Dick asked no questions about the town's number one topic of conversation. Marcie justified not raising any issues in this regard by focusing on the fact that she was signing Dick, and not Allied. And who was to know where the pieces would be on the board at week's end?

They walked outside, into the cool L.A. night air, and Dick kissed her goodnight. Marcie noticed that his Ford still sported New York plates. He promised to be at Allied around eleven the next day to sign papers and meet some of his new agents. As her car arrived, Marcie handed the valet a five dollar bill, and headed home. She was instantly aware of how exhausted she felt. Too many balls up in the air. Too many possibilities. Give it a couple of more days, she thought, and order would be established. But what would that order be?

Chapter IX

Marcie awakened feeling energized and completely alive. So much was going on that it was impossible to predict where things would end up, even at week's end. Instead of being overwhelmed by the anxiety that often accompanies uncertainties, Marcie found herself enjoying the process. She felt centered and open to whatever direction her life took.

She dressed in a dark blue suit with a soft, silk blouse. After an English muffin, a cup of coffee, and a quick read of the *L.A. Times*, Marcie proceeded to the office. Sandy was already at her desk, of course engaged in a spirited phone conversation. Seeing Marcie, she hung up, grabbed a note pad, and followed Marcie into her office.

"Coffee?" Sandy asked.

"Please."

Sandy returned in minutes with Marcie's coffee.

"How was the meeting with Wilhite?"

"It went very well. He's coming in at eleven to meet some of the people. Let's try Valerie Kensington at NBC. Maybe they've got something over there that he'd be right for."

Valerie was Vice President for Comedy Development, one of the few women to hold this post at a network. They had known each other since New York when Valerie had been working in NBC Daytime. They had stayed passably friendly in Los Angeles, crossing paths at parties and industry functions, but had never done any real business together.

There was always a first time, thought Marcie, and maybe she'd turn out to be a Dick Wilhite fan.

Sandy buzzed twice to let her know that Valerie was on the line.

"Valerie," Marcie gushed, "how're you doing? Congratulations on the season. You guys are really kicking butt!"

"Well, it goes in cycles, you know. One day you're a hero, the next day you're looking for a job. Anyway, I'd love to schmooze but we've got a staff meeting in five minutes. What can I do for you?"

"I wondered," said Marcie immediately, "how you and your people felt about Dick Wilhite. I've always been a huge fan of his and I just signed him as a client. He'd like to find the right series, and I thought I'd give you the first shot."

There was a pause and Marcie was convinced her little gambit was about to be shot down. Valerie surprised her with her response.

"This is really weird," she said. "We've just developed a show about a super in a New York building and I'm going in right now to pitch Wilhite for the lead."

"Valerie, that's fabulous. It's exactly the kind of show he's looking for."

"Look, just sit on it for a couple of hours until I see how everyone reacts. Maybe we could grab a quick lunch today and catch up. I should have a better sense of where the temperature is by then."

"Great," Marcie said. "Tell me where and when."

"La Maisonette at one?"

"Perfect. I'll have Sandy make the reservation."

As Marcie spoke with Sandy, she bubbled over with enthusiasm. Maybe her instincts were right. Maybe this was the beginning of a roll. Athletes call it being in the zone. Was this how it felt? Whatever it was, she liked it. The front desk buzzed Sandy to tell her that Lucia Thomas was in the waiting room to see Marcie. Sandy said she'd take care of the reservation and would get Lucia.

Lucia Thomas, an actress client, had just returned from doing an independent movie in Italy. She came in for an extended meeting on the shape of her career. Should she do a television series or hold out for features? Were there any realistic choices? She and Marcie concluded that the best answer would be to see what came up and make decisions at that time.

A young USC graduate whose submitted script had gotten excellent coverage from Allied's best reader met with Marcie to talk about representation. "It's a buyer's market out there," Marcie had told her. "I'd be willing to make some trial submissions, but I'd have to see the level of interest before saying I could sign you as a client." The writer accepted this offer in a heartbeat.

As the young writer left, Sandy said that Tim was on the phone. Marcie waited a beat for the derision she was sure would follow, but Sandy offered no editorial comment. Must be on her good behavior, Marcie thought.

"How're you doing?" Marcie asked. "I'm afraid I don't have your submission together because Ben has been a little inaccessible."

"That's all right," Tim said. "I was calling to ask a question."

"Shoot."

"How well do you know Mark Canton?" asked Tim.

Canton was the erstwhile head of Columbia under Peter Guber, and had taken enormous flak as part of the housecleaning that Sony had done. While he had seemed like a logical scapegoat at the time, the success of the pictures that he began that were released after he was gone called all that into question.

"Not that well," said Marcie. "I didn't cover Columbia when he was running the show, and I didn't know him all that well at Warners. Why do you ask?"

"His name came up today, and I wondered what you thought. I value your opinion."

"Isn't he back at Warners?" asked Marcie.

"Yes, but this was about something else. Thanks for your thinking. We're on for Friday, right?"

"Still good with me," Marcie replied.

"I'll speak to you before. Take care."

"What was that all about?" asked Sandy.

"Truthfully, I'll be damned if I know."

Sandy answered the phone, sitting on the couch in Marcie's office.

"Miss Sandmore's office. Just a second, I'll see." She put the caller on hold and said to Marcie, "It's Dick Wilhite, he wants to move his eleven to four this afternoon."

Marcie checked her calendar. "Tell him that's fine."

As the women looked at each other, Marcie said, "Don't worry, he's not going to be one of those. He's a real sweetheart."

There was a knock on the door.

"Come in!" Marcie said.

Sam poked his head into the room. "Am I interrupting?"

Marcie beamed. "Hell, no."

Sam kissed Sandy hello, to her great satisfaction, and moved to Marcie's desk and gave her a big hug and kiss.

"Are you guys plotting the takeover of the world?"

"How'd you get in past our ace security, anyway?"

"Just walked in like I owned the place. They never batted an eye. Are you mad?"

Marcie laughed. "Of course not. Just curious. Can we get you anything to drink?"

"A diet cola would be great, thanks."

Sandy stood to get Sam's drink, as Sam flopped down in the chair opposite Marcie's desk.

"Everything going okay?" Marcie asked.

"Seems to be. We get new pages soon, and that'll be the test. Hey, did we have a lunch date for today?"

"I thought it was for tomorrow."

"Good, because I lost a filling and the only time I can get in to see my dentist is during lunch."

"Does it hurt?"

"Only when I laugh," Sam said, smiling at her.

Sandy returned with Sam's drink and a fresh cup of coffee for Marcie and retreated back to her desk.

"I've got to go to the Valley for lunch, but let's spend a few minutes now. Have you gotten to know Julia at all?'

"We spent some time yesterday. She's a doll."

"I hear that," said Marcie, "but I don't know her at all."

They continued their conversation with Marcie waiting for some bomb to be detonated. To her delight, it never went off. Maybe this is a banner day for me, she thought. After spending ten minutes with Sam, Sandy buzzed to say she'd better leave if she wanted to be on time for Valerie. Sam checked his watch, rose, and walked with Marcie out the door.

Marcie hurried to the garage, climbed into the Lexus, and swung out to the road. She slipped in a CD of Mozart's 40th, wanting to concentrate on the meeting ahead and the events of the day still to come. She drove to the Valley on automatic pilot, not acknowledging anything she encountered on the way. She got to the restaurant a few minutes late, and was pleased to see Valerie was getting out of a small Mercedes two-door sedan and giving her keys to the Valet. It never failed to amaze Marcie that everyone in town seemed to drive a luxury automobile. It was like some sheikdom or emirate. No wonder tourists couldn't believe the lifestyles of Southern California. But they didn't know that most of the cars were leased by employers, not owned by their drivers.

"Darling, how are you?" Valerie gushed. "It's been forever!"

A leggy blonde, Valerie was a whiz at corporate in-fighting but not blessed with much of a sense of humor. She seemed an odd choice to head up Comedy at a network. Marcie recalled that she would announce in a flat tone, "That's funny," instead of actually laughing. Maybe her gift was knowing what America would laugh at. It seemed unlikely, but so did much of television. To Marcie, the premises of most situation comedies rarely rose above the level of inane.

"It's fantastic to see you, Valerie," said Marcie. "You look absolutely great. You're doing your hair differently, aren't you?"

As they walked toward the Maitre d', Valerie ran her hand through her long blonde hair and said, "Yes, it's Marco, on Sunset right by Le Dome. He's a magician, isn't he?"

They were shown to their table and sat down as Marcie agreed that his work was to die for. They each ordered a glass of Chardonnay and Marcie looked at Valerie expectantly.

"Well, my dear," Valerie began, "this must be your lucky day."

"Really?"

"Uh-huh. They were trying for George Segal and the deal blew today once and for all. When I suggested Wilhite, people thought I was some kind of savior. The Network supports him and we called Levine and Rogers and they think it's a fabulous idea. We're ready to wrap it up this afternoon."

"That's fabulous," said Marcie. "Knowing Dick, he's going to want to see the pilot script."

"I've got it right here," Valerie said, reaching into her bag for two copies of the script. "One for you and one for your client. Get him to read it right away, and we'll put this baby to bed. This is my show, Marcie, and I really want to get it on the air. It has a nice ring doesn't it? Dick Wilhite as *The Super?*"

Lunch was a love fest from then on. Valerie sketched out a tentative deal with Marcie for Dick's services. A fee for the pilot, a commitment to do three years at an escalating salary, a nice equity in the series and a right of consultation on the director for the pilot. Levine and Rogers were well respected and very successful sit-com writer-producers, show drivers as the business termed them, with several on-the-air series already under their belt. They were people that NBC wanted to be in business with, and their support of Wilhite would have been necessary to get the deal to this point.

"Wilhite's not going to get cold feet, is he?" asked Valerie, with a touch of apprehension.

"I assume he's going to like the show," Marcie replied. "As for doing a series at all, we had that talk before I signed him, and he's agreed."

"Fantastic. Let's save the champagne until it's all signed and sealed."

They left lunch vowing to see more of one another, both excited about the mutual good that could come from this situation. As Marcie made the drive back to Beverly Hills, she tried Wilhite on her car phone. She got him as he was about to go jogging on San Vicente, a straight road with a grassy median strip that ran from Brentwood to the ocean. Dick was like a child on the phone, excited and almost disbelieving. He quickly agreed to change his plans from the four o'clock date and meet her in fifteen minutes in her office. "You're a miracle worker," he told her. "Thank god you're *my* miracle worker now!"

When Dick got to the office, he was as charming and funny as she had ever seen him. Sandy fell in love with him at once as he reduced her to gales of laughter with his clowning. Marcie told him to go home and read the script twice and then call her.

There would be time enough to meet some of the other agents and talk about the deal.

In her mind was the notion that there could well be some ambiguities about whether Allied represented Dick. Legally, it seemed pretty clear. She had been acting as an Allied agent when she met with Dick and when she pitched Valerie. But there were no signed papers, and there might be room to negotiate should it happen that the Young Lions discussions proved fruitful. Marcie caught herself fantasizing about how it would be in a small partnership, clawing for a foothold in the town. It was an exciting possibility, and she was conscious of the fact that it had already affected her dealings with Dick Wilhite.

Marcie told Dick that she had a copy of the script as well, and when she had read it, they would compare notes. An excited Dick Wilhite strode out of her office as if walking on air. He kissed her goodbye, fumbled a bit in front of Sandy before putting out his hand to shake hers, and headed for the elevators.

"He's okay," Sandy said approvingly.

"We could get damn lucky here. Please keep all of this very hush-hush. I'm not sure yet whether he would be a client of Allied."

"I wondered how you were going to play that," mused Sandy.

"We'll see. It'll all be clear by Friday."

       *   *   *   *   *

That night, Marcie met Jack Hutcheson for dinner. He had selected this week's trendy trattoria, another in an endless flow of Italian places that seem to stay open about as long as it took to memorize their address. As Marcie walked in, she thought she recognized the Maitre d' from another spot, but couldn't be sure. Do they all look alike, she wondered?

"Signora?" he said as he oozed toward her.

"I'm meeting Jack Hutcheson."

"Si, Signor Hutcheson. Follow me, please."

Marcie followed him to a banquette along the side wall where Jack sat sipping a glass of red wine. He rose to greet her, lightly kissed her cheek and remained standing until she had taken her place. His courtesy was not lost on Marcie.

"A drink?" said Jack.

"Red wine would be perfect," said Marcie. "I'd like it on the light side, if possible."

"Certainly," the Maitre d' promised and headed off to fulfill his mission.

"I'm glad you could make it," Jack began. "You said it best at lunch. We work together, but don't really know each other very well. This will be good for both of us."

Marcie regarded him closely as he spoke. He was very attractive, if a little distant. Unlike many of the married agents, he wore a wedding band prominently on his left hand. There was a grace to his movements that suggested some kind of athletic prowess. She remembered hearing that he was a scratch golfer and made a mental note to ask him about it. He appeared to be very comfortable with her, without the tension she had sensed at lunch.

"How'd a guy like you get sucked into this mess?" Marcie asked, smiling.

"You mean the Young Lions?"

Marcie nodded.

"Randy approached me about it. What he said made a lot of sense. We added Ben to the package, and here we are. Ben suggested that you might be the perfect addition to the team."

"And what do you think?"

Jack smiled, almost seductively, "I guess I'll have a better sense after we get done tonight."

"Fair enough," said Marcie. The waiter arrived with her drink, and Jack lifted his glass in a toast.

"To the fairest young lion of them all," he said as they touched glasses.

"Well you know the way to a maiden's heart," Marcie said.

"Shucks, Ma'am, it weren't nothin,'" Jack replied in a dreadful John Wayne imitation. Marcie had to laugh at how awful it was.

"Jack, if you were thinking about moving on to impersonations, I'll give you some career advice. Keep your day job."

"Don't worry, I save it for special occasions. I know it's not there yet, but it's coming along great."

"Right. What I do hear is great is your golf."

"I am serious about the game."

"And also good?"

"I suppose. I'm playing to a four handicap at Bel-Air. It could be a couple of strokes lower, but my damn job gets in the way."

Marcie chuckled. "So you must have played competitively?"

"Uh-huh. I was number two on the UCLA team, and played a lot in those days. Never quite had the goods, for the tour though."

Marcie thought he sounded a little wistful. It was a feeling she understood very well after her knee surgery took away any professional chances she might have had in tennis.

"Okay," said Jack, turning serious very quickly, "I may not be the next Rich Little, but I'm a pretty damn good agent, and so are my partners. We didn't come to you lightly. We had the whole town to choose from, and we selected you. That must tell you something."

Marcie was happy to get on with the evening's agenda. She liked foreplay as much as the next person, but there came a time to get it on.

Before they could do that, there was the matter of ordering dinner. The waiter had arrived to make his suggestions and take their orders. She asked for a fish dish, while Jack opted for a pasta.

"Sticking with red?" he asked.

"I'd prefer white."

"Me too. Let me get a bottle."

As the waiter left, Jack asked, "Where were we?"

"I was about to tell you that I was flattered. Otherwise we wouldn't have gotten this far. But there are still some things we have to talk about. How do you feel about a woman being an equal in your partnership?"

"My wife, Emily, is a 50% partner in every sense of the word. We share everything, make all big decisions together, and have a wonderful life for ourselves."

"I'm very happy for you. I'd like to meet her."

Jack was looking at her closely, as she knew he would, trying to read her.

"Seriously, I am," she reported. "Everyone says you have a terrific marriage and I'm truly happy for you. You have two children, right?"

"Yes," said Jack. "Hannah is three and Zeke is one."

"You have a Zeke?"

"Uh-huh. His real name is Zachary, after Emily's father, but we prefer Zeke to Zach."

"I love it," Marcie said, with real sincerity.

"All this is about how I am with women, right? I mean that's what I gathered from your speech at lunch."

"That's certainly some of it. I get the feeling that Randy doesn't exactly hold women in very high esteem."

"That's all locker room bullshit. Randy's a professional and, I think, the next Mike Ovitz. We're having dinner tonight because he thinks you're the person for the job."

Marcie reflected on that for a minute. She was vaguely impressed, but felt it was by no means dispositive of the issue. As the food arrived and more wine was poured, she pressed further.

"That's very reassuring," she began. "But I am more than a little concerned about this being a situation of equal partners, with some more equal than others. Frankly, I thought you and Ben were deferring to Randy at lunch. That's not exactly my style. If we're to be equal partners, then I presume that the majority will rule. If we have a deadlock, we'll have to put some mechanism in place to resolve the problem. I don't think I could be happy with the notion that what Randy says goes."

Jack laughed. He had a hearty laugh which lit up his entire face. Marcie found it very attractive, but was grateful when he returned to the discussion at hand.

"I can't speak for Ben on this one, but I can assure you that I'm not walking from Allied to subject myself to Randy's rule. It has sort of been assumed that he would hold the title of president or chairman or whatever we decide to call it, but that all key decisions would be made by the general partners. He's comfortable with that, and so are Ben and I. Shit, Marcie, I don't want to be the one who holds press conferences and fields questions from the Trades. Randy eats that stuff up, so let him do it. I care about building an agency, making Fuck You money, and living happily ever after. Call me crazy, but we have land in Montana and I'd like nothing more than to have the bucks to cash out and disappear from this town forever."

This was a side of Jack that Marcie had no idea existed. Was it genuine, she wondered? It sure seemed to be. She had been thinking about accumulating walking away money, "Fuck You money," as Jack had called it, on her own. Maybe this was the shot she should take. Maybe she and Jack shared the same agenda after all.

"Would Emily like to get out of here, too?"

"In a heartbeat. This is a rough town on women. She knew it when we started, but it's even harder on her than she thought it would be. The kids are great and we've got the money to lead the good life and all that. But Christ, there must be other things to talk about when we go out besides the business. Even when we reach for friends from other fields, all they want to do is gossip. No, this is one dream that we share completely, and I think this move is the best shot to make it happen."

If Jack was trying to romance her into the deal, thought Marcie, he was doing one helluva good job. She had no idea that inside his usual poker-faced appearance was the soul of a romantic. She wondered why they had never become friendly at Allied. His reputation was certainly a good one. Extremely dedicated to his work. Clients who were loyal to him. Not showy, but solid and substantial.

Jack filled the silence with a question of his own. "What about you? I know you were married once in New York. Are you going to go off and leave us and have babies? Do you see yourself being with this venture in five years?"

Marcie bridled at the question, but held herself in check. Was it some bullshit sexist remark or a sincere question about her future plans? She decided that it probably was the latter.

"We make plans with the cards we're dealt," Marcie said. "I fully expect to be working as an agent in five years and not retiring to the bushes to drop children, or whatever other image you see in your mind."

"Whoa," Jack said, "don't turn this into a feminist tirade. I only wondered what your present thinking was. And I don't think it was an inappropriate question."

"All right, I'm sorry," Marcie answered. "You sort of pressed a button. I was out of line."

"No problem," Jack said graciously. "This dinner was to find where the borders were, for both of us. Remember, I'm here to find out about you the same way you came to find out about me."

Marcie nodded and smiled. She felt more and more comfortable with Jack the longer they spoke. She hadn't expected this reaction at all. She had thought he would prove to be a stand-in for Randy. Instead, he was an interesting, sensible man she could enjoy. This made the decision that much more difficult.

"Can you tell me," Marcie began again, "why you think you can make it work with Randy? Ben I know. I have no doubt I could work with him. But Randy, I'm just not sure."

Jack smiled. Clearly he didn't take offense at the question.

"Fair enough," he said. "I think Randy likes to see himself as the tough guy, but I've seen him operate. He's a hard negotiator, but very honest. He's loyal to his colleagues, except when he feels he's being screwed over. In his mind, that's what's going on at Allied. As loyal a friend as he is, he's also that scary an enemy. Randy's not a middle kind of man. He's comfortable playing at the extremes. He thrives on the pressure and performs better the more adrenaline he has flowing. With Ovitz and Ronnie Meyer out of the agency business, my hunch is that Randy's the next superstar agent. He's smart as hell and all over the new technologies. Ben and I both feel he could revolutionize this business the way Ovitz did. Charles is too threatened by him to let him do it at Allied. Does that answer the question?"

"I think so. Certainly from your perspective. What about being his partner and being a woman?"

Jack reached for his glass and took another sip of wine. He pondered the question and then spoke. "That one I have to leave in your hands. I'm not that in touch with my female side that I know the answer."

Marcie nodded. She would take it one step at a time.

"How does Emily feel about him?"

"Good question. She'd heard all the talk about his sexism, but never confronted it first hand. The three of us went to dinner, in fact at this very restaurant, and she worked it out with him. You're certainly welcome to speak with her, but I'd recommend you have your dinner with Randy first."

Jack was a pleasant surprise. She would enjoy working with him and continuing to get to know him. Randy remained a big question mark.

"Thanks," Marcie said, "I'll probably do that. I'd like to get to know her anyway."

The dinner had been cleared away and they were finishing their coffee. Marcie continued to enjoy the conversation which had moved back toward sports and movies. Jack was as curious about her tennis as she had been about his golf. Athletes, especially those who competed in the upper echelon of their respective sports, shared a special kind of intimacy. They knew what sacrifices had to be made to get to that level, and they knew, as fans or less talented players did not, the particular rush that went along with playing a sport particularly well. Odd, she thought again, how she had missed out on being friendly with this man during their years together at Allied.

"One other thing," Marcie said. "Peter Tacy stopped in to ask my advice about leaving to join you. Where does that stand?"

"It's wrapped up in your decision. If you came, we couldn't afford him right away. If you didn't, we'd try to bring him over. What's your opinion of him?"

"I like him. He's just getting started, but I think he's going to be a good one."

Jack paid the check and he and Marcie moved outside, giving their parking receipts to the Valet.

"I enjoyed tonight," Jack said. "I'm sure if you give Randy half a chance you'll find he's not the person you may have heard he is."

"Tonight was great. The fact that you and Ben are partners with him says a lot. Thanks for the dinner. I assume we'll be talking."

Marcie gave Jack a hug, tipped the Valet who held her car door open, got in and drove off. She tried Ben when she returned to her home, but got only an answering machine. Marcie left word that she'd had a very positive dinner with Jack, but that he shouldn't call her back since she was going to bed. Well, not exactly, Marcie thought. First, she had to read the teleplay that Valerie had given her for Dick. God, she hoped it was good.

The pilot script was nothing short of brilliant. Warm, funny, full of the colors of New York and written for Dick. In fact, Dick was so much better than George Segal would have been that NBC should be kissing her ass for bailing them out. She hoped Dick would be as excited as she was. The role had Emmy written all over it; the show looked like a sure-fire hit. She was thrilled for Dick and more than a little happy for herself. With the jockeying for position going on all around her, it certainly wouldn't hurt to have the star of a new series in her stable. She couldn't wait to talk to Dick the next day.

George put her through her paces the next morning, calling her a "wuss" for complaining about the "crunches" for her abs. When she had endured another morning of torture at his hands, she showed him out, showered, and dressed in an elegant Armani suit. She finished her outfit off with her favorite gold and pearls jewelry. Feeling good, she set off for the office.

The minute Marcie arrived, she was summoned to Charles' office by Edith. Edith, ever the benign gatekeeper, warned her that he seemed to be in a rage. "Be careful," she cautioned. "He nearly took *my* head off today." Marcie thanked her for the warning and headed upstairs. It had to be about her discussions with the Young Lions, she thought. There are no secrets in this place.

"Hello, Marcie," Charles greeted her. "I hear you've been talking with Randy and the boys. Anything you want to tell me?"

Marcie concluded that Charles was coming on very strong to intimidate her into submission. She felt she had done nothing wrong and decided at once that honesty would be the best course to follow.

"They've asked me to join them and I told them I'd let them know. That's about all there is to it."

Charles studied her for a minute. He didn't look as if he had expected this kind of candor and was somewhat unnerved by it. For the moment, the balance of power shifted to Marcie.

"Were you just going to walk out without saying anything?" Charles asked snidely.

"Who said anything about walking out? People get job offers every day. You know that. I certainly haven't said yes to them."

"You haven't said no either."

"That's right, Charles, I haven't."

"In case it hasn't occurred to you, this is about loyalty. After the way we've treated you, it's the least we could expect in return."

Marcie exploded. "Treated me! I'll tell you how you've treated me! You've kept me out of the management team; you've paid me less than a man with my business would get; and you haven't shown me one iota of respect. Treated me? My ass!"

Charles recoiled a little at her outburst. He leaned forward and said very quietly, "You've been very well paid by Allied."

"Sure I've been paid well. But salary and bonuses are all comparative. You know and I know that I'm underpaid. My mistake has been that I didn't spend my years fighting about the money the way I should have."

Charles sighed. "What are they offering you? Let's see if we can match it."

"To tell you the truth, we haven't even discussed money. The equity division, sure, but the draw hasn't come up yet."

Charles nodded. "You aren't serious about leaving Allied, are you"?

"I don't know, Charles. It was a complete surprise when they asked me, and I'm playing it out now. I'm not even sure we could all get along as partners. Obviously there are problems, but I'm pretty sure I'll have worked it through by the weekend."

"You have a great future here, Marcie. My advice to you is don't screw it up. You'd be making the mistake of your life if you joined them. Trust me, within two years, three top, they'll be belly up. And you'll have lost all the momentum you have going for you here. Don't do it."

"You act as though I've said yes to them. That's not the case. I'm going to hear them out, as I told them I would, but that's the only commitment I've made."

"It would be a huge step backward for you," Charles persisted.

"I guess the talks between Allied and the Young Lions have broken down."

"Young Lions, you mean little pissants!" Charles bristled. "Yes, they've broken down. I don't think they ever entered into them in good faith. They were on their way out the door from the get-go."

"You know Randy as well as anyone," Marcie continued. "Do you think he could work with a woman and treat her as his equal?"

"Don't be naive, Marcie. You know the answer to that. Randy may be a hot agent, but he's sleaze as a human being. You'd be insane to think you could change him. He'd make your life miserable, and frankly, Marcie you don't deserve that."

Charles paused to let his words register. Marcie stared at him. Finally, Charles broke the silence. "If you decide to stay, there will be a salary review and we'll put together a new financial package for you. We think of you as family, Marcie, and we'd hate like hell to lose you."

Charles rose from his desk chair to accompany Marcie to the door. "Keep me informed, will you?"

"Of course," she said, heading out of his office.

As she arrived at Sandy's desk, she noticed it resembled a small pharmacy. Sandy was nursing a prominent cold, and was making liberal use of the Kleenex on her desk.

"Why don't you go home and get dome rest?" asked Marcie,

In a voice that sounded incredibly nasal, Sandy replied that it sounded much worse than it was, and that she was going to stick it out. "The only thing that pisses me off is that you complain of having the flu, and now you're fine and I'm sick. Where's the justice in that?"

Marcie laughed sympathetically. "Okay," said Marcie, "If you're staying would you try Dick for me?"

"Did you read it?" asked Dick, plunging right in, as soon as Sandy got him for Marcie.

"I did," said Marcie, "and it's a wonderful script and perfect for you."

"I knew it!" Dick exclaimed. "I'm not nuts! *Meshugah*, maybe, but nuts, nah! So what do we do now?"

"Now we finish up a deal at NBC, get you together with Levine and Rogers and get to work."

"I'll be here all day except for 11:30 to 12:30," Dick rattled on. "I've got a little cavity they're going to fix. It's nothing serious."

"I'm glad," said Marcie, chuckling to herself. "I'll get back to you as soon as I can."

"Do you want the dentist's number?"

"No, Dick, I don't think that will be necessary."

"Well good luck, get us lots of money, but don't blow the deal. It's too good a script."

"Don't worry, I won't," said Marcie as she hung up. Whew, she thought, this one could actually be easy. Stash him on a successful series and he'd be fine. Anyway, there was still work to do. This baby wasn't on the air yet.

As she hung up, Sandy buzzed to say that Ben was holding for her.

"Ben, how're you bearing up to the stress?"

"I'm fine, but what about you?"

"I'm hanging in there," replied Marcie. "Charles gave me his sternest warnings this morning about joining you guys. He predicted only doom and gloom for your venture."

"You expected something different?"

"Not really. The interesting thing is he's going to rework my deal for me if I stay here."

"What do you have that's definite?"

"Nothing. It just came up today."

"Watch out, Marcie. If that's the way you go, and I sure as hell hope you don't, you've got to pin him down to specifics and get it in writing."

"Gee, Ben, you make him sound like an agent."

"No shit."

He and Marcie had a brief giggle over this, then Ben asked if dinner was still on with Randy.

"Far as I know," said Marcie. "You didn't hear anything different, did you?"

"No. I know Randy's in, but I hadn't spoken with you since you had dinner with Jack."

"I really like Jack. I'm amazed that I could work with him all this time, and not have a clue who he was."

"He's a pretty neat guy, isn't he?"

"He sure seemed to be. We had a good time together."

"Well, stay open to liking Randy. He's a different sort, obviously, but he's still a very special person. Would you call me when you get home from dinner with him?"

"Sure. Talk to you then. Take care."

As Marcie hung up, the first of a parade of agents trooped into her office to talk about the Young Lions and the rumors that were circulating, linking her to them. Each agent had advice for Marcie, but none of it seemed to carry much weight. Some urged her to take the shot because, for her, there was no real downside. Either she would get rich or the agency would fold and she could come back to Allied or another big agency. Some of the women shared her reservations about Randy. Others were quite taken with him and found his unapologetic *machismo* highly desirable.

Marcie concluded that she had to make the decision herself. It would all turn on whether she could see herself working in close proximity to Randy as his partner. Even speculating on it made her uncomfortable. Don't decide now, she told herself. Remember the pleasant surprise that Jack turned out to be.

CHAPTER X

"I'll be back in a second," Randy said. "I've got to visit the men's room."

Marcie nodded and watched him march off. She thought, not him. Randy can't be disappearing to do blow in the bathroom, can he? She vowed to ask him about it when he returned. God, the last thing she wanted was to become involved with a cokehead.

Randy had chosen L'Orangerie for dinner. It had a well-deserved reputation as one of L.A.'s premier restaurants, although it was not fashionable with the entertainment industry set. Located on a less than trendy part of La Cienega Boulevard, it had more the flavor of an upscale Pasadena restaurant than anything else. Marcie didn't frequent L'Orangerie as a rule, but she was pleased he had chosen it. Judging by how well-known he was by the management, this may have been one of his favorite restaurants. Marcie rather liked his going against the grain in restaurant selection. Especially when it promised major culinary dividends.

"Tell me you didn't disappear to do lines in the john," Marcie demanded, as Randy returned.

"Of course not," he said, laughing. "I had to take a leak, if you must know." Randy's dark eyes sparkled. "I'm afraid I'm not much for drugs. Disappointed?"

"No," Marcie said guardedly. "Just curious."

Randy was dark, with the polished good looks that many would find attractive. He's certainly not my type, Marcie thought. But then, I may be confusing my feelings about him with my judgment of how he looks. He seemed to her to have a sociopath quality, a person not to be trusted. If they were to make any headway at this dinner, she'd have to deal with these suspicions and give him a chance to demonstrate that her instincts were off-base.

"Good," replied Randy closing off this line of discussion. The waiter asked if they'd like refills on their drinks. Randy was drinking some single-malt scotch that Marcie had never heard of, while she was having a Perrier with lime. He nodded that he would like a refill and she did the same.

"Let me fill you in on what's happened," Randy began again. "We got a tremendous deal subletting space from a law firm on Avenue of the Stars. It's a separate suite of offices, all ready to go. We just have to put our name on the door, and we're in business. They've given us a four-month rent moratorium because they're not paying any broker commissions and they're going to represent us as outside counsel. It's the Levenger firm, in case you're wondering, so we'll probably see some clients from them as well. We've got bank financing in place, secured by the earnings of our company and our personal guarantees. Assuming you were on board, and guessing on the commission business you would bring, it looks like you'd gross between $75,000 and $100,000 the first year. There'd be money for a secretary for each of us, but no receptionist in year one.

"As for other staff, Jack may have told you, that if you join us, we've decided against any associates for now. There's time enough for that. We'd have to be very careful about expenses, but there would be a health plan for the partners. Secretaries would have to wait at least a year for benefits. There's parking in the building, and my deal with the Levenger firm is that we split the cost of eight spots for the first two years. We can decide about things like validating guests later."

"What about vehicles?"

"We budgeted for leasing cars for the partners."

"It's a considerable cut, isn't it?" Marcie was doing the math quickly in her head. She could meet her basic living conditions, but the extravagances that she enjoyed would have to be eliminated. Goodbye to the Villas in the Springs.

Randy nodded. "It'll be a problem at the outset, especially for Jack, who's paying for kids in school. You'll have to check out the numbers for yourself, but we think we can get it all back in eighteen months. From there, anything's possible."

"You see the draws and the expenses as being equal?" Marcie asked.

"If we do this together, then we do it as equals. We can always play with formulas for reassessments down the road, but we favor treating everyone alike."

"That's your position too?" Marcie asked dubiously.

"Marcie," Randy turned very serious. "We're past that point. Our talks before were preliminary negotiations. I'm comfortable with an even split, and so are the others. Okay?"

"Fine," Marcie responded. She was conscious of the slight edge that crept into Randy's voice. He was not crazy about being questioned when he made a pronouncement. This was a trait that bore watching. It was hardly a harbinger of happy times to come in the proposed partnership.

"I didn't want to ruin a good dinner by bringing spread sheets with all the projections, so I hope we can find other things to discuss," Randy continued.

"Pardon me," the waiter interrupted. "Are you ready to order?"

"Give us some more time, will you?" Randy was polite, yet decisive. Marcie liked that. He was accustomed to leading, and probably very accustomed to getting his way. Before she probed too deeply into his psyche, especially concerning his feelings about women, maybe she could get him talking about himself.

"You have a place on Wilshire?" she asked.

"Yes, I have the penthouse in one of those high-rises in Westwood. It's a good, safe building and very convenient. It serves my purposes very well."

Marcie wished she could see it. Had he lavished time and money on the furnishings? Was it pulled together by a decorator because he didn't have time for it? Did he collect art? Were there plants, or any other living things besides him in it? Was it as gray and cold as his office? She made a note to see how tonight went, and maybe then finagle an invitation to have a drink there and check it out. There was much to be learned by looking carefully at the interior of a person's home. She remembered the time she'd been invited to the home of a famous movie star who enjoyed a reputation for being unusually bright. Casually examining the bookcase, Marcie had been amazed to see the books were in alphabetical order, all chosen for the statements they might make. Sylvia Plath snuggled up next to Marcel Proust.

"Do you have a significant other in your life?" Marcie asked.

Randy didn't seem surprised by the question. "No, this isn't exactly the right time for that. I'm not afraid of commitments, if that's where this is heading. But I'm quite comfortable living the bachelor life right now. What about you?" he shot back. "Someone special in your life?"

"No one serious," Marcie replied. "I wouldn't be averse to it, but I'm not running around looking for Mr. Right." Her mind raced. She had shied away from deep personal or professional commitments since Rob's death. Even Allied had an arm's length quality to it. She hadn't wanted to take the risks that came with potential rewards. It didn't matter whether it was a job or a man. Maybe she was ready to come off this position. Certainly enough time had elapsed. Could that be the energy that was swirling around her?

Randy had a way of keeping her a little bit off balance. In principle, since the Young Lions were pursuing her, she should be asking the questions and he should be trying to sell her. But in some subtle fashion,

Randy had made the playing field level, if not tilted a bit in his direction. It was a good technique, Marcie observed, one that must contribute to his success as an agent.

"You know you have the reputation of being a real sexist?" Marcie asked, seizing the initiative in the conversation. Randy laughed, finishing his scotch. "What do you think?" he asked.

"If I had to guess, I'd say the reputation is well-founded. You probably don't hold women in very high regard and are inclined to see us more as objects than as individual people."

"That sounds like me," Randy said disarmingly.

"Why should I even consider working with someone like you?" Marcie asked.

"Because I'm a great fucking agent and because you aren't a radical feminist. I'm a professional, and I demand that from my colleagues as well. I don't let my personal philosophy intrude into my work and wouldn't expect anyone else to either. Would we do business with someone whose politics were one hundred eighty degrees away from ours? I sure as hell hope so. Business is business. If I'm out of line with you, I expect to be called on it. And I'll do the same with you. This may come as a shock to you, but there are plenty of women out there who are either unenlightened, in your terms, or who simply like men like me. Either way, I'm not complaining. I can tell you this: there's no way in hell that I'd hold still for your getting twenty-five percent of the action if I didn't think you were worth at least that much to the partnership. I respect your ability to carry your share of the load, and I think the perception of who we are will be greatly helped by having you as a partner. Does that answer your question?"

Marcie sat back. Whew. Answer it, sure, in a most surprising manner. She had expected him to try to weasel out of his reputation. Instead he had taken responsibility for it with refreshing candor. Her decision was going to be more complicated than she had imagined.

"I don't know, Randy. It's nice that you respect my abilities as a professional. I'm having problems setting up a partnership with someone who thinks less of me because I'm a woman. I'm certainly no radical feminist, but I *am* a woman. I can't change that, and wouldn't if I could. I'm not sure I can be the partner of someone who thinks the way you do."

Randy grinned at her. Was he trying to pass himself off as a mischievous boy? While he was youthful, his extremely expensive Italian suit suggested power, not youthful exuberance.

"Fair enough," he said. "Let me tell you a little more about why I wear my image as a sexist as a badge of honor. Believe me, I know very well how politically incorrect it all is. Other than a handful of women I've gone out with, you won't be able to find one instance where I have advocated a sexist point of view in business or in my personal life. Call me crazy, but I use it as a kind of defense mechanism, a shield. It's given me an identity apart from the herd. You don't have to worry about my having dark thoughts about you. I don't."

"Am I supposed to feel good at this point?" Marcie asked.

"I'm not looking for your approval, and it's no great concern to me if you feel good about me or not. My approach to being a good agent doesn't have much to do with caring how people feel about me, except for clients and buyers. And even then, I've learned that whether they like me or not, if I've got something they want they'll deal with me as if I was their best friend. If that sounds overly cynical to you, take a good look in the mirror. You'll see an agent whose clients don't know the meaning of the word loyalty, an agent who works in a business driven by money and power. Anybody who says they see something different is a liar."

Marcie was impressed. Randy was certainly a hardball player. He had used his toughness to climb to the top, whether people were in the way or not. There were only a handful of agents who possessed that kind of constitution and they inevitably succeeded. Could he work with partners?

Was he in it solely for himself? Would she and the others have to be look-ing over their shoulders constantly to be sure he wasn't creeping up behind them to stick a knife in their backs?

"Where do you see yourself in five years?" Marcie asked.

"That's easy. Helping to make this agency pay off like a slot machine."

"And when the studios come calling with the big executive jobs, stock options, and all their other inducements?"

"If they dangle the five hundred mill that Ovitz supposedly got at Disney, that's one set of facts. If it's about sitting in some executive chair with my name on a parking spot, forget it. I'm an agent. I like what I do, and I think working with you, Ben and Jack, we can really light up this town. I'm betting my career on it."

Marcie reflected for a minute. Her mind was reeling with conflict-ing thoughts. She didn't like Randy, and didn't like what he stood for. But he was surprisingly open with her. If she was being put on, then it was one of the best performances she had ever witnessed. It seemed unlikely. No, this was who he was. He was comfortable with that and almost defied you not to accept him. Could she ever be comfortable with who he was? Would she end up having to spend her life apolo-gizing for her partner?

"I'll tell you what's going through my mind," she said at last. "The image of a sexist pig that you enjoy cultivating is an embarrassment to me. I think we could work together in business, but I'm not sure I want to be apologizing for you with clients and buyers. I don't want any place where I work, especially as a partner, to have a locker room mentality. We're equal partners and I want to feel we're joined at the hip. If we feel disconnected before we even open the doors, it's never going to work."

"I agree with you," said Randy. "I would commit to you and the oth-ers that none of that would be a part of our professional life. Most of it is smoke and mirrors anyway, and I'm giving you my word that it won't be an issue. We should dedicate ourselves to bringing this baby home a winner and not have to spend time worrying about shit like that."

Marcie assessed the sincerity of that pledge. He probably meant it, but was he going to be able to live by it? He was looking at her expectantly. He wanted an answer now. "I'll tell you what," she said. "I'll let you know definitively tomorrow."

"I suppose I can live with that," he said, smiling his best boyish smile again. "I hope you decide yes because I know we could kick some ass. Sleep on it and talk to me tomorrow. It's the right thing for both of us. I know it."

       *   *   *   *   *

Driving home, Marcie played back the dinner in her head. It had been full of surprises. As they had waited for their cars, his arrived first. Instead of giving her the obligatory social kiss on her cheek, Randy had given her a firm handshake. Was that a sign of respect or some kind of put-down? And what should she make of his apparent forthrightness about his sexist leanings? He was disarming, bright, surprising, and someone not to be cavalierly dismissed. One thing was certain: she had gone to dinner expecting to be able to dismiss Randy and the Young Lions out of hand. That was all different now. For the first time, she felt as if she could truly make a go of it with that group. For different reasons, she liked and respected all of them and their abilities. She had not expected to see the discussions advance to this point. She was on the brink of a critical decision. Did she want to leave Allied to team up with them? She'd promised an answer the next day. To her astonishment, she realized that if she had to respond that minute, she would say yes.

Arriving home, she made a fast call to Ben to report on her dinner with Randy. He was excited that it had gone well. He assured her that the more she got to know Randy, the better she would like him. He told her that he had looked carefully at Randy's reputation and decided that it was not a problem. "When you cut through all the bullshit," Ben said, "there's no real substance to any of it. I'm betting on the fact that he's going to be a terrific partner."

Ben tried to coax a decision from Marcie, but she held to her promise to respond the next day. She declined to indicate how she was leaning, telling Ben that she needed to sleep on it. He said he understood and looked forward to hearing from her tomorrow. Maybe time for one more call before she turned in. Marcie dialed Jane Pratt, hoping she was still awake. Jane answered and assured her that she was awake and watching Letterman.

"If it isn't too late," began Marcie, "I'm getting to a decision with the Young Lions."

"You want to join them, don't you?"

"How did you know that?"

"You told me you were having dinner with Randy and I know you and I know him. I just guessed you'd hit it off if you gave him half a chance."

"Why didn't you tell me that before?"

"Because it was something you had to find out for yourself."

"Jane, tell me straight out. Would I be making a mistake leaving Allied to go with them?"

"I think you'd be making the smartest move of your career. You'd complete the package and the four of you would own the town."

"You really think so?" Marcie asked, still wavering.

"I know so. There hasn't been this kind of excitement about a new agency since CAA was launched. And you four have more going for you at the start than they did."

"And you don't think people will write me off as a sellout because I joined up with Randy?"

"Only those who were jealous of you to begin with. Randy's a star. Anyone who doesn't see that doesn't understand the business. My best advice to you is to take your twenty-five percent of that business and leave Allied tomorrow. Opportunities like this one don't come around very often."

"Jane, I can't tell you how much I appreciate this. You've really helped me."

"Get a good night's sleep, and knock 'em dead tomorrow."

"Thanks again," said Marcie.

Marcie made herself a cup of tea and got ready for bed. Her mind was racing. She sipped her tea and mulled over the evening. She was excited about the prospect of joining forces with the Young Lions. She knew, when she took stock of her situation at Allied, that she would never move into the top echelon. The glass ceiling was firmly in place. This would be a new beginning, she'd have her hands on the reins. It would be, she was certain, an arduous road to travel, but she was only thirty-five. Pratt was right. This could be the chance of a lifetime. She felt confident she could hold her own with the three men and that together the whole would be greater than the sum of the parts. She still wanted to chat with Jack's wife, Emily, but she could get to that. Call me crazy, she thought, I'm leaving Allied and teaming up with them. Her final thought, before drifting off to sleep, was an anxious one. She couldn't go into this partnership holding anything back. Was she ready for a flat-out commitment? If she did make this move, there would be no holding back.

*   *   *   *   *

The next morning she awakened full of energy. Her trainer arrived and put her through her paces commenting that he'd have to toughen up the drill because she was getting through it too easily. A quick shower, and she got dressed. As she put on her blue suit with white pin-stripes, she smiled remembering the salesperson's comment, "That's a real power suit." Well, damn it, today she felt powerful.

Riding a surge of confidence, she called Randy. No time like the present, she thought.

"Hello," Randy answered.

"Randy, it's Marcie."

"Hey, how are you? Up and at 'em early I see."

"I wanted to catch you before the day gets going. I've thought about our conversation a lot, and the more time I spend on it, the more I'm convinced that joining you guys is the right move for me. So, count me in."

"That's terrific news!"

Randy seemed genuinely thrilled, which allayed the slight anxiety Marcie still felt.

Randy continued, "The guys are headed over here at 8:30 for coffee and bagels. Can you possibly make it?"

"That's perfect," said Marcie. "I want to wrap up the details with the three of you before I see Charles this morning. It would probably be a good idea to make some client calls before Allied sics the dogs on them."

"I'm in the Homestead House, two blocks west of Beverly Glen on Wilshire," Randy explained. "Penthouse W."

"I'll see you in a few minutes," Marcie said.

As she made the short drive from Westwanda to Wilshire, Marcie felt the adrenaline race through her system. It had been some time since she experienced that feeling, and she enjoyed it. What was the name of the new agency to be? It had never come up in their conversations. That was the least of their problems. How long would it take to wrap things up at Allied? A week? Ten days, tops. Would Sandy come? She was sure she would, but some of that would depend on how she got along with the other secretaries. Hell, Sandy got along with everyone. That was her great asset. And her clients? She'd bet anything that they'd all come with her. Other than Dick's series and Sam's current Warners picture, her big clients were pretty open as far as bookings were concerned. Most of their agency papers expired in the next six to eight months, as she recalled. On the whole, she was in damn good shape to make the move. And Dick's series, which was still a dream more than a reality, was very much up in the air. She would need the advice of her new partners on that one.

As she swung into the circular driveway of the Homestead she remembered that she would need to call her attorney, Ira Lang, before the negotiations got too detailed.

Marcie parked the car in a guest spot and took the elevator in the lobby to the top floor. She rang the bell at Penthouse W. Randy opened it, dressed in slacks, an open sport shirt, and Italian loafers without socks. He threw his arms around her and gave her a big hug.

"You've made me a happy man!" he exclaimed.

"I'm pretty excited, myself," Marcie enthused.

They stepped into the apartment and Marcie found herself surrounded by light. The sun poured in and a large bank of windows overlooked the shimmering ocean to the west. The apartment was furnished in magnificent taste. A quick glance revealed signed prints by Jasper Johns, Elsworth Kelly, Jim Dine, and others. Original oils and sculpture were strategically placed around the living room-dining room area. Randy saw Marcie's eyes taking it all in.

"Would you like the one minute tour before the others arrive?"

"I'd love it. I had no idea you collected."

"It's been a passion of mine for as long as I can remember. I just don't feel the need to publicize it. I try to separate my personal life from my business life as much as I can."

This man gets more intriguing the more I know of him, Marcie thought.

"I love your collection," Marcie said. "It's like visiting some of my old friends."

Randy beamed. As they entered the bedroom, Marcie noticed a blank space above the bed.

"That's on loan to the Whitney," Randy said proudly. "It's a Stella that is truly to die for."

The doorbell interrupted Randy's reverie, and he snapped into to his professional persona.

"To be continued," he said. "Let's greet our partners."

Randy opened the door. "Gentlemen, meet our new partner!"

Both Ben and Jack rushed to embrace Marcie. As they told her how happy they were, their voices hopelessly overlapping, Randy emerged from the kitchen with a tray of coffee, sweet rolls, bagels and cream cheese.

"It's from Nate 'n Al's," said Randy, referring to the celebrated Beverly Hills deli, "fresh this morning."

He placed the tray on the glistening white dining room table and they seated themselves around it.

"Marcie called a few minutes ago to tell me the good news. She's decided to become our partner, so I invited her to our first partnership meeting."

Randy paused for a second and said, "Excuse me," and bolted into the kitchen. He returned with a bottle of Cristal and four champagne glasses. "I know we don't usually drink at breakfast, but this is a special occasion!"

Randy popped the cork and poured them each a glass. They raised their glasses, gently clinked them all around and toasted the formation of their agency.

"What are we going to call it?" asked Jack.

"How about The New Agency?" Marcie suggested.

They looked back and forth from one to the other and nodded their assent.

"To The New Agency!" Ben cried, and they toasted once more before settling down to mapping out their strategies. Ben kept notes as they ran through the initial business concerns. The agency would have corporate counsel, the Levenger firm, and they would all retain individual attorneys to represent their own interests. They would have a most-favored-nations clause in each contract that would guarantee that none of their individual deals would be better than any of the others. All corporate benefits would be identical at the outset, with the understanding that they would reexamine the agreement in five years, and then again every three years. It would require three votes to effect changes and all expressed the hope that changes would be the exception and not the rule.

Randy produced the spreadsheets he had alluded to at dinner. Marcie was intrigued to see that all of her clients, their existing deals and the status of their agency papers were scheduled along with those of Randy, Ben and Jack. Catching her surprise, Jack said, "Forgive us, for 25%, we wanted to be sure we were getting more than a pretty face."

"And are you?"

"The numbers tell no lies," said Ben.

As Marcie ran her eye over the projections, she understood immediately that many issues, such as Dick's deal, might be construed as being gray. Talks that hadn't quite matured into deals, discussions that either were or were not formal submissions that might require commissions for Allied, clients who had given indications that they were re-signing, but hadn't gotten around to the paperwork yet—issues that could lead to litigation, which would be both expensive and damaging to a business just starting out. Marcie agreed there was much wisdom in trying to negotiate settlements on as much of this gray area as was possible. Randy brought her up to date on the progress of negotiations with Allied, emphasizing that her business had not yet been introduced into the settlement talks. He told her the talks were ongoing and that her matters would be put on the table as soon as she gave the word. She filled her new partners in on the talks with NBC which, while only for a pilot, still held much promise.

Marcie told them that she would see Charles today, this morning if possible, and call Randy as soon as the deed was done. She suggested she stay for another half hour and make a few calls to her key clients to let them know what was happening. Randy showed her into his study, which was done in traditional dark woods, with floor-to-ceiling bookshelves and muted, red leather furniture. "Use the second line," he said. "If I need to call out, I'll use the first."

Marcie reached Sam, Dick, several actors and actresses for whom she had principal responsibility, and the handful of writers and directors she looked after. It was still early and she got all of them, although several were awakened by her call. Her relationship with her clients was always warm and personal; to a person, they indicated they would, of course, follow her to The New Agency. Most were only dimly aware of the legal consequences of their making the shift to join her, but were greatly relieved to find out that no matter what the outcome of her talks with Allied, they would still have her for an agent, and would not have to pay more than 10% commission. She told them she'd be back in touch with them shortly and would take care of notifying their attorneys, accountants, and business managers. Her last call was to Edith, Charles's secretary, asking when she could get in to see him. Edith set her up for 10:00, a half hour away. Marcie returned to the living room to find her new partners poring over catalogues of office furniture. "You guys free for lunch?" she asked.

"We're free as they come," replied Jack. "You're the only one still getting paid."

"At least until ten," Marcie interrupted. "That's my appointment to see Charles."

"How about Madame Wu's at one?" Randy asked.

Again, Marcie noted, the choice was for fine food and little likelihood of encountering industry people. They agreed on the place and time, as Marcie made a quick tour of the room, kissing and hugging each of the men in turn. Ben whispered to her, "I'm really happy this worked out." Marcie gave his hand a special squeeze.

In ten minutes, she was at Allied with a little time to spare before going up to see Charles. She asked Sandy to come in and close the door. Carrying her note pad, Sandy followed and sat down on the sofa in Marcie's office.

"You're running a little late today, aren't you?"

"Sandy, I'm due upstairs to see Charles in a few minutes. I want you to know that I'm going to resign and join up with the Young Lions. We'll be opening our own shop, called The New Agency, in Century City. I'd love for you to come with me, but the deal may be somewhat less than you're making here. At least at first."

"Hey, you're my main man," Sandy said, ignoring obvious gender problems. "Where you go, I go."

The women shared a warm hug. "I'll be down in a moment and we'll go over everything," Marcie said. "Do me a big favor, please, keep it to yourself for a few hours. You'll still have the scoop. I promise."

Sandy smiled and said, "Good luck with Sir Charles."

      *   *   *   *   *

Charles looked up as she sat down. "You wanted to see me?" There are no secrets in this town, she thought. His network has already reported to him. I'm no longer one of the good guys. I've moved over to the bad guys' camp.

"Yes, Charles. I wanted to tell you, as I promised, that I've made up my mind. You've been very good to me, and I've been happy at Allied. But the time has come for me to make a change. I decided today to join forces with Randy, Jack and Ben."

Charles stared at her for a moment, then coldly said, "You're making a terrible mistake. Everything looks so glamorous when you're drawing up dreams. It's like those stunning press releases when new studios announce their fantastic plans. But when the smoke clears a couple of years later, they're out of the goddamned business, and those bright executives don't look so fucking bright anymore."

"I know there's a risk in doing this," Marcie said, hoping to cut Charles's observations short.

"You don't know shit," he continued. "If you did, you would have listened to our new offer, negotiated a little bit, and walked away with a deal that would have made your head swim. Instead, you get suckered into joining those second stringers, taking a pay cut, going into debt, and for what? To have Randy piss all over you? To be able to say you're out there on your own? Let me tell you something, Marcie. It's plenty fucking cold out there. When your people are paying their commissions to Allied, or any other shop you steal clients from, you better have some way to pay your bills. Forget those fancy dinners and Lexus cars you've grown so fond of. You're moving to Siberia. A couple of years, you'll be begging to come in out of the cold."

Charles looked down at the copy of *Variety* he had been reading when she entered the room. Was she dismissed, she wondered? Is this really how all these years ended? Well, damnit, she wasn't going to sink to his level. She stood up and extended her hand. "I want to thank you, Charles, for the time I've spent here. You taught me a lot and I wish you continued success."

Charles again looked up, almost puzzled at her relentless cheeriness. For the moment, he reminded her of the aging Charles Laughton. His face suddenly thawed, and his eyes looked warmer, more human. Just as quickly, his face clouded over. He stood up and came around to Marcie's side of the desk. "Life isn't about having it both ways, Marcie. From now on, Allied is out to bury you and your treacherous friends."

Charles started back toward his desk. "See if you can talk some sense into those new partners of yours, and we'll wrap up these negotiations this afternoon. They can't want to keep paying the damn lawyers any more than we do."

"I'll do what I can. I know they'd like to finish it up as quickly as possible."

Marcie turned to leave.

"One more thing, Marcie," Charles said. "A free piece of advice. Keep your eye on Randy. He's your greatest strength and your greatest weakness."

Marcie walked back to her office thinking about the meeting. Not as bad as she had expected. No demands that she be out by noon, or threats to take her clients away. He had said Allied would bury them, but that was to be expected.

Sandy was waiting in Marcie's office, pointedly fighting her instinct to get on the phone and spread the news about Marcie. She looked up as Marcie entered, saying, "I didn't tell anybody. It's killing me, but I swear I didn't tell a soul."

Marcie smiled. "I always knew you could keep a secret."

"It was hard with Beverly. She came in to see you when you were upstairs. She's like all teary because she got popped for possession of a couple of joints last night. Big deal. It isn't even a criminal offense."

"How did it happen?"

"She was driving down Sunset and a plainclothes cop in an unmarked car saw her torching one down. Anyway, they booked her last night and let her go on her own recognizance."

"What did she want from me?"

"The name of a lawyer, and how to keep it out of the papers. Don't worry about that, 'cause I fixed her up on both."

"Really? She's okay?"

"She's fine. Trust me."

Count on Sandy, thought Marcie. It was comforting to know that she could be relied on for drug-related problems, on top of everything else.

"I'm glad you took care of it. I would have had to turn to you if she had come to me first, anyway."

"How was it with Charles?"

"A little stiff at first, but not too bad."

"I guess that's about all you could hope for."

"I'm going to meet with Randy and the guys for lunch and we'll probably work out the details. This is something you want, right?"

"I told you before, you're not fucking leaving me here. Got it?"

Marcie laughed. "Yeah, I got it. Do yourself a favor, though, and take a good look at your finances while I'm out. The money's going to be short at the beginning. You'll get the same as the others, and I'm sure it will increase as time goes on. But you've got to figure out if what you need to get by."

"Will you please not worry about me? If you must know, Miss Busybody, I've still got some of my grandmother's inheritance that I haven't spent. I'd rather invest in us than put it up my nose."

Okay, Sandy. An answer for every problem. Marcie still had her concerns about looking at it as an "investment," but it was certainly better than wasting the money on cocaine. One thing for certain, she'd be terrific at The New Agency. And they'd be lucky to have her around. Things had progressed so quickly that she hadn't thought about organizing her move. She was thankful that she kept her own contracts and deal memos file. It would be much easier to track her clients' business arrangements instead of having to avail herself of Allied's corporate files. As she thought about it, Marcie concluded that she could be out of Allied, paperwork stashed neatly in boxes, in less than forty-eight hours. Again, she experienced a rush of adrenaline that made her feel excited and strong.

CHAPTER XI

By noon Friday, Marcie's years at Allied were reduced to a neatly labeled stack of boxes. The packing had gone smoothly, despite interruptions from other agents and staff dropping by to say how much they would miss her. She already felt removed from her comfortable office, which had lost its identity the more she packed things away. Even her attire, jeans and a T-shirt, set her apart from her colleagues, who were dressed for their normal day's work. Marcie's new associates had done their packing earlier in the week, under the watchful eye of a security guard. No such constraints were imposed on Marcie.

After much discussion, she reluctantly consented to a going-away cocktail party to be held that afternoon in the large conference room. The party could delay the date she had made with Tim. She resented that and also detested the contrived and artificial nature of such functions. Sandy, as usual, made the most convincing argument.

"Who the fuck wants to spend their Friday afternoon in a conference room?" Sandy asked. "You'll be out of there before you know it."

As four o'clock rolled around, agents and secretaries assembled to bid Marcie farewell. People hung back in the hall, rather than getting wedged into the conference room. Sandy walked past Marcie, on her way to get another drink, and whispered, "Think Sir Charles will deign to come?"

Before Marcie could answer, Charles appeared, Derek by his side, holding a large, blue Tiffany box. He didn't have to ask for quiet.

"As you all know," he began, "Marcie has decided to leave us for what she hopes will be greener pastures."

Nothing like starting with a little dig, thought Marcie. Charles's remark had evoked a polite laugh from the assembled employees. He seemed impervious to the response, as if he couldn't have cared less what his colleagues were thinking.

"On behalf of all of us," he continued, "I'd like to present Marcie with this token of appreciation for a job well done."

That was it. Impersonal and to the point. Marcie flushed slightly as she moved through the group to accept the box from Charles. Charles had assumed his habitual position at the head of the table, and Marcie now found herself looking out over the faces of her former associates.

"Thank you, Charles," Marcie said. "I'm better at selling things than at saying thank you. But I am going to miss all of you and I hope we can all continue to be friends. There are enough clients to go around, and enough commissions out there for all of us."

Marcie looked toward Charles who seemed to recoil slightly. "Aren't you going to open your present?" Derek asked, as Charles shot him a withering look.

Marcie sincerely wished she could say no, but she untied the red ribbon and opened the box. Pulling back the white tissue paper, she found a Tiffany vase, simple, but always in good taste. Marcie carefully removed it from the box and read the etched inscription: TO MARCIE: FROM ALLIED. As she held the vase up. She wondered how they had gotten the inscription done so quickly. Perhaps that accounted for the all-purpose, impersonal text they had chosen. Nine years in the trenches, and that's all they had to say. Sandy stepped forward to hug her and place the vase back in its box. Charles, followed by Derek, was out the door without a backward glance.

In minutes, it was over. Hugs and kisses and good wishes from agents and staff, and then it was only Sandy and Marcie. To Marcie's amazement, Sandy now began to weep. Sandy? The toughest of the tough? "I'm sorry," she said. "I can't believe I'm being such a wuss." Her arm over Sandy's shoulder, Marcie walked with her back to their office. The movers were due at eight o'clock Monday morning and there was nothing left to pack.

"Thanks for all your help," Marcie said.

"Piece of cake," Sandy replied. "Get some rest this weekend. We've got to be sharp on Monday."

Marcie was glad that Sandy thought of the move as their move. It would make things easier if things got tough down the road. No question about it, Sandy was a prize.

Marcie drove home to shower, change, and await Tim's arrival. She had been rushing to get to Randy's that morning and hadn't had time to really digest the meaning of the single yellow rose that greeted her when she opened her front door. "SEE YOU TONIGHT AT 6:00: DRESS SEMI-FORMAL" the note had said. Other than the curious hour, it was a damn romantic gesture, Marcie thought.

At exactly six o'clock, Tim rang the bell to Marcie's house. She answered it, seeing a limo behind him, the back door being held open by the driver.

"I take it you don't want to come in."

"No time. We've got to get rolling."

"Well, I'm all ready. Do you have to be home by nine?"

Tim laughed, saying, "Nothing like that. Our schedule's a little tight, is all."

They headed down Benedict Canyon and turned west on Sunset. Marcie's curiosity was growing by the minute.

"Can you give me a clue?"

"You'll see, it's a surprise."

They turned on the San Diego Freeway, heading south. Now Marcie was really at a loss. Only Orange County was in this direction, and no one went there for dinner. The driver took the Century Boulevard Airport exit.

"We're picking up your ex-wife at the airport and all going out to dinner," Marcie guessed.

Again, Tim laughed, but offered no additional information. The driver passed the commercial carriers and pulled into the charter area. He parked on the tarmac by a twin-engine private jet with its engines running. On the side of the aircraft was the name BRADEN INDUS-TRIES. Tim jumped out of the limo saying, "Hurry up, we're going to be late."

A uniformed man, Marcie presumed he was the pilot, assisted them up the stairs leading to the interior of the cabin. He followed them and moved forward into the cockpit. Marcie was duly impressed and a bit excited.

The cabin was luxuriously appointed, and a flight attendant was the only other passenger. "Good evening Mr. Garland," she said breathily. Marcie hated her at once.

"Hi Monique, this is Marcie Sandmore."

"Very pleased to meet you. May I serve you champagne and caviar?"

Marcie looked over at Tim. "Do we have time?"

Tim smiled.

As the plane taxied into position for takeoff, Marcie asked, "I'm being sold into slavery by Braden, and you're brokering the deal. Right?"

"Close," said Tim. "We're trying a new restaurant in San Francisco that got great notices."

"A bit extravagant, isn't it?"

"Not as bad as it seems. Jimmy Braden is a close friend and the plane was idle tonight. I'd do the same for him."

As the plane took off to begin the short hop to the Bay Area, Tim turned serious. "I hear you've cast your lot with the group that broke away from Allied."

"Yes, you hear right. Your information's pretty good. It won't break in the Trades until tomorrow."

"It's really a small town when it comes to gossip."

"I don't know if you still want to see material from me, but Ben and I have some exciting properties we'd like to show you."

Tim laughed at her efforts to agent him. "I think we should put that on hold for a bit. I'm pretty tied up in another matter anyway."

Marcie looked closely at him. He was relaxed and easy with her, with none of the pressure of a business situation. No, this was a date. The yellow rose, the romantic trip to San Francisco, this was not about business at all. She suddenly felt a beat behind the action. Events had swirled so quickly in the last forty-eight hours that she hadn't been processing other information as rapidly as she usually did. Better tune in now if this evening is to have any chance of succeeding.

Tim continued to surprise her by next bringing up Randy.

"He's quite extraordinary, isn't he?" Tim asked.

"Yes," Marcie said warily. "He's a helluva talent."

"Do you think he's through tripping over his own cock?" Tim asked.

Without missing a beat, Marcie responded that she certainly hoped so. "He's promised not to let his personal life interfere with the business. We're gambling, I guess, that his word is good. I want very much to believe it is."

"I think it's a good bet," Tim replied.

"You seem to be pretty plugged in on what's going on," Marcie said.

Tim smiled. "You develop a network if you're interested in a business. I'm still watching from the sidelines though."

"It doesn't sound as though you expect to stay there too long."

Tim looked at her, then turned to look out the window of the limousine that had picked them up at the San Francisco airport.

"We're here," he said.

Tim's choice of a restaurant, L'Oasis, proved all he had suggested it would be. Run by the son of the proprietor of the same-named restaurant in Cannes, the food was fantastic. An associate of Tim's, an impeccably dressed Italian man, named Carmen Savaglio, joined them for a drink. Carmen and Tim spoke about some business between them in what seemed to Marcie to be code. Carmen apparently had something to tell Tim that concerned the availability of funds, and Tim was pleased with the news. No dinner invitation was extended to him, and Carmen politely excused himself, kissed Marcie's hand, and left.

"What was that all about?" Marcie asked.

"Just a deal I'm working on," Tim said.

"Forgive me, but Carmen seems almost like Mafia."

"You watch too many movies," Tim said smiling. "He's Italian, but he's just another businessman."

But Marcie wasn't so sure. As charming as Tim was, his penchant for never answering any questions about his business was a little troublesome. Was he just circumspect, or were there other reasons he preferred not to share that aspect of his life with her?

The flight home saw conversation again focused on the picture industry. Tim was casually offhanded in his efforts to probe Marcie's assessment of the strengths and weaknesses of each of the studios. Yet again, there seemed to be an agenda of which she was not aware. As the plane was in its approach to LAX, Tim steered the conversation around to more personal subjects. Marcie felt more at ease as they climbed into the waiting limousine.

"I'd like to show you my house," Tim suggested as they headed back to the freeway.

"Sure," replied Marcie. She only knew he lived somewhere in Beverly Hills. They turned off Coldwater at a corner Marcie didn't know. The "Not a Through Street" sign at the corner shed no other light on his specific address. The road immediately ascended until they reached a gated compound at the summit. The driver pushed a button, and the gates swung open revealing a dramatic, wood-and-glass home with a sweeping circular driveway. Tim felt her curiosity.

"It was designed by Neutra, although I've done some work on it."

"It's fantastic."

"Let me show you the inside."

The driver opened the doors for them. Tim showed her to the front door where he entered his code into a keypad before opening the door. Stepping into the house, Marcie was overwhelmed. "I have the oddest sense I've been here before."

"Maybe you saw it in *Architectural Digest* last year. I let them talk me into doing a big piece on the house."

"That's it! I thought that spread was a knockout!"

Tim swept Marcie up in his arms. "So are you, Marcie. I'd given up finding a woman like you."

Marcie felt supremely happy in Tim's arms. They stayed that way for several seconds, swaying gently, their arms wrapped around each other.

"Let me show you the grounds."

Tim took Marcie's hand and walked with her toward the rear of the house. A large picture window looked out over the twinkling lights of Beverly Hills below. Tim switched on a bank of lights, and suddenly the back area was illuminated. The knoll that comprised the property was much deeper than Marcie had realized. Stretching out in front of her were exquisitely landscaped grounds leading up to a lap pool surrounded by a brick and redwood deck. Off to the side were a tennis court and a guest house.

"Come on," said Tim, ushering Marcie out the french doors. The night smelled of jasmine, and they toured the property, keeping to the brick paths.

"I'm being a dreadful host," Tim said. "I haven't even asked you what you wanted."

Marcie looked into his eyes. "I want you. Why don't you tell the driver to go home? He's done enough for one night."

Tim walked inside and continued to the front to have a word with the driver. He returned to find Marcie examining a Rothko painting hanging over the fireplace. Marcie was completely lost in the shimmering bands of color and didn't hear Tim come up behind her.

"It's amazing, isn't it?" Tim said.

"It's the most incredible painting I've ever seen."

"I'm very lucky to have it."

Marcie looked up at the man beside her, in front of this remarkable painting, and smiled.

"No, I'm the lucky one."

Tim led her upstairs. She had only an instant to take in the master suite before she was lost in his embrace. While her passions raced, time seemed to slow down. All she was aware of was the touch of his lips and the feel of his skin.

Her breasts seemed unusually sensitive, but he was gentle and sweet. His kisses moved down her abdomen, between her legs. "Fuck me," she whispered.

He entered her, moving in the same unhurried fashion. Soon, she heard herself cry out as the waves of her orgasm came crashing down upon her. He held her closely to him, and she could feel him savoring the moment. His rhythmic movements began again, and his breathing became more labored. Responding to his growing urgency, Marcie began to climax again.

"Come with me!" she said, her voice raspy and not recognizable as her own.

Tim emitted a deep, animal-like sound as he drove deeply into her and climaxed. Marcie felt herself pulled into a deep vortex as uncontrollable tears coursed down her cheeks. Tim held her close, comforting her, giving her soft words of assurance. Her eyes were heavy, her body entwined around his. She had no thoughts, just a warm, profound sense of being one with him.

*　　*　　*　　*　　*

The next day, a package from Cartiers arrived at Marcie's home containing a massive, gold link necklace. The card read: "FORGIVE ME. I KNOW NOT WHAT I DO, ONLY THAT LAST NIGHT WAS VERY SPECIAL." Marcie tried calling Tim at home, using the telephone number he'd given her the night before. When she got the answering machine, she left a message that the necklace was beautiful, and thanking him for his consideration.

She had promised Ben she would meet him at the new offices at eleven, and was looking forward to seeing the space her partners had rented in Century City. Marcie drove to Century City shortly before eleven, proud of herself for being on time. She parked in the nearly empty lot below ground and took the elevator to meet Ben. At the twenty-second floor, she was surprised to see that the office already had discreet gold letters on the door proclaiming it the home of The New Agency. We didn't even have a name until Friday morning, she recalled. Now that's getting things done quickly! The door was open and Marcie walked in calling, "Ben."

Ben emerged from an office to the right and rushed to greet her. "Here it is!" he exclaimed. "The New Agency and a new deal for all of us!"

Marcie's eyes swept the bright, nicely decorated office. It was corporate, yet with a bit of panache. She liked it at once.

"Where did all the furniture come from?"

"We made a deal with the law firm and added a bit of our own. Pretty neat, don't you think?"

"I think it looks great. I'm very impressed."

"Let me show you your office," Ben said, leading Marcie to a corner office at the far end of the hall. "This is yours, Randy is at the other end, and Jack and I are in the middle two offices. It's great, isn't it?"

Marcie was indeed impressed. Her office looked west and she could see the Pacific glistening past Santa Monica. The decor was bright and cheery, with a yellow and white color scheme. Everything was in nearly new condition and she thought she'd need to bring little if anything, other than a VCR, DVD and a CD player.

"The law firm had a woman litigation partner in this office. We thought it would be perfect for you."

"You thought right, Ben. It's wonderful. Let's look at the rest."

Ben showed her through the other offices, which were equally bright and well furnished. All the offices were the same size and presented, she felt, the perfect image for a small, prestigious talent agency. Marcie conveyed her satisfaction to Ben as he showed her the secretarial stations, and what would one day be the receptionist's desk. Marcie knew Sandy would be happy with the warm, attractive surroundings.

"I'm going to really enjoy this," said Marcie. "I have something to show you that you won't enjoy."

"What's that?"

"Our loan papers covering the money we borrowed to finish off this place and the expenses before we turn cash positive. We are all on the hook for it; the phrase they use is 'jointly and severally liable'. We've already signed it to get going and you might want your attorney to look it over."

Marcie gave Ben a hug, and took one final look at her new office. After Ben locked up, they rode down to the parking area together. He reported that the negotiations with Allied had gotten rid of the easy issues, but that some of the ticklish problems were still on the table.

"What's the status of *The Super*?" he asked.

"I should know more on Monday," Marcie said.

"If it goes, it looks like we've got a real good shot at splitting the commissions," Ben said.

"I'm on it, first thing," Marcie said.

As she drove home, she regretted her commitment to Wes to go out that night and to play tennis the next day. She wondered how he'd respond to splitting the difference—playing in the tournament, but skipping their date. After her night with Tim, she wasn't up for a reprise of their evening at the Villas. Tennis, sure, but she'd pass on the rest. Marcie called Sandy to tell her how terrific the offices were. Sandy was excited about the move and said she'd meet Marcie a little before eight on Monday at Allied. Marcie could hear a male voice telling Sandy to hang up and come back to bed. Marcie thought better of asking Sandy anything about it, and said goodbye. She wondered who Sandy was involved with, but knew that she would soon hear if it was more than just a weekend diversion.

*   *   *   *   *

Marcie had no way to reach Wes, so she decided to swing by the location of his commercial, a tennis club on Motor Avenue in Culver City. As she gave her car to the attendant, she could see the television production team straggling out the door. They must have wrapped for the day. She asked the receptionist where the production crew was working and was directed to one of the outer courts. At the center of the group walking toward her was Wes, looking handsome in his tennis whites and a smart, sleeveless tennis sweater.

"Marcie!" he called out, leaving the others and rushing over to her. His eyes were sparkling and he seemed delighted to see her. As he reached her, he opened his arms and kissed her warmly on the lips.

"How did it go?" she asked.

As if on cue, the group caught up with them, and a man with a viewer around his neck said, "You were terrific today, Wes. We'll give you a call when we get another commercial that you're right for."

"Fantastic," Wes replied.

The group continued in the direction of the clubhouse, leaving Marcie and Wes alone on the walk.

"Now, where was I?" said Wes.

"It went well, huh?" asked Marcie.

"Tremendous. I love this work."

"They sounded happy with you."

Wes beamed. "They seemed to be, didn't they? Do we have a plan?"

Marcie jumped in. "I know this is late notice, but tonight's not going to work out. Since we talked, I've resigned at Allied, and start at a new shop on Monday. If it's all right with you, I'd like to take a raincheck on our date and still play in the tournament tomorrow."

Wes's eyes mirrored the disappointment he felt. "I understand," he said. "I can crash with my friend for one more night and meet you at the Malibu Tennis Club tomorrow. You're sure you still want to play."

"We're going to kick ass."

He reached over and clasped her to him and gave her a kiss. "I've got my car in the lot, so why don't we just meet at nine at the courts?"

"See you then," Marcie said, wondering how much Wes had been able to read between the lines.

*   *   *   *   *

The tournament was for the benefit of an AIDS organization. Marcie paid the entrance fee, which entitled them to a day of tennis, lunch, and prizes if they reached the semi-finals. They would play single set matches until the finals, which would be the best of three. Marcie and Wes entered the Open division where they could expect to find other club pros and "A" players. There were always a few players who hopelessly over-classified themselves, but they were usually eliminated in the first matches. All pairings were mixed doubles, and Marcie knew she'd be able to hold her own against most of the women. She expected to encounter some hotshots from the local college teams, who had youth, two good knees, and probably a playing edge. Well, she thought, those were the teams where Wes would have to carry the day.

They won three matches before lunch, each one a little more difficult. Marcie felt good on the court, and she and Wes teamed nicely. Her strong backhand enabled her to play the ad court letting Wes swing away in the deuce court. The other teams they encountered all positioned the man on the backhand side, which limited his effectiveness. Marcie's experience playing with men always helped her in returning serves.

By lunch, they had reached the quarters. They took their meal to a shady spot and sat down to eat.

"How would you feel about a quickie?" asked Wes.

"I never indulge in the middle of a tournament," deadpanned Marcie. "I once took on the first four USC singles players between matches and it ruined my tennis for the afternoon. Never again."

Wes looked at her with a curious expression. Marcie couldn't keep a straight face any longer and exploded in laughter. Wes joined in, relieved that she'd only been putting him on.

After lunch they met the other surviving teams before taking the court for their quarter-final match. Wes pointed out two blonde youngsters he identified as the number one men's and women's singles players at nearby Pepperdine University. "They're both All-Americans," he said, "and they'll both be playing on the circuit. If we get that far, they're going to be very tough."

"We'll outsmart them," Marcie responded.

Wes just grinned.

They sailed through the quarters and the semis, as a buzz began to develop among the spectators in anticipation of the finals. As expected, the Pepperdine players also cruised through the afternoon competition, setting up the finals match that Wes had anticipated. He took Marcie aside for a brief strategy session.

"We'll never outrun them," he said. "Those goddamn kids could run all night. I think our best chance is to overpower them. Go for the passing shots and crunch them at her body."

"Take-no-prisoners tennis?" Marcie asked.

"Exactly," Wes nodded, and smiled evilly.

As they took the center court to warm up, Marcie noted that the two hundred or so spectators seemed to be pulling for her and Wes. The match hadn't even started and already they were the underdogs. Maybe it had to do with the average age of the spectators, which was much closer to their own than to the Pepperdine undergraduates. When Marcie looked at the scoreboard, she noticed that their opponents had the same last name, Medford. "Brother and sister?" she asked Wes.

"Twins," he responded.

Then it all clicked in. She had read articles calling them "the future of American tennis."

"You weren't going to tell me who they were?"

"I didn't want to freak you out. Just play your game, and we'll do fine," Wes said.

Marcie won the coin toss for their team, and Wes served first. With Wes nailing three of four first serves, they took an early 1-0 lead. Both Marcie and Wes found the going exceedingly tough. The points were hard-fought and the match turned on one service break in each set. The Medfords triumphed 6-4, 6-4. At the awards ceremony, Marcie learned that the Medfords were the tenth-ranked mixed doubles team in the country. She asked Wes if he knew that. "Sure," he said. "It's in all the tennis magazines."

"But you didn't want to freak me out."

"You got it."

As they packed up their gear, film director Norman Jewison wondered over to say hello to Marcie.

"Hey, Norman," Marcie said. "How're you doing?"

"Fine, thanks. I wanted to congratulate you and your partner on your showing. The Medfords are tough."

"Thanks," said Marcie. "Oh, I'm sorry, Wes Snyder, this is Norman Jewison. Wes is the club pro at the Villas in the Springs."

"Well done," said Jewison, shaking Wes's hand. "You gave them a great match."

"I've also been doing some acting lately," Wes blurted out, "and maybe you have something I'd be right for."

Jewison seemed surprised by Wes's boldness, murmured something about having his agent call, looked curiously at Marcie, and left abruptly.

Marcie unleashed a torrent of rage at Wes.

"How dare you pitch yourself to someone who comes over to congratulate me? He even thought I represented you! We have enough problems getting The New Agency off the ground without cleaning up messes with important directors that you get us into."

"Jeez, Marcie, I was only trying to do myself some good."

Marcie was disgusted. She addressed him venomously. "Have you ever thought that maybe there are some moments that aren't about you? I'm sorry, you were way out of line."

As Marcie put her things in her tennis bag, Wes made a few abortive attempts at conversation. But Marcie wasn't to be placated. She knew that the pressure of the tennis matches coupled with the stress of the week may have heightened her reaction to Wes's words. Yet, she felt no inclination to let him off the hook. Time for him to grow up. As they headed for the parking lot and their cars, she suggested that she needed a little time alone.

When Marcie arrived home, still upset with Wes, she turned her attention to her answering machine with its relentlessly flickering red light. Many callers were congratulating her on the move. Marcie made a list and decided to answer them all with a note later.

There were several business calls, including one from each of her three new partners. Ben wanted to know all about the tennis tournament, while Jack wanted to tell her how excited he was that everything had come together, and to find out what she thought about the offices.

She returned Randy's call first. He was friendly, but quickly swung the conversation around to business. He wanted to know if Marcie knew Sandra Dunning. Marcie told him they'd met on several occasions, and she knew her well enough to say hello. Randy had heard that she was unhappy with her present representation and had agreed to have lunch on Monday. Would Marcie be willing to join them?

"Of course," Marcie answered. "That's pretty exciting. She's drifted off the "A" list and I'm not surprised she's vulnerable. Do you think we have a shot?"

"I wouldn't be taking up our time if I didn't. This is where the two of us can make a big impression. I want to sign this broad, Marcie, and I'm sure we can do it."

"I'm sure she'll really be impressed by being called a broad."

"It's just an expression," Randy said. "It's nothing to get bent out of shape about. If I offended you, I'm sorry."

"No big deal," said Marcie. "As long as you don't speak that way when we're having lunch."

"I'll be cool, I promise. I'll see you Monday morning. Take care, partner."

If that's as bad as it gets, thought Marcie, I know I can get through it. But suppose he does embarrass me? Where does he get off using a word like "broad" anyway? Marcie decided to keep focused on the big picture and not become preoccupied with every word that fell out of his mouth. She had made her decision, and this was no time to go back on it.

CHAPTER XII

Marcie arrived at Allied at seven forty-five on Monday. The front desk was staffed from seven-thirty on because of the number of callers from different time zones. The morning receptionist had already been instructed to show the movers to Marcie's office and have them use the freight elevator. Two burly men showed up promptly at eight o'clock and Marcie told them what stayed and what went. Soon after, a breathless Sandy arrived muttering about "some damn gardeners" who had tied up traffic when their truck rear-ended a van. She saw the movers piling boxes onto a hand truck and went to get Marcie coffee.

The movers completed their task by eight-thirty. Only a handful of secretaries and agents had straggled in, so Marcie and Sandy were able to head off without undue ceremony. The movers were familiar with the Century City building, and Marcie agreed to meet them there.

As the two women rode the elevator together in Century City, Sandy announced, "I'm in love with the drummer for Leaking Faucets." Seeing the blank look on Marcie's face, she continued, "They're a new group that are making a big splash in the clubs. Like, really hot!"

Marcie nodded, not sure how to react.

"The drummer, Bobby Imhoff, is truly awesome!"

As Sandy gushed her opinion of the drummer, a woman in the elevator with them rolled her eyes prompting Sandy to give her the finger. Marcie tried to keep a straight face while this little drama played out, but was not successful. As the woman got off and the doors slid shut, Marcie and Sandy burst out laughing. They were still laughing as the doors opened on the twenty-second floor.

Sandy knew the other three secretaries who had made the trip over with their bosses. To a person, they all got up, along with Marcie's partners to welcome the newcomers to The New Agency. Sandy quickly moved through the office, hugging her co-workers and claiming her position in this universe.

When the movers arrived, Marcie left Sandy to deal with them while she joined Ben and Jack in Randy's office. The news was good.

Randy said, "I closed with Fisher and Sudaway yesterday. The Morris Agency is going to be really pissed. Their papers expired on Friday, and they were being dicked around over the language in the packaging agreement. We'll go to CBS with them this week, and everything will be at a full ten percent."

Jack announced he had signed a "B" list actor, who "was one picture away from returning to the 'A' list."

Even so, thought Marcie, he was grossing $1.5 million annually, which threw off a fast $150,000 in commissions. This was a new way for Marcie to see the business world. Instead of the money going into the corporation, which would reward her at year's end, all moneys earned went first to meet expenses and retire their debt, and then went directly to the four partners. It made life both simpler and more exciting.

They pooled all the information they had on available parts for leading women, in both television and film. Randy and Marcie would have to convince Sandra Dunning at lunch that a small, boutique agency would be in her best interest, both short-term and long-term. Randy had uncovered a Liam Neeson picture at Universal that was, he had heard from the director, going to be greenlighted that morning. The director thought Sandra would be perfect for the leading female role and Randy was confident that the studio would go along with the idea.

As if on cue, Randy's secretary buzzed him to say that the director, Ron Underwood, was on the phone.

"Fantastic!" exclaimed Randy, on being told that the picture was a "go." "I'm having lunch with her in a little while and I'll call you as soon as it's over. Hold off 'til lunch is done before you pitch Universal. I want to be sure I can deliver her."

As Randy hung up, he smiled and announced, "Slam dunk!"

They spent the balance of the meeting talking about other on-going situations, clients who might be worth pursuing, and work that was suitable for those who were now in house. Ben brought up the subject of taking an ad in the Trades to announce the opening of their office. Jack could get the ad designed without charge by a graphic artist who owed him. They all agreed the cost of placing the ad would be money well spent.

Marcie returned to her office to find Sandy finishing up with the movers. They looked as though they would be very relieved to get out from under her firm hand. While there was much still to be unpacked, Sandy had organized their basic tools so that they could conduct business as usual.

"And what do you think, Miss Sandy?" Marcie asked.

"It's fucking off the page!" Sandy answered, in what Marcie interpreted to be high praise indeed.

As Sandy looked at her, she noticed, apparently for the first time, the gold necklace that Tim had given her. Her eyebrows raised. After dispensing with the movers, she returned to Marcie's office.

"Whew," she exclaimed, casting an envious eye at the necklace. "Where did that baby come from?"

"Like it? It's a gift from Tim."

"It's fucking awesome. What do you have to do to score a necklace like that?"

"Oh, you know, salad oil, whipped cream, the usual stuff."

"Maybe you'll let me in on your secrets someday. Maybe I was wrong about him being a little light on his feet."

Marcie smiled. "We better get some work done if this place is going to make it. Would you try Valerie for me? Let's see if they've moved Wilhite's show along."

"Hi, Valerie," Marcie said, after Sandy buzzed twice. "How's it going?"

"We truly must be in sync," Valerie replied. "I just asked my temp to call you. Great news! We're fast-tracked for a startup on the pilot. We'll need to get at least the deal memo signed today, but the guys are genuinely excited. I mean if this clicks, it might anchor Wednesday night!"

"You're set with a director?" Marcie asked.

"We just signed David Martinson. He's from New York originally, and is great with comedy. He loves Dick's work and has a great feel for the material."

"And the other casting?"

"Why don't you swing by after lunch? We can put the finishing touches on Dick's deal and talk about anybody else you have that may be right. Oh, I almost forgot. Congratulations on your move. It sounds like a great shot."

"Thanks, Valerie. It's very exciting. I've got a lunch in Beverly Hills, and could be in Burbank by two-thirty. How's that work with your schedule?"

"It's perfect. I'm having my nails done at lunch time, and I'll be back by then."

Perfect, thought Marcie. I'll be hustling a new client, and she'll be getting her nails done. "Thanks for everything, Valerie. We're on to something wonderful here."

Marcie made a quick call to Wilhite, after notifying her partners of the good news from NBC. Wilhite was thrilled with the news and found the sudden quickening of his career almost hard to believe.

"It must be you, Marcie," he said, "because I'm the same old *putz* I always was."

"NBC didn't buy my comic genius, they bought yours."

He laughed. "Okay, I guess you're right. Call me when you get back from seeing Valerie, will you?"

"I will, for sure."

Sandy poked her head in. "Tim called and said he'd call back. He's not reachable now. I hope you don't mind, but I told him I'd look great in the bracelet that matches the necklace he gave you. I told him if he thinks you know tricks, wait 'til he sees me work."

"But you're in love with a rock star, or at least a rock star-to-be," Marcie protested.

"Oh, we have an open relationship, at least from my side."

"How convenient," replied Marcie. "What else is going on?"

"Your buddy, Horace Anderson called from Paramount. He said he had to go out to a location and would you please call him tomorrow morning?"

"Problems with the Lent deal?"

"He didn't say."

"Oh, and Sam called, but said no message."

"How'd he sound?"

"Now that you mention it, pretty shitty."

"Damn," said Marcie. "Remind me to try to find him when I get back from Burbank."

Some dictation and a host of congratulatory calls took up the rest of Marcie's morning, until Randy popped in to say it was time to leave for lunch. Riding together to the Grill in Beverly Hills, Marcie told him, "I think this setup feels very good. I know this is the honeymoon period, but I really believe we can make this thing take off."

Randy assured her that he was certain "their timing was impeccable. The business is in a state of flux. This is the moment for a new alternative, and we're it."

They arrived before Sandra and were shown to a booth where they each ordered a mineral water. Randy scanned the room with his experienced agent's eye. "Isn't that your client Sam over there with Fred Specktor from CAA?"

"It certainly is. He didn't waste much time checking out CAA, did he?"

"No. What are you going to do?"

"I'll go over and say hello. I doubt if he's contemplating a move, probably just window shopping."

"Collect the chip by letting him know you saw him at his game."

Marcie walked across the restaurant to Sam's table. He saw her approaching and sprang uneasily to his feet. Sam gave Marcie a big embrace and awkwardly asked, "Uh, do you know Fred Specktor?"

"Of course," said Marcie, leaning down to give Fred a kiss on the cheek. "I just stopped by to say hello. I'm having lunch with my new partner, Randy Goldberg."

Specktor looked over to where Randy was sitting in time to see CAA client Sandra Dunning sitting down at his booth. Marcie caught the quick look of dismay as he realized who Sandra was meeting with. Specktor feigned a friendly tone and wished Marcie luck with The New Agency.

"We'll need it," Marcie said. "These waters are shark-infested."

"Are you going to be there this afternoon?" asked Sam.

"Sure am. At least, after four."

"Okay if I drop over?"

"Great. You know the address?"

"I do. See you later."

Marcie kissed Sam goodbye and walked back to join Randy and Sandra, who gave her a big hello. Marcie was surprised that Specktor didn't find a reason to visit their table, and concluded that Sandra must have already announced her intention to go elsewhere.

Their lunch followed the prescribed regimen for seducing the vulnerable artist. She was told that they were her biggest fans and always had been. Nothing against CAA but somehow she wasn't getting the parts that someone of her stature should be offered. Again, nothing against CAA, but they had so many women to represent that it was no wonder that major artists like her didn't get the attention and career guidance they deserved. Why, for example, how about the Underwood picture at Universal? Had she met with Underwood? She hadn't? Did she know it was greenlighted and she would be perfect for it? She didn't? Well if she were ever thinking of making a move, The New Agency would be thrilled to represent her and could guarantee that she'd be meeting on the Universal film as soon as today.

Sandra was hooked. She'd been considering a change ever since Mike Ovitz and Ron Meyer went over to the studios. It was so hard for her, living out of town, to know which way to go. But a small, select agency run by people she knew and trusted, sounded perfect. She reported that her agency papers with CAA had expired and, although they had sent her new ones, she hadn't signed them. She must have known somewhere in her subconscious that a meeting like this was going to come along. "Yes," she concluded, "I'd be proud to make the switch and to do it today."

"That's fantastic," said Marcie.

"I know you're going to be very happy with your decision," echoed Randy. "Incidentally, could you meet at Universal this afternoon?"

"Yes, I guess so. I'm in town for the next couple of days."

"Excuse me for a second," said Randy and headed over toward the men's room. He stopped, out of sight of the table, and took a cellular phone from his pocket.

Marcie filled Sandra in on Ben and Jack and the philosophy behind a small agency as opposed to a large one like CAA. "It's almost like having a personal manager," Marcie said. "It will be intimate and you'll have lots of personal attention. Randy and I will be your principal agents, but you'll get to know Ben and Jack, as well. Think of the four of us as representing you."

Randy returned and told Sandra she had a meeting at Ron Underwood's office on the Universal lot at 3:00. "If it's all right with you," he said, "I'll drive you over and give you a sense of what they're looking for. I have a very good feeling about this one."

"I'd appreciate that very much," said Sandra. "I'll be outside the Chateau Marmont at 2:30. Okay?"

As Sandra left, she either didn't see or didn't acknowledge Fred Specktor.

✶   ✶   ✶   ✶   ✶

Driving from Beverly Hills to Burbank, her mind racing with deal points to discuss with Valerie, as well as other possibilities, writers, directors and actors, to talk about with her, her train of thought was broken by the sound of the car phone.

"Yes, Sandy," Marcie said automatically.

"It's not Sandy," said Wes. "It's an apologetic tennis pro you used to care something about."

"How'd you get this number?" Marcie asked angrily.

"I told Sandy it was an emergency. Did I do something wrong? I feel so badly about what I did on Sunday. I'll learn, I promise. It's all real new to me now."

Marcie thought it was hard to stay mad at him. He had the winsome naiveté of a child. Maybe some of it had been her over-reaction with Jewison. Maybe she should have told him she'd met someone else. Was she ready to say something like that about Tim? It all seemed to be going so fast.

"I'm acting in a little film those guys on Friday got me," he went on. "Is my career 'taking off'? Does this mean the industry will think I'm 'hot'?"

"If you're truly serious about acting," Marcie said, "I'd start taking classes right away. Good looks and a good backhand can take you only so far in this business."

He listened carefully and thanked her with great earnestness. She found that quality endearing.

"And what about us?" he asked. "Have we been apart long enough?"

"Wes," Marcie laughed, "it's been less than a day."

"I know, but I miss seeing you."

"Let me get back to you on that. Everything's spinning very fast right this minute."

"I'll be waiting for you. I know that timing is everything."

Wes hung up as Marcie turned into the NBC Burbank parking lot.

The meeting with Valerie turned out to be a love fest. After Marcie was shown into Valerie's office with its decorations featuring the signs of the Zodiac, and seated around a coffee table, Valerie launched into an excited summary of the passion NBC felt for *The Super*.

"I mean it's being talked about as our *anchor* for Wednesday night. Do you know what that means?"

Marcie nodded expectantly.

"It means," Valerie went on, "that the full weight of the network would be behind making that show a hit. Like it's really fabulous! Aren't you thrilled?"

As Marcie opened her mouth to reply, Valerie noticed her necklace. "God, Marcie, that necklace is gorgeous!"

"It's a gift."

"Well, hang on to the guy who gave you that! It's a knockout!"

Marcie assured Valerie that there would be no trouble completing Wilhite's deal. Pulling out a yellow pad, Valerie led Marcie through the arrangements on the basic pilot deal for a star in a sitcom. Fees and points were not an issue. Options with the network for three years, in case the show were a hit, even though both of them knew that these prices were inevitably subject to re-negotiation if the show took off, and the right to direct one or two shows in the second season.

As an afterthought, Valerie said, "Oh, I almost forgot. Congratulations on your new partnership. I think it's wonderful! You must be thrilled."

"I'm very happy." She smiled. "Of course it's only day one! I did want to run through our client list with you in case you think any of them are right for the show."

Marcie had made up a three by five card with their clients neatly typed on it. In time, this wouldn't be necessary. But it *was* only the first day. Valerie passed on the names Marcie suggested, but did indicate interest in two of the directors, should the show get picked up. She stared at Marcie, as if collecting her thoughts.

"I shouldn't tell you this," she began. "But, there's a damn good chance they may give this show an on-air commitment before the pilot is shot. Do you know what that means?"

Marcie's first thought was in terms of a large infusion of commission revenue into the agency. She doubted that this is what Valerie had in mind.

"Like it's such a shot to my career, you can't even imagine! You have to keep this between us. I trust you, Marcie, you know I do. Otherwise, I'd never have told you this."

"It would be wonderful for you, for my client and even for the agency if it happened," said Marcie. "You can count on me to keep my mouth shut about it, and hope like crazy to hear from you that you've pulled it off."

Marcie saw Valerie's eyes glow at the suggestion shat *she* would be the one pulling off the feat of getting the network commitment. In truth, she would be informed about it, if it ever occurred, as the decision would come from executives considerably higher on the corporate ladder.

The meeting ended with Valerie rising and moving to Marcie to bestow air kisses on each cheek. No risk of smudging her makeup with that show of affection. Marcie left Valerie's office and returned to the parking lot to retrieve her car. As she presented the attendant with her validated parking receipt and headed back to the office, the car phone rang.

"Hey, Sandy, what's going on?"

"Disappointed, it's me?" Randy asked.

So much for my system of outgoing calls only, thought Marcie. Better get used to having partners.

"Not at all," Marcie said. "what's up?"

"Just calling to say you're really kicking ass at NBC."

"What have you heard?"

"Just that they've given *The Super* a commitment for thirteen shows. Not bad."

"Did Valerie call you?"

"No, her boss. As soon as she reported she'd closed with you on Wilhite, they pulled the trigger. He called me a couple of minutes ago. Pretty exciting, huh?"

"Do we have a shot at any of the commissions?"

"That's the best part," Randy said. "We signed a deal memo with Allied this morning. We split commissions fifty-fifty in year one, then it's all ours."

"Why the hell would they agree to that?" asked Marcie, as she turned onto the freeway heading back to the office.

"Because they thought there wasn't a chance in hell of any show starring Wilhite getting close to being on the air. It's you, babe, that pulled this rabbit out of the hat. Congratulations, it's a major coup!"

"Thanks," said Marcie, ignoring his referring to her as "babe". "I'll see you when you get back from Universal. Good luck with Sandra and Underwood."

Marcie drove back to Century City feeling pretty damn good about her first day in her new partnership. Obviously every day wouldn't be a mirror image of this one, but it was a fabulous beginning. It was also gratifying, she thought, to have Randy be as warm and congratulatory as he had been. Nice to know that the speech she had made to Sandra at lunch was not just lip service, but had some foundation in real life.

*   *   *   *   *

Returning to the office, Marcie took a minute to fill Sandy in on the lunch with Sandra and the meeting with Valerie. Randy's news of the NBC pickup was not common knowledge at the office, but Marcie let Sandy know, asking her to keep it to herself for the moment. She then had Sandy place a call to Wilhite.

"Oh my god, oh my god!" he exclaimed, on hearing Marcie's news. "I can't believe it! You're really something else!"

"They're not buying me, it's you," Marcie said. "I'd keep it all to yourself until they make their official announcement, but it sure seems to be a done deal."

"When can we celebrate?"

"As soon as it's official. In the meanwhile, be a good soldier and get close to Levine and Rogers. They and you are the locomotives that drive this train."

"Count on me," Wilhite said. "I'm their new best friend."

Marcie hung up and decided to take advantage of the momentary lull in telephone calls to visit the ladies room. As she returned to her office, she discovered Sandy in conversation with a young man in torn jeans, a marijuana tee-shirt and more visible body piercing than Marcie had ever seen. "Marcie Sandmore, Bobby Imhoff," said Sandy, in a short-hand introduction.

"Hey," offered Bobby, in Marcie's direction.

"Hey," said Marcie, as Sandy looked on, growing increasingly concerned. Was this the drummer, Marcie wondered? Had Sandy told her his name, or only the name of the group?

"You guys are doing all right for the first week," Bobby observed. "You booking any rock acts?"

"Not right now," replied Marcie.

"Yeah, well," continued Bobby, "I did some acting in high school, and I'd be willing to do some movies if that's what you're into. The kind of stuff that Sting does. Know what I mean?"

"I do, Bobby, believe me, I do. Get a picture to Sandy and I'll keep my eyes open. It was nice meeting you, but if you'll excuse me, I have to make some calls."

Marcie entered her office feeling very old. Not much chance that she'd be representing Bobby Imhoff. And, hard to see the "hunk" quality that Sandy had described. Oh well, they're a generation younger, and she hoped they were happy with one another. As she sat down, Sandy entered her office.

"I'm really sorry," she said. "I don't know what made him come by here. He just got out of a recording session and thought he'd say hello. I promise it won't happen again."

"It's not a problem," Marcie said. "Forget about it."

"Thanks. And I'll straighten him out about the acting thing. He's usually not that kind of pushy jerk."

"He's an artist," said Marcie. "He was just taking a shot. No harm in that."

Sandy looked gratefully at Marcie. "Thanks," she said, and returned to her desk.

Sandy buzzed a second later to say that Jenkins from Fox was on the line.

"Hi," said Marcie. "I'm sorry, but Sam hasn't gotten to the *Beef Jerky* script yet. The Warners picture has him swamped."

"It's not that. There's some actor at the Pico gate insisting that you sent him over to meet for *Beef Jerky*. Do you know anything about that?"

With a mounting sense of dread, Marcie asked the actor's name.

"Wes Snyder," came the reply. "I've never even heard of him."

Marcie felt her skin flush as her worst fears were realized. "Neither have I," she lied. "He must have read my name in the Trades and thought he'd bluff his way onto the lot. Sorry about that."

"No problem. It happens all the time. Sometimes we even have to tell the police to physically remove them. Anyway, good luck with your new shop, and get back to me as soon as you can about Sam. We think it's a great situation for him."

"I'll do that," she said. As she hung up, she realized her hands were shaking. How could he? All that bullshit on the car phone, and now this. Sandy buzzed to say Tim was on the line. She started to tell her to get a number, but changed her mind, and picked up.

"How're you doing?" she asked, hoping her voice wouldn't betray the anger she felt.

"What's the matter?" Tim asked, sensing her mood at once.

Before she could stop herself, Marcie had filled Tim in on Wes Snyder's exploits of the last two days.

"And he's the tennis pro at the Villas?" he asked.

"Yes, he was fine down there. Maybe it's this damn town that does something to people."

Tim suddenly sounded very serious, almost grave. "No, it's not the town, it's him. But don't give it another thought. I'll take care of everything."

"What do you mean?" Marcie asked, a chill passing through her.

"Just leave it to me. The reason I called was to tell you I have to go back to New York. I'm actually at the Admiral's Club at the airport right now. I did want to tell you how much I liked Friday night."

"So did I."

"I'll call you from New York, and we'll get together as soon as I get back. Okay?"

"Sounds good to me. Have a safe flight."

"Thanks, and don't give that Snyder person a second thought."

Marcie put the phone down and stared at it as if imploring it to tell her more about Tim's reaction to the Wes Snyder story. This whole business unnerved her, and Tim seemed as much of the problem as the solution. She got up, feeling very anxious, and opened the door to her office to speak with Sandy. Standing next to Sandy's desk, an orchid plant in her hands, was Jane Pratt.

Marcie looked at the orchid. "For me, Jane? It's beautiful, you know I love orchids."

"This one's originally from Thailand. The named translates into 'Good Luck Orchid.'"

"Thanks, Jane. You're really terrific."

Jack walked out of his office. Seeing Jane, he volunteered, "Hi, you're Jane Pratt, aren't you?"

"Uh oh, he's on to me," Jane smiled. "You're Jack, right?"

Marcie introduced her to Jack, and Jane continued, "You guys have the town talking. You must be doing something right."

"It's all smoke and mirrors," said Jack.

"No, that's what I do for a living. The word is this place is for real. And I better let you get back to work if you're going to keep it that way."

She shook Jack's hand, gave Marcie a hug, and headed out.

"Sam's on the line," Sandy said, as Marcie returned to her office.

"What's up?" Marcie said.

"Peter called and wants to see Julia and me. He really wants to meet now, so I'm afraid I have to take a raincheck on visiting your new office."

"That's fine, we signed a long lease. Is everything okay?"

Sam hesitated for an instant. "Oh you mean Specktor? No, everything's fine. He'd been bugging me for a lunch for months, and this was the day. No, if I can settle everything with this picture, the rest of my life is great."

"We'll talk soon," Marcie said, as she said goodbye. She wondered how truthful her client was being.

*   *   *   *   *

The four partners met the next morning in Randy's office. Randy volunteered to do the honors with the coffee, as none of the secretaries had arrived. Part of the new order, she was told by Jack, was that anyone wanting coffee could get it themselves. Marcie detected a slight grimace on Randy's face as the egalitarian edict was proclaimed.

Randy began by emphasizing the importance of working extra hard to secure industry information. "We don't have the legions in the field that we had at Allied. The Underwood film is a perfect example. Sandra got the picture and we got Sandra, signed, sealed and delivered." Randy had let Marcie know the night before, but this was the first Ben and Jack heard the news.

"What did you get for her?" Jack asked.

"A million, five percent of net, and second star billing," replied Randy.

"Whew, not bad, especially considering that CAA wasn't having any luck at all with her," said Jack.

"She's coming in at ten o'clock to meet you and Ben before she takes off for Montana. If possible, I'd like our clients to get to know all of us. It'll save our asses in the long run."

"I think that's great," said Ben. "How about signing people? Should we discuss that too?"

"I'd be in favor of that," said Marcie. "It doesn't necessarily mean we'd need a unanimous vote to sign someone, but I think it's a good idea to get the benefit of everyone's thinking."

The partners nodded.

"See how well we all get along?" Randy offered. "This is like a well a well-oiled machine."

Marcie added, "I think these meetings are key. We ought to hold them at least three days a week, and probably at eight-thirty before the phones start ringing."

"We hope the phones will be ringing," said Jack.

"Amen," said Ben.

"Monday, Wednesday and Friday at eight-thirty okay with everyone?" asked Randy. He looked from one to the other before adding, "Let's go to work."

As she walked to her office, Marcie felt content. Her impression of The New Agency, even though it had just opened its doors, was that the team concept was more than an ideal. It seemed to work, and it certainly felt good.

Just after ten, Randy's secretary, Nancy, walked in to tell Marcie that Sandra had arrived. They walked back to Randy's office where the other partners were gathered. Sandra rose and gave her a warm embrace. Marcie was aware that Randy had known instinctively that Sandra would be comfortable with a woman. No doubt about it, his agent moves were first-rate.

The meeting was warm and friendly. Jack and Ben carried the early discussion so that Sandra could get a feel for who they were. The partners then pressed Sandra on what kinds of roles she was seeking, whether she'd do quality cable movies or television movies, and where she'd like her career to be in five years. She was a smart woman with a secure sense of who she was and where she stood in the Hollywood firmament. Her ambition was to be considered more mainstream and less special. She pointed to the career of Sally Field as one she'd like to emulate. Sally had moved into a position of respect and stature playing leading roles. There were an increasing number of good parts she felt she'd like a shot at. The partners of TNA reiterated that they were proud to represent her, thrilled that she had gotten the Underwood picture at Universal, and would be searching very aggressively for the right roles for her.

Marcie walked her to the elevator, as Sandra said to her, "I feel very good about this. Can I call you if I have any concerns?"

"Of course," said Marcie. "The service has our client list, and instructions to forward calls to us any time." They kissed goodbye, and Marcie walked back into the office. Sandy was waiting by the door for her.

"I've got Horace Anderson on the line. He seems really wired."

"Okay, let me find out what his problem is."

"Can you come right over?" he said, as soon as Marcie picked up. "I mean they're really on my case."

Marcie checked her watch. "Sure, I'm on my way."

Horace Anderson, a Production VP at Paramount, had closed a rich deal with her for one of her writers, Michael Lent. According to the settlement with Allied, the commission was to be split fifty-fifty, with any servicing to be done by TNA, since it would then have Lent as a client. Anderson had bought an original Lent idea for an action-adventure film, ideal for any of the major leading men, from Harrison Ford to Jean-Claude Van Damme. Paramount had gone nuts over the concept and committed $500,000 for a first draft and a set of changes. Bonuses could bring the grand total up to $2 million. Marcie wondered what the hitch might be.

"Marcie," Horace began, as Marcie entered his office. "We've got a big problem."

"What's that?"

"Sherry came back to town and hates the idea. She knows that John loved it and where we are on it, but she's not going through with it."

Sherry was Paramount's female topper, Sherry Lansing, a well-respected, savvy film executive. John was John Goldwyn, a relative of the distinguished family of Goldwyns that had been active in the film business for decades.

"That sounds more like your problem than mine, Horace. I've got a memo from your office confirming the deal for a half million. What did you have in mind?"

Horace paused. He was the only African-American member of the Paramount executive team. Marcie knew this put untold amounts of pressure on him. The fact that there were few minorities in Hollywood's executive suites was one of the town's dirty little secrets. Horace had been hired from USC film school and his progress through the ranks at Paramount had been steady to his present position of Director of Production. The town believed he was already over his head, but the studio proudly pointed to him when pressures on minority hiring became pronounced.

Marcie let her gaze move quickly around his office. She noticed the familiar accents, pictures with "A" list stars, a basketball autographed by the Lakers, and a large photograph, hung behind his desk, of Olympic record holder Michael Johnson. The connection between Johnson and Horace remained unclear.

"Okay," said Horace, filling the awful silence, "we're not able to make the deal you and I discussed."

"Don't you mean confirmed in writing as a Paramount officer?"

Horace winced. "Come on, Marcie, these things happen. My ass is way out on a limb on this one. Sherry won't even discuss it and John has run for cover. She said make it go away, and goddamn it, that's what I have to do. You know it's nothing personal."

"And you know I have a duty to my client. We made a deal and you signed off on all the major points. If you're saying that Paramount wants to renege, then it goes to the lawyers, and we'll let the chips fall where they may."

Horace's face took on a hard countenance. "You're forcing my hand on this. If you don't play ball here, I'll see that TNA does no further business at Paramount. You're a new company. Can you really afford to kiss off a major company like this one?"

Marcie stood her ground. "What we can't afford is to let ourselves be bullied, by a studio, another agency or even a client. I'm not a lawyer, but it doesn't take a genius to know that what you sent me is an enforceable agreement. If we have to sue on it, so be it. If we're locked out of here because of it, that'll last until we represent something you want, then all will be forgiven."

Marcie stood to leave.

A long sigh came from Horace, like air escaping from a balloon. "Just a minute. We've got a couple of books in the same genre that we're putting together with writers. Suppose we take Lent's deal and flip it into one of these books. Same dollars, same points, same deal. Can you live with that?"

Marcie smiled. "I think so, and I'd certainly recommend to Lent that he take it. Of course, you give up all claim to the original."

Horace nodded.

"Horace, you're a genius. You've found a way to make everyone happy."

Marcie put out her hand to shake his, and Horace, trying to gauge her sarcasm, resentfully shook it. "You'll send the two books and a confirming letter by messenger? My client is a wee bit anxious at the moment," Marcie said.

"No later than the morning," replied Horace, standing and walking Marcie to the door.

Chapter XIII

One Month Later

The honeymoon ended, as Marcie knew it must. The first glorious days had been about signings, sales and widespread support for the new kids in town. While the base of new clients and old virtually assured The New Agency of a first year that exceeded all expectations, the partners knew the year would not be without its bumps.

On the personal front, difficulties began with a telephone call from Wes. Marcie had told Sandy that she didn't want to speak with him again. On this occasion, Sandy had gone to the ladies room and Marcie answered her own phone.

"Hello," she said.

"Don't hang up, please," Wes implored, "I'll be off in less than a minute."

"What is it?" Marcie said, her voice expressionless.

"I wanted to tell you goodbye. I didn't know you played that rough."

"What are you talking about?"

"You needn't play the innocent. I can understand what you did and why. Okay, so I'm not at the Villas, but I value my knees too much to stay in California. They gave until today to leave the state, and I'm headed to Florida. Have a good life." Wes hung up.

Marcie was shaken by the call. There was certainly no love lost with Wes, but the threats he described seemed out of a bad novel. This must be what Tim meant when he told her he'd take care of it. Should she ask him about it? Did she even want to know?

While she was turning these options over in her mind, Sandy walked in looking unusually grim.

"What's up?" Marcie asked.

"I got some bad news from a friend in New York."

Happy to get her mind off Wes, Marcie pressed Sandy for details.

"It's hard for me to tell you this."

"Don't be silly. You can tell me anything."

Sandy took a deep breath and began. "Do you remember Maryanne who used to work for Bob Feldman in the New York office?"

"Not really. I may have met her once. Why?"

"That part's not really important. She's a good buddy of mine and we talk all the time."

"Uh-huh."

"Well, not that it matters, but she's a lesbian and last night she was at this gay club in Manhattan with her roommate and this guy was buying drinks for them. She thought it was a great deal because he was like all over this guy he was with. Somehow, when it came time to introduce each other, well, he said his name was Tim Garland."

Marcie gasped audibly. "My Tim Garland? How did she even make the connection?"

"I'm afraid I told her you were seeing him, and that I was way off base on my read because I thought he was gay."

"And Maryanne wouldn't be bullshitting you?"

"No way. She's like one of my closest friends. If I liked chicks, she'd be my choice. I mean we're that close."

Marcie tried to process this latest piece of information.

"I shouldn't have told you, should I?"

"No, Sandy, you did the right thing. Obviously you know we've been getting closer and closer. It's pretty important that I know about this, assuming it's true."

As Sandy looked at her, seemingly distraught by the conflict within her, Marcie was reminded of her insistence that Tim was gay. Sandy's devastatingly accurate eye could well have been off by only a smidgen. Maybe Tim wasn't gay, maybe he was bi. He had been spending increasing amounts of time in New York working on what he described as "the deal of his business life." He wouldn't discuss it with her, claiming that it had nothing to do with how he felt about her or the trust he had for her. Although this bothered her, and provoked more than one heated discussion, she reluctantly accepted his position. Tim was due back from New York in a day or two. Marcie considered confronting him on the telephone, but decided it would be better to wait until she could talk with him face to face.

Sandy picked up the phone in Marcie's office told her that Valerie was on the line "and sounded plenty pissed."

"Hi Valerie! What's up?"

"I hope nothing serious," she answered gravely. "We lost time yesterday when Dick kept challenging the director about how the scenes should play. Martinson's a terrific comedy director, for Christ's sake. This better be just opening jitters and not some humongous problem."

"This is the first I've heard of it," said Marcie. "Dick is a very reasonable guy who knows how important this show is to his career. Let me talk to him, and I'm sure it'll all be straightened out."

"Do that, Marcie. If we've made a mistake, it's not too late to change horses."

"I'll call you back later," Marcie said.

"Try and get me Dick on *The Super* set at NBC, Burbank," Marcie asked Sandy.

Marcie glanced at the headlines in the Trades before Sandy buzzed twice on the intercom.

"Hi Dick, how's it going?"

"Hiya Marcie. Oh, you know, some things to work out, actor stuff."

"Look, when it comes to dealing with my clients, I'm very straight-ahead. You won't get a lot of bullshit from me."

"That's why I'm with you."

"Fine. I have to tell you that I heard from the network this morning and they're very upset at whatever went on yesterday between you and Davidson. They say they lost time and they're making noises about replacing you if this is the way it's going to be."

Dick gasped. "Goddamn it, Marcie, I ought to know how I can be funny. I've been doing it long enough. What the hell's the matter with talking to the director about other ways to shoot the damn scene? Is that such a crime?"

"Dick, slow down. The network is understandably nervous. If this were the thirteenth show, no problem. But it's the pilot and they're looking at it under a microscope."

"So what are you saying?"

"Clean up yesterday's mess and make a fresh start today. Ask to see Martinson and apologize for yesterday. Tell him you don't want to slow down anything, but you'd appreciate the chance to discuss things with him before the scenes are shot. You've got to convince him that you know he's directing the show, and not you. He'll be very open to that because his ass is on the line as well."

Dick reflected on Marcie's advice.

"Maybe I was a bit too aggressive yesterday," he conceded.

"Be cool today," Marcie went on. They'll probably have execs around checking things out, so be charming. Make nice with the suits. You're the greatest at that when you want to be. Don't let this get blown out of proportion."

"Deal," said Dick. "I'll be fabulous, trust me."

"I know you will, and if you need me, I can be there in a half hour. Just call. Okay?"

"You got it. I'm going to hang up and see a director about a show."

Marcie buzzed Sandy and asked her to get Valerie Kensington at NBC.

"Coming right up."

Valerie listened to Marcie's description of her phone call with Dick but was guarded in her response.

"We'll see what today brings. I'm telling you, Marcie, the guys are very serious about replacing him if he fucks up. This is too hot a property and Dick should be kissing our asses for casting him. The last thing we need from him is trouble."

"Valerie, there's no argument. Trust me. Today will be a whole new ballgame."

"It better be," said Valerie.

Marcie sat back in her chair, hoping that Dick wouldn't shoot himself in the foot. She'd try to get out to the studio this afternoon, although the drive to Burbank was far from her favorite pastime.

That afternoon, Valerie Kensington called. Marcie picked up, hoping for the best.

"You've done it!" Valerie gushed. "Dick has been marvelous, and they'll make up the time they lost yesterday. You should have seen him. He had Ohlmeyer in stitches."

Marcie let the feeling of relief wash over her. Don Ohlmeyer was the president of NBC and the most important suit they could have put on the case. Dick must have made a shoe-string catch, and saved his ass.

"I knew he would, Valerie. It was all a misunderstanding yesterday. Dick's a big pussycat. He won't be a problem."

"I don't think you understand," she continued. "He was brilliant. The network is going to the mat for this one. This is the hit of the new season. I've never seen Don carry on like this. He thinks I'm a genius for putting this together."

But of course, thought Marcie. It's fine for NBC, fine for Dick, even fine for America, but let's get real. It's really fine for Valerie and her

career. That's all right with me. Let Valerie climb the highest peak in tel-
evision-land, so long as Dick is part of her support team.

"I was on my way over there," Marcie said, "to check in with Dick.
He's still shooting, isn't he?"

"For sure. They'll be shooting for at least three more hours. Stage 4.
And it's one happy set."

"I'm delighted. Do me a favor and ask your girl to leave me a drive-
on." As the words were spoken, Marcie thought how Randy-like to refer
to Valerie's secretary as "your girl".

"Will do," Valerie said, and hung up the phone.

An hour later, Marcie bumped into Valerie as she was heading toward
the stage where *The Super* was being taped. Like most three-camera tape
shows, the plan was to do second unit photography to establish the
location as New York, but do the week-to-week taping in Burbank.
There were cost savings as well as a larger pool of creative talent available for taping in Burbank instead of New York. It was also more convenient for the network executives, which factor played an important
role in the decision.

The two women kissed hello, making certain neither left lipstick on
the other.

"You must be a happy camper," Marcie said.

"The word from the set is that they're zooming along. By the end of
today, they'll be ahead."

"That's wonderful. I'm really happy. Were you going to watch a bit?"

"You bet," said Valerie. "Let's go back to the booth."

From the booth in the back of the stage, above the live audience filling
the bleachers, Marcie and Valerie were able to watch the performances as
well as see how the show played on the monitors. The laughter of the
audience would probably be mechanically "sweetened" in postproduc-
tion, but the audience response was still a good indicator of how the show
was doing. In this case, it was doing fabulously well. Wilhite was domi-
nating the stage as the eccentric superintendent of a New York apartment

building. The part fit him like a glove and he seemed sublimely comfortable going through his comic turns. Joke after joke met with wild bursts of laughter and applause. Other network executives were congratulating Valerie as they proclaimed the show a certain hit. From their mouths to God's ears, thought Marcie.

The director called for a fifteen-minute break to set the lights for another scene. Marcie turned to Valerie saying, "I'm going to go back to Dick's dressing room and say hello."

"Would you mind if I joined you for a minute?" asked Valerie.

"Of course not. Come along."

They worked their way to the dressing room area behind the set. Marcie knocked on the door with Dick's name. "Come in," he said.

Wilhite rose, a huge smile on his face, to greet Marcie. "You did come, I'm really glad to see you."

"Dick, you know Valerie Kensington from NBC?" said Marcie.

"Of course," said Dick. "How's it look today?"

"Just fabulous! You're going to be the hit of next season. Everyone thinks so."

"Should I be asking for a raise?" Dick asked, directing the question to both Valerie and Marcie.

"We'll wait a touch," Marcie replied.

Valerie ignored Dick's question and rolled onward. "I knew yesterday was nothing to worry about. I told the guys you'd be great today, and I was one hundred percent." Valerie threw her arms around Dick's neck and gave him a big kiss. "Keep it up, Dick! This show's a smash!"

Her words tumbled out in staccato bursts. Without missing a beat, she turned and hurried off.

"My God," said Dick.

"Shh," counseled Marcie. "Don't even try to figure it out. Just be happy that she's happy."

"I am, but still…. That woman is certifiable."

"Be comforted in the fact that she helps choose the television that America watches."

"You mean like *The Super*?"

"Exactly."

"My God."

"Trust me, Dick," said Marcie, "it's a dead-end worrying about people like that. She's into numbers and you're doing a show. Let the budgets and the ratings take care of themselves. You be funny, cooperative and your most brilliant self, and everything else will fall into place. Now, let me wipe her lipstick off you before they all think you were doing me in your dressing room."

Dick beamed and thanked Marcie for coming out to Burbank to see him. A production assistant knocked on the door and said they were ready. Marcie kissed Dick goodbye, making certain not to repeat Valerie's mistake, and left.

She telephoned Sandy from the car to get her messages. Sandy reported that Sam had called sounding very agitated.

"Did you get a number?"

"He said he wouldn't be reachable until tonight and asked you to call him at home."

"No idea what's eating him?"

"I even asked him if there's anything I could pass along to you for him. He wants you, toots."

"Great, I'll call him tonight."

"Hey," Sandy said. "Why don't you come see Bobby tonight at the Big Pink? The Faucets are doing a set at twelve, and I think you'll really like it."

"Too late for me," Marcie replied. "Maybe next time."

"Deal."

"I think I'm going home and make some calls from there," Marcie said. "Jane's coming over for drinks."

How nice it would be, Marcie thought, to have the whole day to prepare to be gracious for cocktails. But maybe not. She saw the women who shopped on Rodeo Drive in Beverly Hills all the time, and they certainly didn't appear happy and fulfilled. They were always dashing to a hair appointment or a fitting and appeared to have the same pressures she had, without any of the challenge or satisfaction.

A little later, Jane arrived, warning Marcie that it was likely she'd be getting a telephone call. One of her clients had been arrested in a prostitution sweep in the manner of Hugh Grant. Only in this case, her male client was involved with a young man and not a woman. The street name for professionals of this kind was a "chicken hawk" and Jane worried that the press was going to have a field day outing her client.

"How are you going to handle it?" Marcie asked. "Research for a part?"

"I don't think there is any way. We'll probably take the 'seeking medical treatment' route, but this has to play itself out. The public finally gets tired of stories. They did with Hugh Grant and even with O.J."

Marcie poured wine for both of them and served hors d'oeuvres. They were seated in the living room, both on the sofa.

"So how's life with your new partners? Still think you made the right decision?"

"I think it's going to work out fine," said Marcie. "Everything seems to be moving along very well."

"And Randy?" asked Jane.

"He can be a bit abrasive, but he's one helluva good agent. He's actually a very interesting man."

Jane smiled. "I'm glad you gave him the chance to show that side. I've worked with a lot of hot agents who turned out to be just flavors of the month. I think Randy is the real thing. Probably the best this town has seen since Ovitz. My guess is that you're in a really good seat."

"We'll see," Marcie said.

The phone rang, interrupting the conversation. As Marcie reached over and picked it up, she glanced at Jane, noticing her face had clouded over, as if fearing the worst. After hearing the voice at the other end,

Marcie pointed towards Jane. Shrugging resignedly, Jane got up to deal with the caller. An expert in handling the media, she gave them what was public record, which they already knew, but nothing else. She offered the medical treatment angle, but declined to provide any details. It was handled professionally and undoubtedly proved frustrating to the gossip-crazed media person. When Jane hung up, her face seemed sad.

"Are you okay?" asked Marcie.

"I'm fine. I just hate to see someone's stupidity bring their life crashing down around them. The public forgave Hugh Grant because he was straight. I'm not so sure that'll be the case here."

"Wouldn't you think he could have used a bit of common sense?" Marcie said.

"I know," Jane said, "but then I wouldn't be paid the big bucks to help smooth out the messes." She sighed wearily. "I guess I ought to go back to my office. There's going to be a lot more calls. I'll just change my referral number, okay?"

Marcie nodded and Jane finished her wine, and trudged out the door. We've all been there, bailing out our clients, thought Marcie. But it never seems to get any easier or more pleasant.

Marcie warmed some pasta and sat down with *The New Yorker* to catch up on some reading. It was still early, so she could have a quiet moment before calling Sam. She had just begun to scan the table of contents when the phone rang again. Sure it would be for Jane, she was surprised when it turned out to be Sam.

"Hi," Marcie said. "Sandy said you called this afternoon, and I was going to wait a bit and then call you. Is everything okay?"

"It's week goddamn one of the picture, and Peter doesn't pay me the slightest bit of attention. It's all about Julia! How she feels in the scene. What's the subtext of her scene. How radiant she looks. It's like I'm completely in the background."

"Sam, have you talked to Peter about your thoughts?"

"Try all lunch yesterday! He said it's important that she nails the character before our relationship develops. So that's the only reason he seems to be working with her. He said I already owned my character."

"So, what's the problem? It sounds as if he paid you a big complement."

"That's what he wants it to sound like. He's very clever."

"Sam, get a grip. You're saying he's deliberately ruining his own movie. Think about that for a minute. It doesn't make any sense."

"Goddamn it, Marcie! I'm not crazy! Come by the set and see for yourself. I'm not making this shit up."

"Where are you shooting tomorrow?"

"We're still on Stage 24 on the lot."

"I'll be there tomorrow. I'll talk to Peter, and we'll work this whole thing out. You don't have to worry about this anymore."

Marcie hung up wondering how much was actor paranoia and how much was on the money. She suspected the former, especially in light of her experience with Sam to date. She knew he would be a handful, but if this picture worked, he'd be a monster star to go along with it. She got up to put a kettle on to make tea thinking it did her no good to complain. This is the nature of the beast. The servicing of clients is a good bit of what agentry is about.

Pouring the hot water over a mint tea bag, her mind moved to Sandy's report on Tim. What the hell was he about? She ran through the modest alarm signals that had come up in the short time she had known him. His secrecy, his toughness that apparently lay just under the surface charm, the many rumors that placed him with the "funny money" folks from Vegas—these were disturbing enough. Now, if Sandy's source was reliable, there was a sexual preference question. Who and what was he? Marcie knew herself well enough to be certain that sexual preference was not an issue in her professional or personal lives. She had had too many close friends in both spheres to think anything otherwise. But she had never knowingly gone out with a bisexual, and she wasn't at all sure how she felt about sharing Tim's affections with a man. Indeed, the attention that Tim had showered on her led her to believe that he was a one-woman kind of guy. She felt a bit strange about sharing Tim, and especially with a man. This was competition with which she had no experience. Sipping her tea, and picking up *The New Yorker* again, Marcie decided that this was something to be worked out as soon as Tim returned from New York.

*   *   *   *   *

After a solid night's sleep, Marcie was put through her paces the next morning by her trainer. George was his usual sadistic self, but she didn't engage him in banter, as she usually did. He adapted easily to her new attitude and pushed her through her regimen, even adding a new exercise for her abdominals. As she finished and toweled off, the phone rang. Waving goodbye to George, she picked it up to hear her mother's voice.

"How are you, darling?" she asked. "This is a good time, isn't it?"

"Actually, I'm rushing to get into the shower and dressed. Can I call you later from the office?"

"Of course. I just wanted to chat."

"I'll speak to you later then. I love you, Mom."

*   *   *   *   *

When Marcie arrived at TNA, Sandy was already there looking bright and cheery.

"Did you go to hear Bobby last night?"

"I sure did. He was fabulous! The place went ballistic for the Faucets. You should have seen them."

"I'm happy for you," said Marcie. "I just don't know how you party all night and come in ready to go the next morning."

"Piece of cake," said Sandy, as she poured Marcie a mug of coffee. Randy appeared at Marcie's office door.

"Hey, babe, how are you?" asked Randy.

Marcie recoiled slightly at being called "babe," and noticed the glimmer in Randy's eye. It's all a big game, she thought. He enjoys baiting me. No way that he would know this isn't exactly the best day for games.

"I'm fine, what's up?"

"Allied's getting a little cute on a television package that they have no right to commission. Charles is saying that unless we split it 50-50 with them, they'll queer the whole thing at the network."

"Can they do that?"

"They can sure as hell try."

"What are you going to do?"

"It's what are *we* going to do? I think it's time to take off the gloves and play hardball. If we stand up for our rights on this case, I doubt if they'll fuck with us any more."

"What do the lawyers say?"

"They agree. Allied's trying to nickel and dime us out of what we agreed to last week. I say stick it to them now, and let them know who we are."

"You've got my vote," said Marcie. "Do we have to pay the lawyers a retainer?"

"No, they're being pretty good about it. They'll handle it without one unless it goes to trial."

"We're a long way from that, aren't we?" asked Marcie.

"We fucking well better be," Randy answered. "I'll run it past Jack and Ben and let you know."

"Great," said Marcie.

Marcie met Fred Sherman for lunch at Le Dome on Sunset. It was far from her favorite place, but Fred had wanted to go there. It was frequented by record people, and Marcie found both the food and the service inadequate. Fred was the Australian director who had led the invasion to the U.S. He had preceded Peter Weir, Bruce Beresford, Philip Noyce, Gillian Armstrong and all the others who came to the

States where budgets and fees dwarfed what was available in Australia. Fred had been married several times and was the father of many children. Raucous and wild, Marcie thought, and very talented. While he always kept working, he hadn't picked the projects that would allow him to break out as an "A" list director. This fact gave Marcie her agenda for the lunch.

Fred arrived ten minutes late sporting an Outback hat, and complaining about the traffic that had prevented his being on time. He promptly ordered a beer from the "mate" who waited on his table, and turned his complete attention to Marcie.

"So, my girl, what's all this I hear about a new agency?"

"It's all true, Fred. TNA, The New Agency. Four of us broke away from Allied to set it up."

"Do I know any of the others?" he asked.

"Randy Goldberg, Jack Hutcheson and Ben Kloster. You tell me."

"I bloody know Randy and I've met Jack before. But Ben, what's his area?"

"Literary mostly. Writers and directors. He's a damn good agent."

"Are they treating you okay?"

"Sure, we're all equal partners. So far so good."

"I never thought Randy would go for a deal like that."

"You mean with a woman as an equal partner?"

Fred grinned. "You got it."

"He puts on a good show in that area."

"He sure had me fooled," said Fred.

The waiter arrived and they both ordered. They kept up their banter until the food arrived. Starting to eat, Fred asked her when she was going to make her pitch.

"Now, if you'd like. You know I've always been a fan. Since I saw UNDER A NIGHT SKY, before I knew you."

"I appreciate that," said Fred.

"My feeling is," continued Marcie, "that with your talent and experience, you should be getting better material and packages to work with. Frankly, Fred, I think we could do a better job for you. You work steady. That's not the problem. We think you should be right at the top of the 'A' list, and we think we can get you there."

"I'm flattered, Marcie, I really am. But what makes you think that the four of you can do a better job than ICM has done for the years I've been with them? I've made a lot of money, worked with big stars like Meryl, and had choices about what I wanted to do."

"Have you had a studio production deal?" Marcie retorted.

Fred looked closely at her. "What makes you think you could deliver that?"

"It would be that important to us that we'd make it happen. I wouldn't mention it if I didn't think we could deliver."

An impish look came over Fred. "You're an attractive Sheila, you know? Do you fool around?"

"Oh Fred," said Marcie, "be serious, will you?"

"It was getting too bloody serious there. But okay, I'll give you an answer. I'm sure you know my papers are up. You agents always seem to know shit like that. I'll give you a week to nose around and see if you can turn up a deal like the one you described. It has to be at a major and they have to be willing to start negotiating with my lawyer right away. No 'definite maybes.' If my lawyer tells me they're for real, I'll sign with TNA. That way you've got me whether we ever close or not. Is that fair?"

"I think it's more than fair," said Marcie. "What do you say we have some champagne to celebrate?"

"Just a glass for me, I'm still editing this afternoon. And you still haven't answered my question about whether you fool around."

"You're married, aren't you, Fred?"

"To a very friendly woman," said Fred, lifting his glass in a toast.

Marcie wondered as she sipped her champagne whether Fred was drinking to his wife or to her. She decided it didn't matter.

As Marcie walked into her office following her lunch, Sandy told her that Ben wanted to hit some tennis balls with her after work.

"Is he in his office?" Marcie asked.

"He was a minute ago."

Marcie walked to Ben's office and looked in the open door. Ben was just wrapping up a phone call, and smiled warmly at her.

"How'd it go with Sherman?"

"Pretty well, I think. If we can find a studio willing to start negotiating a production deal with him in a week, he's ours."

"Wow, do Randy and Jack know?"

"Uh-uh, I just this second got back from lunch. Are they here?"

"No, they're both out of the office, and probably won't be back."

"No problem, we'll talk about it at the meeting tomorrow. You say you're looking to get beaten up on the courts tonight?"

"That could happen," said Ben, "but I sure need the exercise."

"Great," said Marcie. "Let's check with each other around six."

The day continued at a frantic pace. At one brief lull, Sandy asked, "Do you want to talk about the Tim situation?"

"No, but thanks for asking. I'm going to try to clear the air when he gets back to town. Until then, I don't know what to think, or how to react."

"It's a tough one, isn't it?"

"Not as tough as it could have been if we'd been seeing each other for a longer time."

"I mean," said Sandy, "that you haven't gotten seriously involved with anybody for a while. This seemed like it might happen for you."

"We'll see," Marcie said, anxious to change the subject.

Sandy got the message clearly and nodded, walking back to her desk.

At the end of the work day, Marcie and Ben rode out in separate cars to Riviera Country Club for their tennis match. Ben lived in Santa Monica, a little west of the club, while Marcie had to head back toward town to get to her home off Benedict. They warmed up for nearly a half hour before agreeing to play a set. While Ben played a fair game, he was no match for Marcie in singles. She conserved her energy, and her knees, by her superior placements and her ability to make Ben run from one side of the court to the other. In the end, though the set score was 6-3, in favor of Marcie, the match really wasn't that close.

They walked off together, Ben with his arm over her shoulder.

"Got time for a drink?" Ben asked.

"Loser buys?"

"Of course."

"Sure," Marcie said. They walked toward the clubhouse and the bar.

Inside and seated at a table, Amstel Light beers in front of both, Ben asked how she thought things were going so far?

"Ben, I think we've been blessed. We've scored some extraordinary commissions, we all seem to be getting along, and my concerns about Randy haven't amounted to anything."

Ben beamed. "I know. It makes me ask myself why we didn't do it sooner."

"You know that timing is everything. This was the moment. CAA was vulnerable, there was no hot new kid on the block, Allied was becoming too stodgy. It all came together."

"Pretty damn exciting, isn't it?" asked Ben.

"For sure. But no time to get complacent. We're still going to have to hustle to build momentum. We are starting from scratch."

"I know," Ben said. He took her hand. "I just want to say that it means a lot to me that you decided to join us. I mean not just for the good of TNA, but personally."

"Thanks, Ben." Marcie didn't pull her hand away, but she was conscious of the fact that Ben hadn't released it. Was this a new drama unfolding in her life? He let her hand go, although he continued to stare at her before picking up his beer. I'm not going near this now, thought Marcie. Better to play dumb on this front.

*   *   *   *   *

To her surprise, Marcie received a mid-morning call the next day from Charles. Edith told her that he was very anxious to speak with her.

"Hi Charles," she began, "what's up?"

Without a pretense of courtesy, he took off after her. "I don't know if you're aware of it, but your fucking company served papers on Allied late yesterday."

"The partners authorized it, but I didn't know you had been served."

"Cut the shit, Marcie," he growled. "Don't you fools have enough to worry about? We'll beat your brains out, and you'll end up paying lawyers up the kazoo!"

"That's our business, Charles. I think you'd be better off having your lawyers talk to our lawyers. That's how it's done, isn't it?"

Charles exploded. "You ungrateful bitch! After all Allied did for you, after all I personally did, this is how you repay us? Fine! The day of the boutique agency is ancient history anyway. The beating you're going to take will only speed along the inevitable."

Marcie was tempted to simply hang up. Better to bring closure to this inane discussion, she thought. "You know, Charles, you're always telling me what you and Allied have done for me. I was overworked and under-paid my whole time there. And you know that goddamned well! So you can take your tough-guy attitude, and shove it! Goodbye!"

Marcie looked up and saw Sandy standing in the doorway, probably attracted by the level her voice had risen to.

"God, he pisses me off," Marcie said.

"You get 'em, girl!" Sandy said supportively. "He's had that coming for a long time."

Marcie stood up saying, "I'd better let the others know Charles is playing hardball."

Randy told her that Charles was only sniffing around for weakness, trying to drive a wedge between the partners. "You did great," he said. "Show the bastard a united front."

Jack and Ben echoed Randy's sentiments. Jack followed Marcie back to her office, closing the door behind him.

"He can be very abusive, can't he?"

"I guess I took it there for too long."

"I just wanted to say that you were appropriately tough in your dealings with us, and you seemed to have returned Charles's best serve with a passing shot of your own."

Jack's compliment made Marcie feel good. The friendly hug he gave her before going back to work reinforced that feeling.

Marcie had little time to revel in her good feelings, as Sandy buzzed her to say Sam was on the line.

"Hey, how's the picture going?"

"It's a fucking nightmare."

"You've got to calm down, Sam. You're only going to make things worse carrying on like this. What time have they been breaking for lunch?"

"One o'clock."

"I'll be there a little before, and we'll get with Peter and work this out. Lots of pictures have these problems coming out of the gate. Call them growing pains. We'll fix it, I promise."

Sam sounded none too sure as he said goodbye. Damn, Marcie thought. I could almost write his dialogue for him. Why couldn't the children play nicely together? But they rarely did.

*   *   *   *   *

Marcie arrived on the Warners lot around 12:30. They were between takes on Stage 24, so she was able to walk in. She came close

to clobbering the director, Peter Weir, with the door, as he was stepping outside for a breath of air.

"Peter," Marcie said, "how's it going today?"

"Fine," he said guardedly.

"I'm glad. I wonder if I could have a minute of your time?"

"I'm due back in a sec."

"I know you're having problems with Sam. He's like a big puppy.
Scratch behind his ears, and he's your friend for life. He doesn't think
you care about his performance and what he thinks. If you could spend
a little more time with him, give him his confidence back, I promise
he'd bust his chops for you. He's really a good kid."

"Look, Marcie, I went way out on a limb for him. Warners wanted a
bigger name, but I insisted they take him. Considering that it's his second picture, he's got a pretty inflated idea of his importance."

"He's young, but you're right. Peter, your instincts in wanting him
were right on. He can deliver all that and more. That's got to be best for
the picture, doesn't it?"

Peter smiled broadly. "I feel like I've been agented by one of the best.
But you're right. I've got to get him in harness and pulling in the same
direction as everyone else, especially Julia. Without some chemistry up
there, we've got nothing. I'll be more patient and supportive of him,
and anything you can do behind the scenes will be greatly appreciated."

"Deal!" exclaimed Marcie.

"I won't get to him before lunch," Peter said, "so you can meet him
now in his motor home, if you want."

"Thanks," Marcie said, as Peter kissed her lightly on the cheek and
disappeared onto the stage.

Marcie knocked on the door of Sam's motor home and was ushered
in by a client very happy to see her. She outlined her conversation with
Peter, emphasizing that he was committed to work diligently with Sam
to pull this picture off successfully.

"He's hustling you, Marcie. Goddamn it, I told you he'd try some shit like that. Can't you be strong enough to protect me in this situation?"

Marcie laid down the law. "The truth is you're as hot as your next picture. You haven't been around as long as the other "A" list actors, and you sorely need to solidify your position. I'm your biggest fan, but I'm also your agent. You get a reputation on your second film for being unprofessional, and you're yesterday's news."

"Whose side are you on?" Sam blurted out.

"Yours, of course, but part of my job is to tell you the truth. You want smoke blown up your ass, there are plenty of agents in town who'll do that for you."

Sam gave ground. "No, I guess I was out of line. If Peter will pay more attention, I'll be there for him."

"Bring a positive attitude to the set, and I think you'll be pleasantly surprised. Both of you want the same thing—for the picture to work."

Sam nodded and gave her a half-hearted hug. He was becoming his own worst enemy right in front of her, and she seemed unable to slow the process. Goddamn actors, anyway, she thought.

CHAPTER XIV

Driving back to the office from lunch the next day, Marcie had a call from Ben on the car phone. So much for my system of outgoing calls only, she mused.

"Hey Marcie," Ben began, "we just got an offer for Sandra to star in a mini for ABC."

"That's wonderful news. What does Randy think of the project?"

"That's just it. No one can seem to locate him. He went off to some kind of meeting real early."

"And the time pressure?"

"ABC knows she got the Underwood film and needs to hear right away whether she'd consider a mini. They'd hold for her if she'd commit."

"Tell them she'd be happy to consider it, and get us the material right away. She can always not like it down the road."

"I know that, but she's your baby, and I wanted you in on the decision."

"Thanks, Ben, but she's all of ours. What do you suppose is up with Randy?"

"No idea. It's very unusual for him to be out of touch."

"It's probably something major like a dentist appointment. Hang in, I'll see you in a few minutes."

Fred Sherman rolled in to TNA a smart thirty minutes late for his three o'clock appointment. He blamed an editing problem for his tardiness and was pleased that no one challenged him. In truth, Marcie,

Ben and Jack were vamping themselves, hoping that Randy would return from wherever he was. When Fred arrived, they had little choice but to start the meeting without him.

"My lawyer tells me," Fred began, "that Universal seems damn serious about the deal you guys began."

"We could be helpful on that, if you'd let us," offered Marcie.

"Well, mates, that's why I'm here. I thought Marcie was making conversation, but it seems you've moved quickly enough to impress my lawyer, and that's not easy to do. If you still want me, then this is the place for me."

Marcie beamed. "We couldn't be happier, Fred. You never have to worry about agency politics here. All four of us will be working for you, and you can speak to any of us at any time."

Ben caught Marcie's eye and gave her a barely perceptible nod. Marcie continued. "Ben has signed a new writer whose script took second prize in the Nicholls Competition. Why don't I let him tell you about it?"

Ben quickly sketched in the plot of the script titled *Silk*. It was a 90s version of the classic 40s "bad girl" scripts, written for a mature female lead. Ben described it as a "relentless thriller, full of twists and turns."

"Who's seen it?" asked Fred.

"No one. They'll all know about it on Friday when they announce the Nicholls winners, but for now, no one. The writer's a young woman from USC who I've been talking to for a couple of years. I signed her Friday. She's so talented, it's scary."

"You're thinking of bringing it to Universal, if that deal comes together?"

"Absolutely," said Ben. "It's Ronnie's kind of picture," he said, referring to Universal film boss, Ron Meyer.

"Do you think it's right for Meryl?" asked Fred. "We're looking for something to do together again."

"She was made for the part," said Ben.

"What do you think?" Fred asked Marcie.

"I think it's dynamite. It's special, but hugely commercial."

"Did you read it too?" Fred asked Jack.

"Absolutely. I agree wholeheartedly. With you and possibly Meryl, it could be a monster."

Fred was excited. His energy level increased as he contemplated the screenplay.

Ben produced a copy of *Silk* and handed it to Fred. Marcie noticed that it had a white cover with a red border, and large block letters on the front reading TNA. Ben didn't waste a lot of time, Marcie thought.

Fred also took notice of the new cover saying softly, "TNA. The New Agency. Not bad. Let's wrap this up. Bruce Ramer, my attorney, has a date at Universal at two to lay out the deal. I'd like one of you to be there with him."

"That should be me," said Jack, "I've had the most experience at that studio."

"Fine," said Fred. "You might also prepare agency papers and bring them along for Bruce to review."

"I'll get on that right now." Marcie smiled.

Getting up, Fred said, "I think I'll go work out and then get my hair cut. Might as well look good if my career's going to take off."

Marcie took Fred to meet Sandy on his way out. As she validated his parking receipt, she asked "Didn't you direct *Under a Night Sky*?"

He nodded, a smile playing on his face.

"One of my favorite flicks. Truly awesome."

"Thank you," said Fred, pleased with Sandy's take on his movie.

Marcie walked Fred to the elevator, very happy with the meeting. He seemed particularly warm as he said goodbye.

✶   ✶   ✶   ✶   ✶

That evening, Marcie fell asleep watching the eleven o'clock news. The telephone awakened her with a start, leaving her very disoriented. It was Jane.

"I'm sorry," Jane said. "I woke you up."

"That's all right. I was kind of napping. What's up?"

"I'm afraid there's a little problem with Randy. He and his lawyer just called me. He was arrested in a prostitution ring, kind of like the Heidi Fleiss operation."

"Oh no!"

"Seems he's used the service before, but this time the girl had a wire and set him up. It's part of a crackdown on johns. I think there are a bunch of celebrities involved."

"He's out on bail?"

"Yes, and there's no way in hell to keep it out of the papers."

"Randy Goldberg's not Hugh Grant, Jane. Who else got busted?"

"We don't know yet. I'm sure you're right, though. It'll be a chuckle for a while, but it'll pass over."

"What kind of damage control can you do?"

"Not much. He's a single guy, and it's really a victimless crime. I think the best approach is to do nothing at all. That's what I told them when they called. Ride out the storm. Business as usual."

"Was this a regular thing with him?"

"I have no idea."

"Thanks for calling. I know you'll do whatever can be done."

Marcie hung up and tried Randy, getting his machine. She left word, telling him she'd heard from Jane, and offering any help she could deliver. Marcie then called Ben and Jack. Neither had heard, and both were shocked with the news. They agreed to meet at seven thirty the next morning, and see how it was treated in the *Times* and the Trades.

They met in the office, keeping the service on to pick up calls. Randy took fourth billing in the papers behind two series actors, and an up-and-coming movie star. Marcie and her partners were thankful for that.

"What about our clients?" asked Jack. "I can't believe Sandra is going to be too enthralled with the news."

"I agree with Jane," Marcie suggested. "It'll blow over. Randy's an agent, not a clergyman or a politician. Let's play it cool for a couple of days and let the town get its laugh. Soon enough, it'll be old news."

"I agree," said Ben. "It blew over with Hugh Grant."

"Pun intended?" offered Marcie.

"Let's go to work," said Jack.

Sandy kept the reporters and the inquisitive at bay, as callers seemed a bit more plentiful than usual. From Universal came word that the Sherman deal was making good progress. They were hoping to have a Deal Memo to execute the next day. Apparently the news from Universal also reached Fred, for he called moments later.

"Looks good, doesn't it?" he asked.

"Sure does. Is Bruce happy?"

"For a bloody lawyer."

"And *Silk*? Have you read it yet?"

"Does a bear shit in the woods? Of fucking course I've read it."

"And?"

"And it's bloody marvelous, that's what it is. It's hot, commercial as hell, and probably the best piece of material I've ever had."

"Oh Fred, I'm glad you're excited about it."

"Excited isn't the word. I'm fucking knocked out. And it's great for Meryl! I've already called her and she can't wait to read it. Her picture's pushed back, and if she likes it, which I know she will, she'll do it next."

"Terrific. If you give Sandy her address, we'll FEDEX a copy to her right now. She'll have it in the morning."

As Marcie put Sandy on, she reflected that should Meryl say yes, with Fred attached, the script would go for a bundle, maybe seven figures. Not bad for a first-time writer. Except for Randy's nonsense, things couldn't be going better.

Jane called later that afternoon to check in. "Have you talked to Randy?" Marcie asked. "We haven't heard from him all day."

"No, his lawyer is keeping him incommunicado. They've gotten a criminal lawyer, he said, and they're hoping to walk it through. Not too easy to deal with, is it?"

"You're telling me."

Jane anticipated where Marcie was heading. "Does this change your thinking about having left Allied?"

"Not at all," Marcie said. "We always knew Randy was the wild card, so no surprises there. I was just thinking that I'm not feeling any sense of panic. I'm well out of Allied, and whatever happens now' I'll make the best of."

"If you keep things in that perspective, you're going to be fine. I'm off to NBC to sit with a nervous client at the Leno show."

"You do earn your keep," Marcie said.

"Don't we all."

*   *   *   *   *

Marcie's sleep was again disturbed by an early morning phone call. As she answered the phone, she was amazed that so many people were now calling her this early. Chances are, she thought, nothing good could come from this. It turned out to be Randy, offering to bring breakfast by in a half hour.

"Why not go out?" Marcie asked.

"I'm kind of laying low," Randy answered.

"Make it forty minutes, and you've got it. I'll put some coffee on and take a fast shower."

"See you," Randy said, and he was gone.

As she showered and dressed, Marcie wondered why Randy wanted to speak with her. Had he already met with Ben and Jack? She doubted it, believing she would have heard from them. As the doorbell rang, she thought she'd know soon enough.

"You don't look any the worse for wear," Marcie said, giving Randy a friendly hug.

Setting the bag from Nate 'N Al's on Marcie's kitchen counter, Randy said, "I'm doing okay. I guess I was in the wrong place at the wrong time."

"What's the likely outcome?"

"Probation, with maybe some community service. Not too bad."

"Was this a regular thing with you?"

Randy chuckled. "Maybe you'd call me a regular."

"Forgive me, but why?"

"Why not? No involvements, no arguments, only fun and fantasies. What's wrong with that?"

"I don't want to argue with you about the pros and cons of hookers. But you assured us that your personal life wouldn't get confused with your professional life. And this little caper has embarrassed the agency."

"And I'm genuinely sorry that this happened. It seems to be dying down. The press don't give two shits about me. Would you agree?"

"I think so."

Randy heard her indecision. "Did you have something else in mind? Like dissolving the partnership?"

"No," Marcie replied, "that never occurred to me."

"Good, because we're on a great roll and I'd hate to cash in at this juncture."

"I agree," Marcie said. "You coming in today?"

"You bet. I see my lawyer at nine, and I should be at TNA by ten."

"Have you brought the others up to speed?"

"Not yet. There was something else I wanted to mention to you. I talked to a friend of yours the other day, Tim Garland."

"I don't know as I'd call him a friend, more of an acquaintance. Where'd you run into him?"

"Just a coincidence. I was talking to our banker, and his name came up. One thing led to another and we ended up spending a few hours chatting on the phone. He's an interesting guy."

Marcie nodded, feeling somehow wary of this situation. She couldn't put her finger on what troubled her, but Randy seemed less than forthcoming. Maybe it was the whole arrest problem with Randy that had her on guard.

"Are you planning to meet with Ben and Jack?"

"Of course. Hopefully, this morning, as soon as I get through with my lawyer. I asked Beverly to set it up, and if you could try to be there too, I think we can get past this business."

A little after ten, Randy assembled his partners in his office, asking all secretaries to hold calls. He expressed regret for having dragged his personal life into his professional life and promised to work doubly hard to be sure that didn't happen again. "I was hoping that we could take this time to air any concerns any of you may have with me or my lifestyle, and then see if we can put it behind us. We're off to a great start with TNA, and I'd like to keep the momentum going."

The others exchanged quick looks, before Jack spoke. "We haven't discussed this to reach a consensus, Randy, so I'm speaking for myself. I think we are off to a great start, and we do make a good team. I have no opinion about your personal life. It's yours and I hope it makes you happy. But I damn well care when it slops over into TNA. It affects me, Emily, and my sense of trust in you. I look at it as completely unprofessional and unacceptable."

Randy looked to Ben, who seemed a bit shaken. "I can't add much to what Jack said. I see all this like a wakeup call. We're not a big corporation, but a four person partnership. If one of us fucks up, it can't help but reflect on all of us."

"Marcie?" said Randy.

"We've talked briefly about this earlier, and I'm still feeling a little uneasy. I don't think this partnership can make it if one of us is a loose cannon, operating without regard for the others. I know it's not what I want it to be."

"Is that it?" asked Randy.

Everyone nodded.

"Okay," Randy began. "I want to apologize again for bringing this trouble into the partnership. None of you bargained for it, and you're all correct saying it could bring the whole house of cards down. Thanks for sparing me the moral lectures and keeping the focus on the professional side. I'm truly sorry it happened, and you have my word it won't happen again."

Jack shook Randy's hand, saying, "I'm glad."

"Me too," said Ben.

Marcie gave Randy a hug. "You screw up again, and I'm calling my friend Vito. Let's consider it history and go forward."

As the day wore on, it was readily apparent that the media interest in Randy's escapade had already waned. A single man, with a Peck's Bad Boy reputation, Randy's image didn't seem to suffer from any of this. Even Sandra, who called in that afternoon, had heard about it and took it in stride. Jane was correct, thought Marcie, it will blow over in short order. The public's appetite for juicy scandals needed highly charged celebrity power, like a Hugh Grant or an O.J. Simpson, to stay alive. If this were as bad as it got, they'd probably sail through without the ship sinking.

*   *   *   *   *

Tim flew back to Los Angeles the next day. He telephoned Marcie, suggesting he drop over around seven and they could play it by ear from there. Marcie put out some cheese and crackers, opened a bottle of wine, and was prepared to find out where things stood when, at exactly seven o'clock, the doorbell rang. Glancing at her watch, on her way to open the door, she wondered how people could go through life being this punctual.

"God, it's good to see you," Tim said, as he entered her house. He seized her in arms, and was instantly aware of the fact that Marcie was far from responsive to his embrace.

"Is something wrong?" he asked.

"I don't know," Marcie said. "We have to talk. Do you care for some wine?"

"Sure." Tim sat down on the sofa. "What's going on?"

"This is a little hard for me."

Marcie sat across from him in an easy chair. She could see his uneasiness when she didn't sit next to him. She poured Tim and then herself a glass of wine, sat back, and looked at him.

"Talk to me," he said. Tell me what's going on. Is it that I've been away too long? You know I was working on this deal."

"No, Tim, it's not the deal, whatever the hell the deal is." She heard the edge in her voice, and took a breath to get control of herself. This was not the time to become overly emotional.

"Whatever it is, put it on the table and let's talk about it."

"Okay," Marcie began. "I got a report that you were seen in a gay club in New York with some guy. They said you were all over each other. What the hell is that all about? I think you can understand that it's a bit tough for me to deal with."

Tim looked at her for a minute, collecting his thoughts. "Yes, I can understand that. I was at a club with Jerry, a special friend of mine. I used to live with Jerry, when I split up with my wife."

Marcie felt the color drain out of her face. She wanted to tell him to stop speaking, to tell him to please leave. But she couldn't. She was unable to say anything. Tim went on.

"I bumped into Jerry completely by accident. It was like a reunion. That's all."

"What do you mean 'that's all'?" Marcie said, her voice rising. "You tell me you used to live with some man named Jerry, and dismiss it as just a reunion! What the hell's going on, Tim?"

He again took a beat before responding. His voice was calm and evenly modulated. "I guess you'd say I was attracted to both men and women. Bisexual, you know? I'm fundamentally a monogamous person, and I think of myself as being in a relationship with you. Nothing happened with Jerry in New York. As I said, it was only a reunion."

"Were you not going to tell me you were bisexual? Was this your idea of a little surprise to drop on me over dinner one night?"

"It didn't, and doesn't, have anything to do with my feelings about you. I understand that it's caught you off guard, and if it's upset you, I'm truly sorry. But it doesn't have anything to do with how I feel about you."

"I'm afraid it does have quite a bit to do with my feelings about you," Marcie said. "You can't just drop this on me and expect me to take it all in stride."

"Believe me, I understand how you feel. But you have to understand about bisexuals. It's not as though I fantasize about men when I'm with you. My relationship with you is completely fulfilling and satisfying for me. I don't have a roving eye, and I'm not looking for other men or women. I think we have something very special together, and my hope was that we could let it develop and see where it took us."

Tim looked closely at Marcie, apparently expecting some kind of response.

"I'm supposed to respond to that?" Marcie asked.

"Not if you don't want to."

"Look, Tim, the minimum I've got to have in any relationship is trust. And, frankly, that's the thing I find precious little of with us. You don't talk to me about your business deals. You pump me for information about the movie business, but it's all a one-way street. Everything about you is so damn mysterious, that I don't really know who the hell you are. And now this! Truthfully, I don't know how I feel about you being bi. What I do know is that I resent like hell finding out as gossip and not from you directly. If you're so cool about it, and expect me to be as well, then why didn't you tell me? Were you planning on hiding it, or is this your idea of a good joke?"

Tim reached toward Marcie, trying to take her hand. She pulled back, unwilling to make physical contact with him. He sat back in the sofa and exhaled slowly.

"I've lived with being a bisexual for a long time. It hasn't always been easy. Most people are horrified and even frightened about what it means. You're right, of course, I should have talked to you about it. The truth is, I was afraid. I never expected to find myself involved with someone like you, and I didn't want to risk seeing it come to an end. As things have worked out, I guess I handled it wrong."

Marcie thought he seemed very vulnerable at this moment. His tough guy persona had given way to an attractive, boyish quality. Careful, thought Marcie, you've been taken in by this kind before.

"I think I understand," said Marcie. "I'm going to need a little time to think about everything. It's hard enough for a woman to compete with other women, but a whole new ballgame to also compete with other men. I have to think about all this."

"Okay," Tim said. "But it's not about competition. Any more than I'm competing with your ex-husband. Those are only facts about people. Give it some thought. I'll call you in a couple of days. I'm here any time you want to talk to me, and I hope, more than anything, that you can make peace with this part of me. It's not a problem for you and me, and it needn't ever be."

Tim put his glass down and stood up. Marcie got up as well, feeling very awkward. She allowed herself to be hugged by Tim, although he made no effort to kiss her. She had turned her head away from his as he held her, not wanting any intimate contact at that moment.

"Let's see what happens, Tim," Marcie said, as she showed him to the door.

"I'm here when you want to talk," he said. Tim closed the door behind him, and Marcie heard his car start up and drive off.

*   *   *   *   *

The next morning, at the office, Sandy brought Marcie a cup of coffee, letting the door close after her.

"Jesus, Marce, you look worse than I feel."

Marcie tried to decipher her message. Marcie knew she'd been dumped by her rock drummer, Bobby Imhoff. Sandy told her Bobby was now seeing one of the continuing characters on *Baywatch*. "It's not so much the bimbo," Sandy had told Marcie, "or even that she's cornered the market on silicone, it's that Bobby didn't have the decency to tell me himself. One day he's there, and the next day he doesn't show. He had his goddamn roadie tell me we were finished. My fault for thinking he was different," Sandy concluded.

"You're right, things aren't too red hot this morning."

"It's your wacko partner, Randy, isn't it? What kind of shit is he into? He's got to buy hookers? Is he some kind of freak?"

"It's kind of hard to say. He wishes for our sake that he hadn't been caught, but there doesn't seem to be a whole lot of remorse."

Sandy reflected on the situation. "I don't know, I can't bring myself to trust Randy at all. For your own sake, be careful, okay?"

Marcie nodded.

"And what about Tim?" she asked. "Did he ever come back from New York?"

"He did, and I saw him last night."

Now Sandy's interest was really piqued. "And?"

"And I guess your friend's story was accurate."

"You're saying he *is* gay?"

"I'm not saying anything just yet. He says he's bi, but that he wants a relationship with me."

"Man, I just knew it," Sandy said softly. "So what are you going to do?"

"I don't know. It scares me how little I really know about him. I feel like Alice in Wonderland."

"Trust me, walk away. You don't need this kind of shit in your life." She paused. "Even if you have to give back the necklace."

*　　　*　　　*　　　*　　　*

Her mind awhirl with personal problems, Marcie was still riding the crest of the wave of success at TNA. From nowhere, their partnership had become the little agency that could. Prospective clients were beating a path to their door, and Marcie and her partners were suddenly forced to become very selective if they were to preserve their small, boutique quality. Charles's prediction that the era of the small agency was over appeared completely off the mark. After much discussion, the partners rejected the idea of growing rapidly in favor of keeping their original concept of a small, alternative agency intact. It was decided to add another agent to help handle the unexpected business. With Ben's urging, they chose Elinor Villadsen, a young hotshot from CAA's literary department. They talked at length to Allied's Peter Tacy before choosing Elinor. Her existing client list and experience outweighed the present value of Tacy. He returned to Allied with the promise he would be reconsidered within the year.

Marcie continued to weigh the whole relationship with Tim in her mind. She kept coming back to the word "trust." The truth was, she told herself, she didn't trust him. It wasn't only his sexual preferences, about which she became far less uncomfortable, it was more fundamental than that. Unanswered questions, shadowy references to his past, a general sense of being closed off to the idea of letting her share his life all contributed to her feeling of distance and separation from him.

Jane had put it succinctly, "Do you think he'll ever let you be really close to him?"

"I doubt it," Marcie answered.

"Is that important for you?"

"It's at the top of the list," Marcie responded.

Jane looked at Marcie without saying anything.

*   *   *   *   *

One of the shining successes Marcie and TNA enjoyed was the Wilhite show, *The Super*. It proved to be the hit that NBC had predicted, and much more. Slotted in a great time period, between two existing hits, the show and Dick became the talk of the new season. For Wilhite, it was a complete renaissance. The network was only to happy to let him direct several shows, as many as he wanted, as long as he re-upped for additional seasons. His new deal with NBC included the right to produce, direct and star in movies of the week, as well as a development deal to create and package comedy programming. Movie offers flooded in for his hiatus period, and Dick was now as hot as he had been cold before. In his interviews, he was lavish in his praise of Marcie and TNA. That kind of press favorably impacted the creative community and further contributed to the momentum that TNA had built up.

*   *   *   *   *

As time went by, Sam's picture never managed to hit its stride. Marcie worked hard to keep the lines of communication open. Still, Sam was never able to forge the desired relationship with either Peter Weir or Julia Ormond. There were good days, but more often hopeless misunderstandings. It became one of those projects that had a bad aroma to it, and the whole town knew it.

Peter invited Marcie to look at the rough cut with a handful of friends, the day before Warners saw it. Making all the necessary allowances for a temp music score, no effects and no opticals, the film was a disaster. The chemistry between Julia and Sam, the backbone of the film, was totally absent. As the last reel ended and the projection room lights came up, the invited guests stared at the blank screen in horror. There was a smattering of applause, a few token compliments, followed by the audience fleeing, lest they catch whatever affliction the film had. Marcie stayed, along with a couple of Peter's industry friends, to talk about editorial options that could be explored. Some suggestions made sense, but Marcie sensed that it was like putting makeup on a corpse. The film simply didn't work. Even Sam, so electric in the Pollack film, was flat and uninteresting in this one. If Sam and Julia appeared uncomfortable together on the screen, how could the audience root for them? There was no movie magic, only movie tedium.

Peter screened for Warners the next day, and the reaction was the same. Warners had been guarded after seeing the dailies, but after screening the rough cut, they were resigned to writing the whole project off.

Sam took it very hard, lashing out at Marcie for ever having forced him to get involved with this project. The Warners publicity people wanted Sam to help plug the picture on television and radio, but he flatly refused. He washed his hands of this film and everyone connected with it. Marcie tried to get him interested in a new project. *Beef Jerky* was still in search of a male lead, along with two other major studio projects. Marcie held firm offers for Sam, all between a million five and two million. Sam went through the motions of reading the scripts and considering the offers, before turning them down. On a day when Marcie was supposed to have lunch with him, a registered letter arrived for her at TNA. It was from Sam's attorney instructing the agency to cease holding itself out as Sam's agent. They were dismissed. A couple of phone calls later, Marcie learned he had signed with Jimmy Wiatt at the Morris office.

Ben and Jack sat with her to discuss Sam's action.

"How do you feel?" Ben said, gently.

"Not really surprised, but a little disappointed. He should have been enough of a *mensch* to tell me himself."

"The more actors change, the more they stay the same," said Jack.

"I know, but you always hope this one will be different." As she said the words, Marcie was reminded of Sandy's words when Bobby Imhoff broke up with her.

Ben gave Marcie a hug. "We still love you."

"You too, Jack?" Marcie asked.

"Absolutely," Jack smiled.

"Before we conclude this love fest," Marcie said, "has anybody seen Randy?"

The subject of Randy had become very delicate again. He had been true to his promise to stay out of trouble. That wasn't the issue. It was as if he was distracted, no longer the driving force that the other partners knew him to be. Jack identified the problem first. Finding a moment when Randy wasn't in the office, he asked Ben and Marcie to join him.

"I've known Randy a long time," he began. "Something's up, I can smell it."

"Have you spoken to him?" Ben asked.

"Sure, we're supposed to be partners."

"And?" Marcie said.

"And he denied there was any problem at all. 'Have you looked at my bookings and signings lately?' he had asked. Well, they're terrific, no way they're not. But I know Randy. Something's going on."

"Do you think he'd say anything different to me?" asked Marcie.

"I have no idea," Jack replied. "Take your best shot. I think we all have to try to get to the bottom of this as soon as we can. Maybe it's nothing. I sure hope so. But I tell you, something's going on."

Chapter XV

Ironically, Marcie was feeling very good about her life. As if emerging from a long holding period that began with her son's death, she now was living life to the fullest, and completely enjoying the sense of participation without holding anything back. She had dealt with Sam, she could deal with whatever Randy threw at her, Tim was on hold, and the agency was continuing to throw off staggering commission business. It soared past the first year's projected earnings in six months and seemed headed toward achieving more than twice projections. Marcie felt alive in a way she hadn't in many years.

Sitting with Jane at her house, Marcie reflected on the possibility of Randy leaving TNA. Jane picked up her thoughts and asked, "If that did happen, do you think you guys could keep it all together?"

"Funny, I was just running that question through my mind. I've made a real emotional commitment to TNA, and you know, it feels pretty good. It's a lot different than anything I've done with my life for a long time, and I like it. I was thinking of the worst case scenario where Randy screws everything up for all of us, and I think it's still going to be okay."

Jane smiled at her and touched her arm with her hand. "You sound like you're on top of your game, kid. Now, tell me what's going on with the mysterious Mr. Garland."

"Mostly smoke and mirrors."

Jane smiled and gestured at Marcie to keep going. "More information, please."

"Well, he keeps calling, hoping we can resume where we left off. I honestly think I'm past the bisexual thing now. It's something else. Kind of hard to put into words. It's almost like he's some kind of weird robot. No feelings, no conscience, almost like he's sociopathic."

"You're describing most of the moguls in this town," Jane quipped.

Marcie laughed. "You're probably right. And that's not a Mr. Right that I could be happy with."

"Have you talked to him about your feelings?"

"Sure. He says all the right things, but I'm not buying it."

"Give it some time," advised Jane. "Everything always gets clearer with time."

*   *   *   *   *

Matters had become more strained at the office. The early morning partners' meeting, once a time of excitement and enthusiasm, now seemed shrouded in distrust and uncertainty. Randy continued to insist it was business as usual, and the earnings continued to skyrocket. Whatever the problems were, they were confined to TNA, and were not known outside the office.

As one such meeting came to an end, and the partners rose to leave Randy's office, he said to Marcie, "Spoke to Tim this morning. I guess his deal is just about closed."

Marcie tried to maintain her composure. What did Randy know about Tim's deal? Was Tim confiding in him when he had refused to talk to her? Why was Randy speaking to Tim in the first place? Marcie's mind raced. Was she jealous of Randy's relationship with Tim? Could they possibly be…?

"What were you speaking to Tim about?" asked Marcie, keeping her voice even and modulated.

"Some business stuff," Randy said evasively.

"Randy, what the hell's going on? Don't give me some line of shit about 'some business stuff'! I asked you a simple question."

"Maybe you'd better ask Tim. He gets in around two-thirty."

Randy terminated the conversation the way Charles used to by reaching for the telephone and asking Beverly to get started with his calls.

Marcie looked at him for a beat, but his eyes were on the papers on his desk. She walked out, went in to Jack's office, and closed the door.

"What's up? Didn't we just have our meeting?"

Marcie filled him in. He listened carefully, then slumped back in his chair.

"Whew! That is food for thought."

"Any ideas?" asked Marcie.

Before Jack could respond, there was a knock and Ben poked his head in.

"Come in, Ben," Marcie said. "This concerns all of us."

Marcie recounted the story to Ben who indicated he hadn't a clue what was going on. "Maybe it's just a coincidence," he suggested.

"Wait a minute, guys," Marcie said. "We've got one of the town's great information sources right down the hall."

Jack and Ben exchanged questioning looks as Marcie asked Sandy to join them. In response to Marcie's question, Sandy said, "My friend at Tri-Star tells me the company's about to be sold."

"Would she know?"

"She's a he," sniffed Sandy, "and he works for a real biggie. They're expecting to have a new boss before the end of the week."

"Anything else?" asked Ben.

"The rumor is some hotshot agent's coming in to take over the movie division, but that's always the rumor. Oh yeah, the joke over there is that it's more Asian money. Haven't they learned their lesson?"

Sandy looked from face to face. Suddenly, her eyes lit up. "You think it's Randy, don't you? You could be right, but I'm pretty sure no one over there knows that. If they did, I'm sure I would have heard."

Jack and Ben regarded Sandy with a new respect. For Marcie it was further confirmation of Sandy's unique talent.

Marcie thanked her saying, "Do me a favor, please keep this conversation to yourself."

"No problem," replied Sandy, as she left the room.

Jack dialed Randy, but Beverly said he was out and not expected back today. She didn't know how to reach him.

The pieces, it seemed, were starting to come together. Playing devil's advocate, Ben suggested that they had no corroborating evidence about any part of this. "It's speculation built on speculation."

"Maybe so," said Jack, "but it all fits together too nicely. I'm always suspicious of that much coincidence."

Marcie's face looked dark and resolute. "I'll try to reach Tim when he gets in. I've got some private numbers for him. Let's keep each other informed."

Like Jack, Marcie had never put much stock in coincidences. The scenario she had sketched with Jack and Ben seemed all too real. Randy's growing aloofness, his conversations with Tim, the hot rumors about Tri-Star, it all made too much sense. She left word for Tim on his cellular and on his private, unlisted home number. At his downtown office, his secretary said she would be hearing from him when his plane touched down. Marcie left word, saying it was important.

Her mind ran through their many conversations about the shape of the movie industry, now and in the future. It all made sense. She was part of his "due diligence." And Randy? Was this what Charles had warned of? What had Charles said? Randy's "your greatest strength and your greatest weakness." Would it turn out that Charles was in on this too? She had met Tim through Charles. It was certainly possible. And Randy's doing battle with Charles? They were cut of the same cloth.

Game players who reveled in locking horns, and then doing a one eighty and putting some profitable deal together. She was certain now.

Sandy buzzed to say that Jane was on her way in. Marcie wasted no time. "What have you heard, Jane?"

"Not even a hello?"

"I'm sorry. We're a little bit crazed today."

"Well," Jane continued, "there's no official word yet, but the talk is it's a done deal. Your ex-guy Tim is the new chairman, and your ex-partner, Randy, the new president."

"And Charles?"

"Wow," said Jane, "I didn't hear anything about that."

"I didn't either, I just wondered. He may be working behind the scenes. There are suddenly more conspiracies than an Oliver Stone movie."

"You're saying you didn't know any of this?" Jane asked. "I came over to chew your ass out for not clueing me in."

"Me? It's just the guy I went with and my partner. Why should I be in the picture?"

"I thought you would be up to your ears in it. Like already headed to Tri-Star as Head of Production."

"No, I'm the chick with no taste in lovers and none in partners."

Jane reflected on Marcie's words. "Where do you go from here?" she asked.

"I still have to speak to both of them. It's all kind of hearsay. But, look at the bright side. Tim pissed me off but didn't break my heart. And, whatever happens with Randy, TNA is a success. It's the right agency at the right time."

Jane beamed. "I'm glad to see you with that attitude. Let me know how I can help." Jane gave Marcie a hug and left.

"Guess what?" Sandy said, entering Marcie's office.

"Believe me," Marcie replied, "at this point, I don't have the foggiest."

Sandy leaned forward conspiratorially, "Tim and Randy just pulled into Tri-Star in a big limo and are meeting with the top execs as we speak."

Marcie stared at her, the news sinking in.

"My friend said it's like a funeral over there. No one even makes eye contact. Pretty scary, huh?"

Before Marcie could respond, the phone rang and Sandy answered it.

Putting the caller on hold, Sandy said, "It's Tim's secretary."

Marcie took the phone, listened for a minute, and said, "Tell him I don't want to see him in a restaurant. I'll be at his house at eight-thirty." She hung up and looked at Sandy.

"A restaurant?" asked Sandy.

"An old trick," replied Marcie. "When guys break up with you, or give you some awful news, they take you to a public place so you won't make a scene."

"My friends welcome a scene," Sandy said.

"Not the Tim Garland types."

While Marcie filled in Jack and Ben on Sandy's latest news bulletin, Beverly said she'd heard from Randy who'd like to have breakfast with them at the Bel-Air at eight the next morning. They agreed, deciding also to speak with their individual attorneys and then meet beforehand in the office at seven.

"Might as well go in as prepared as we can," Jack suggested.

At eight-thirty that night, Marcie pressed the doorbell outside the gates of Tim's house. The heavy gates opened immediately, and she drove up to the front door.

Marcie thought Tim looked totally exhausted as he opened the door to greet her. He moved forward toward her, but she walked past him into the house. Tim was instantly aware of Marcie's coldness, but followed her into the living room where he graciously offered her wine and food. Marcie accepted the wine and indicated that the cheese and crackers already on the table were fine.

"I guess you've already heard," said Tim, sitting down on the sofa.

Marcie sat across from him on a chair. "I guess I have."

"I feel terrible that I couldn't fill you in, but I hope you know I had no choice. I can see you're upset, and I don't blame you, but you have to know that Tri-Star is a public company, and the SEC and the lawyers..." His voice trailed off.

"Are you finished?" asked Marcie.

Tim was surprised at Marcie's question.

"I mean is that your whole speech, or is there more you'd like to say?"

Tim spoke softly and earnestly, "Tell me what you're feeling right now."

Marcie looked at him coldly and spoke without emotion. "I feel like a pawn in your game. You fucked me over for the deal, or your new associates, or the money. It doesn't much matter. You used me, you involved my partner, and all the while you kept me on the string with a series of lies. Tell you what I feel? I feel like shit. But I'll get past it. It's refreshing to finally see you for who you are. You're a cold man, Tim, with a great act. I feel damn happy to have you out of my life, once and for all."

Tim poured himself another drink. Marcie shook her head when he offered a refill. "You've got it wrong," he said finally. "You became involved with my personal side, not my business side. I've never been in a spot where they overlapped, and it did create real problems here. It doesn't change my feelings about you. I care for you, and I'm hoping we can get beyond this misunderstanding, and maybe even work together. Randy and I would love it if you'd consider coming over as VP for Production. If you think we should keep our professional and business lives separate, I understand. But don't throw away what we have together. It's too special."

"You fucking don't get it, do you?" Marcie said, her voice rising.

"What do you mean?"

"Christ, Tim, unless you're insane, you're not two people. You're the same Tim Garland in business and in your personal life! The good, the bad, the whole goddamned package! I have no interest in working for you, and less than any interest in maintaining a relationship with you. We are, as they say, history!"

Marcie walked out to her car and drove off. Making her way home, Marcie felt angry, but not devastated. She wanted to stay an agent, not become a studio exec. Even without Randy, she was excited about the prospects of TNA. She smiled as she thought she had just moved to a third share from her hard-fought one-quarter. Randy would probably do well with Tim. The same ice water ran through both of them. For her part, she was well out of it.

Marcie's answering machine had no less than twenty-seven messages stacked up for her response. After fast-forwarding through them, she first returned the call from her attorney, Ira Lang.

"You're really okay?" he asked.

"Doing fine. Cleaning house is all. Goodbye Tim, goodbye Randy. Hello, a new partnership with Jack and Ben."

"You really okay?" Lang said, doubtfully.

"Really, Ira, fine. What'd you find out when you read the partnership papers?"

"It's the way I remembered. You leave before a year, you walk away clean. No assets, no liabilities. Randy comes off the loans and the lease, but he's not entitled to any distributions after the day he leaves, presumably today. Are his people saying anything different?"

"I don't think so, but I won't know until breakfast tomorrow. We're all having breakfast with him."

"Do you want me there?"

"No thanks, Ira. It's just the four of us. No lawyers."

"Well, you know the drill. Listen carefully and commit to nothing. Okay?"

"Okay, coach. And thanks."

Marcie then called Jane, who informed her that this would be all over the Trades tomorrow. She advised the remaining partners not to speak with reporters about the future of TNA. "I keep hearing," Jane said, "that Charles is up to his eyeballs in all of this. I'm not sure what I believe, but I'd watch out for Randy. He, Tim and Charles make quite a team."

"They tried to enlist me."

"What do you mean?"

"Tim offered me a job at Tri-Star a few minutes ago."

"Perfect. What'd you say?"

"Among other things, no thanks. It's business as usual for him."

"You sound together," Jane said.

"I think I am. A lot of this caught me by surprise, but I think I've adjusted to it."

"I feel terrible about being an advocate for Randy."

"He was a little spooky during all of this, but the truth is it was probably pretty new territory for him too. We're having breakfast with him tomorrow, and that should be pretty interesting. He certainly might have been more forthcoming, but it would have been very awkward for him if it hadn't worked out."

"Call me if you need me," said Jane. "I have a client opening at the Taper tonight and I've got to go the opening party."

"Lucky you."

"Yeah, right."

As Marcie hung up, she decided that there'd been enough excitement for one day, and that she would turn in. Just then, Sandy called.

"How're they hangin', toots?" Sandy asked, with her customary disregard for gender identification.

"It's all okay," Marcie responded.

"Did you see Tim?"

"I did, and put an end to all of that."

"Do you get to keep the necklace?"

"Sure, it was a gift."

"Cool," said Sandy.

"Any more bulletins from Tri-Star?"

"Nothing I've heard. So, are you going to go over there?"

Did Sandy know Tim had offered her a position? Or, was she only exercising her ability to construct scenarios? Marcie decided it didn't matter.

"No way," she said.

"I'm glad," Sandy said sincerely. "I'll see you tomorrow. I'd like to talk, but I'm going to a club with this dreamy bass player from Peanut Butter."

"Is that a group?"

"God, you're old," Sandy said, as she hung up.

*   *   *   *   *

The next day, at seven, Marcie met with Jack and Ben. They had spoken with their attorneys as well and received similar advice.

"Let's leave the numbers crunching for the accountants," suggested Marcie.

"I agree," Jack said. "I'm hoping we can sail through this meeting without a lot of hassling."

Ben produced the morning's Trades which carried bold headlines announcing the doings at Tri-Star. Randy was profiled in both *Variety* and *The Reporter*. Both papers mentioned his being a founding partner of TNA, and neither speculated on the impact on the young agency of his departure. A quote from Randy described TNA as being "in very solid shape, with wonderful long-term prospects."

"That sounds pretty supportive," said Jack.

"It does, but it could be just a negotiating tactic," Marcie said.

"One other thing," Jack added. "Ben and I had a talk last night, and we think it would be best for TNA if you took over the president's job. Oh, one other thing. Neither of us wants it."

His serious look caught Marcie a little off guard. This wasn't something she expected, but their good-natured laughter made it clear that she could comfortably accept the title.

"I assume that would mean a 40-30-30 split."

Ben and Jack exchanged panicky looks.

"Just a joke," Marcie said, laughing. The air cleared at once, as Marcie thanked them for their support and said she'd be happy to take over that role.

"The unstated assumption is," she continued, "that it's business as usual for TNA."

"Right," said Jack. "We'll find out what Randy has in mind, whether we can hold on to his key clients, and get back to work."

The remaining partners rode in Jack's car to the Bel-Air Hotel, where Randy was already sipping coffee and reading the accounts of the previous day's events. He greeted them warmly and seemed undeterred by the wariness exhibited by his erstwhile partners. Small talk was unnecessary, so Randy got right to the point.

"I know," he began, "that I told you I wasn't looking for a studio job when we began TNA. And that was true. What I was offered was so extraordinary that I had to look at it as a once-in-a-lifetime shot. I'm sure you think I should have confided in you before you heard it on the street, but it was all speculation until the deal finally closed in New York yesterday. The truth is I wasn't at liberty to talk about it, even with you, until it finalized. Believe me, I wish I could have been more up front."

Randy paused for more coffee, checking out the reactions of his former partners. They were paying close attention, but remained guarded. He went on.

"You must have already talked with your attorneys, and I'm sure discovered that there is no buyout, just a payoff of what was due through yesterday, and a release from all corporate obligations."

Again, he paused, and again there were no comments. Clearly, they were waiting for him to get to the crux of what he wanted to say.

"I wish," Randy went on, "that the rest was as easy. I'm afraid that all but one of my clients has decided to return to Allied. Of course, you're protected on the new deals, but they feel more comfortable in more familiar surroundings."

"Cut the shit!" said Marcie. "This is the pound of flesh you're giving Charles for putting you into the Tri-Star deal with Tim."

"No comment," said Randy, taking another sip of coffee.

"Nothing surprises me anymore," said Jack. "But I will say that you disappoint me Randy. When I signed on with you, I did assume you had some semblance of decency. I see that I was wrong."

"Don't be naïve," Randy replied. "Business is business."

Marcie looked from Jack to Ben, then back to Randy. Standing up, she said, "I don't think there's anything else to say. We have a business to run."

Ben and Jack also rose, walking out of the dining room, leaving Randy still sipping his coffee and perusing the Trades.

The three remaining partners left the hotel for the drive back to Century City. At the office, they assembled the secretaries, Elinor Villadsen and two interns, and discussed the events of the last twenty-four hours. There were now three partners, and not four, Marcie had replaced Randy as president, and their continued support and loyalty were sorely needed as TNA made the transition.

Ben followed Marcie into her office. "You were great at breakfast."

"Thanks, Ben. Any one of us could have said the words. It's what we agreed to."

He smiled at her. "No, I mean it. You were terrific. Could I interest you in dinner tonight?"

"I'd like that," Marcie said.

"Later," Ben said, and walked back to his office.

Sandy slipped in as Ben left.

"You okay?" she asked.

"Fine."

"Did you guys settle up with Randy?"

"Not really. He's sort of in bed with Charles as well as Tim."

Sandy nodded, as if none of this came as any surprise.

"And how was your guy from Peanut Butter?"

"Total loser. The kind of dude who gives drugs a bad name."

Marcie smiled at the description.

"How come we keep ending up with loser guys?" asked Sandy.

"It happens, but it'll change. If you stay in the game, at least you've got a chance. Otherwise, what's the point?"

Sandy wrestled for a moment with Marcie's pronouncement.

"So you're saying it's all about going forward?" she asked.

"You got it."

Satisfied, Sandy got up and went back to work.

THE END